DARLINGTON
CIRCUS
THE VELVET DECEIT

Published by Darlington Publishing
ISBN: 979-8-9908912-4-1

Printed in USA

First Edition July 30 2025

DARLINGTON
CIRCUS
THE VELVET DECEIT

SK HINKLEY

CONTENT WARNING

This series contains mature themes, explicit content, and sensitive subjects, including:

- BDSM and DOM/SUB relationships
- Scenes of rape and kidnapping

Reader discretion is advised.

Dear Reader, This tale precedes the events of Eternal Act. Feel free to enter our world through either doorway but be sure to experience both before indulging in the secrets of Immortal Greed.

Happy reading, and welcome to the circus!

—Bellamy Darlington

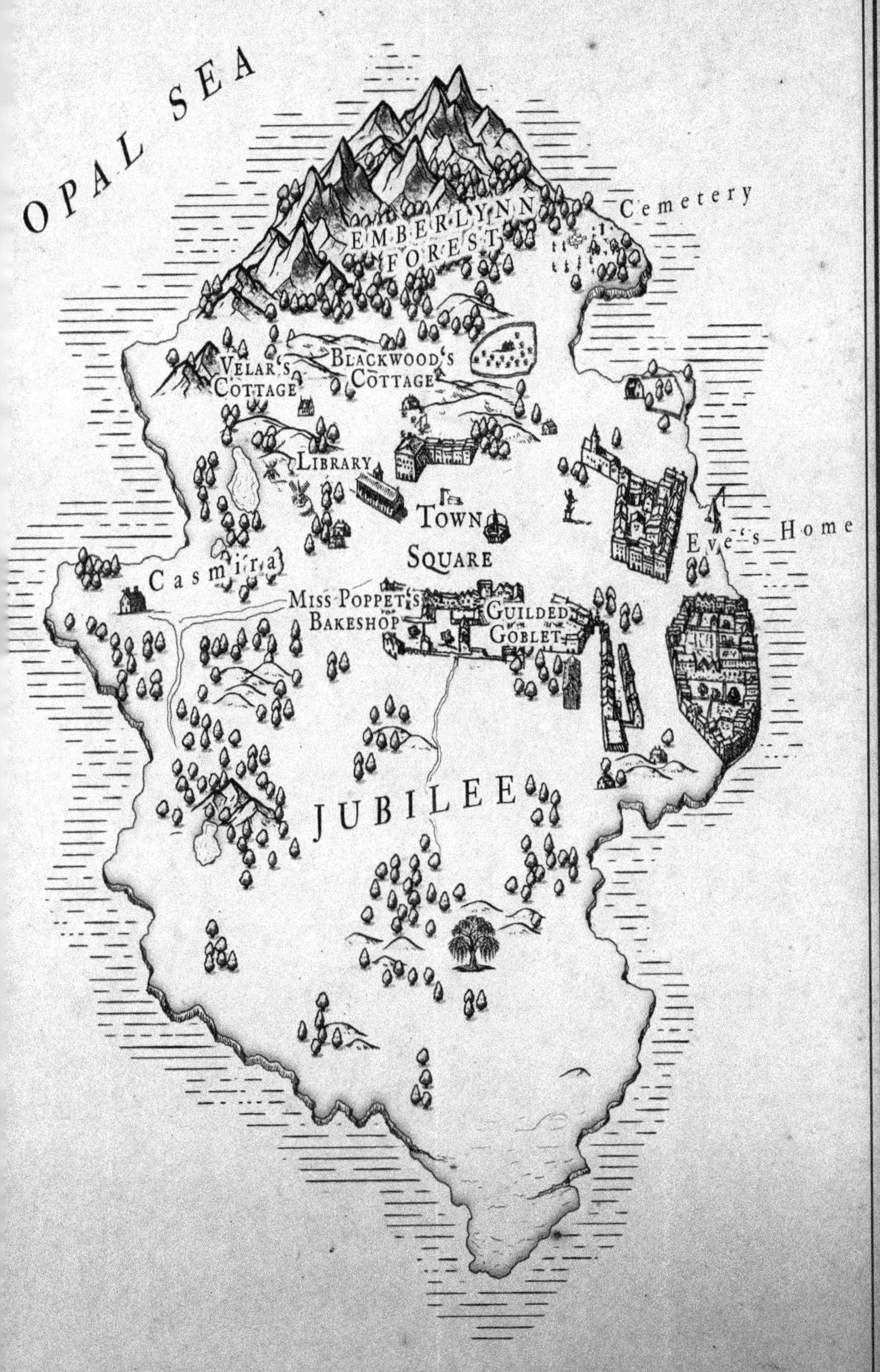

OPAL SEA
EMBERLYNN FOREST
Cemetery
VELAR'S COTTAGE
BLACKWOOD'S COTTAGE
LIBRARY
TOWN SQUARE
Eve's Home
Casmira
MISS POPPET'S BAKESHOP
GUILDED GOBLET
JUBILEE

PROLOGUE

As I stood on the windswept hill, the weight of my grief threatened to consume me. Before me lay the freshly dug grave, a poignant reminder of my failure to protect the love of my life. Nicole, my sweet, gentle wife, had been torn from my arms once again. The cruel fate that had been ours to bear for so long seemed determined to crush me beneath its heel.

Velar, my loyal friend and confidant, approached with a solemn step, his eyes red-rimmed from tears shed for our collective loss. His presence was a bittersweet comfort, a reminder that I was not alone in my sorrow. Together, we gazed upon the coffin, our hearts heavy with the knowledge that Nicole's radiant smile had been extinguished, her laughter silenced once again.

The Samsara ritual ensured her return, but the agony of her absence remained. Oh, how I yearned for her to be like us, immortal and forever bound to our side! Because of the curse, fate had other plans, and I was left to deal with the aftermath, my mind lingering on the memories of our time together.

As I raised my eyes to meet the sympathetic gaze of our friends and family, Eve's nod from the front row was a gentle prompt to begin the eulogy. My voice trembled with emotion as I spoke the words,

"Beloved friends, gathered here today to bid farewell to our beloved... Nicole, my love, my heart, my everything..." The words faltered, lost in a sea of tears, as the grief I had held at bay came crashing down upon me like a tidal wave.

"We will find her again, just as we always do. And so, we must content ourselves with the knowledge that we will be reunited once again. In her next life, we will find her, and we will hold her close." Velar's hand tightened on my shoulder. I took a deep breath and looked at the coffin where she rested.

"I will find you again, I promise baby girl."

CHAPTER
ONE

1965

It was a sweltering summer day in July, and the city was alive with the vibrant rhythms of the sixties. The concrete jungle pulsed with energy, as the sun blasted down the Great White Way. The air was thick with the smells of hot dogs and pretzels from street vendors, but also the pungent aroma of urine-soaked alleys, exhaust fumes from yellow cabs, and the sweet scent of blooming flowers in Central Park, struggling to overpower the stench of garbage and decay. The sounds of honking horns, chattering pedestrians, and wailing saxophones filled the air, creating a symphony that was quintessentially New York City.

As I strolled through the streets I stepped inside my favorite library, basking in the cool air, I could not help but feel a sense of tranquility. The only escape from this heat wave was the air conditioning in restaurants, stores and my favorite place, the library. The nonfiction section was my first stop, but as I was reading a back cover, I noticed a woman gazing at me with a hint of curiosity.

Her bold geometric pattern top with tapered pants caught my attention, and I wondered why she seemed so interested in me. I quietly compared my shift dress to her style, admiring her pulled-back brown hair. I shrugged it off and headed to my favorite section, fiction.

Shelf by shelf, I examined the covers and read the back of the books, seeing what adventure I wanted to go on next. As I reached for a book, I sensed someone approaching. I turned around to see Gary strutting towards me, a smirk on his face.

"There you are," his tone teasing. I rolled my eyes, knowing he would find me. My high school boyfriend often teased me about my love for books, and I was not in the mood to see his friends today. His unrelenting persistence won out, and so I agreed to grab a milkshake at the diner with them.

As we walked towards the front, Gary snatched "The Feminine Mystique" from my hand, raising an eyebrow. "What are you reading this for?" His tone was playful but slightly condescending. I grabbed the book back, asserting my love for all genres.

At the counter, the woman from earlier approached, and we struck up a conversation about the book. "I'm Nicole Sullivan" I introduced myself. We chatted until Gary grew impatient, urging me to hurry up. The young woman did not pay any mind to my obnoxious boyfriend. Instead, she seemed to be intrigued with me. *Maybe because we both enjoy books.*

Reluctantly, I bid her farewell, but not before asking if she lived in the city. She shared that she was visiting New York City for the weekend, and I was about to ask more questions when

Gary pulled me away. Before I was dragged out of the door, I turned back to ask her name, and she smiled sweetly. "Eve."

Outside in the heat, I turned to Gary and halted in defiance. I was embarrassed by him dragging me away like that. "That was rude, you didn't have to act like that in front of that lady." I crossed my arms as he hailed a cab. "Come on, I'm getting hungry." Before I could speak, a cab pulled up to the curb we were standing on.

The ride to the diner was silent, with Gary and I not exchanging a word. I was still irritated with him for hurrying me out of the library. But my mind was preoccupied with Eve, wondering who she was and what she wanted to discuss with me. Her enigmatic presence lingered in my thoughts. I found myself contemplating a return to the library the next day, hoping to cross paths with her again and continue our unfinished conversation.

As we pulled up to the diner, the neon sign casting a colorful glow on the pavement, I could already see my boyfriend's friends huddled inside. They strutted around in their slim-fit jeans, their sleeves rolled up in a style that seemed to shout 'status quo. I couldn't help but feel like they were stuck doing the same thing every day and night without a care or ambition to venture beyond the upper west side.

My own dreams, on the other hand, were bursting at the seams. I longed to leave the nest, to spread my wings and soar into the unknown, to explore the world beyond this city and make my mark. For now, I was stuck in this diner, surrounded by the same old faces, the same old stories, and the same old malted milkshake.

I had graduated early, a feat my boyfriend's friends loved to rip me about, as if being smart was something to be ashamed of.

But I knew I was destined for greater things, and I couldn't wait to break free from this cycle next month when I start school.

As I drained the last drops of my chocolate malt, I gathered my books and slid out of the cozy booth, the vinyl creaking in protest. Gary and his friends were standing around the jukebox, but when they spotted me making an exit, Gary's eyes widened in disbelief. "You're bailing on us already?" His hands shooting up in the air.

I fabricated a hasty excuse, my words tumbling out in a rush, "I've got to get home, my mom needs me for something." I aimed for a quick peck on the cheek, but Gary caught me off guard, his lips locking onto mine in a sloppy, wet kiss that left me breathless and mortified.

His friends guffawed and catcalled. Their taunts and teases are familiar as a worn-in shoe. I forced a laugh, my cheeks burning with embarrassment, and extricated myself from Gary's grasp. I bid them a hasty farewell. My words were swallowed up by the diner's hubbub and pushed out into the sweltering heat, the sidewalk radiating like a griddle.

I skipped the cab line and hurtled down the subway stairs, my feet pounding the pavement in a frantic bid to escape the stifling atmosphere, both inside and out. I squeezed onto the train just as the doors were closing, the car's airless interior encircled me like a suffocating shroud. But I didn't care, I was headed home.

As I emerged from the subway at seventy-sixth and ninth Avenue, the sun was sinking slowly below the Manhattan skyline, casting a warm orange glow over the city. The sky was a kaleidoscope of pinks, blues, and purples, a breathtaking sunset unfolding like a canvas of vibrant hues.

I sauntered down the sidewalk, the summer air thick with the scent of blooming trees and freshly cut grass from the park across the street. I reached the familiar facade of our apartment building on seventy-second street. The brick exterior, worn to a warm golden brown from age.

I bypassed the steep stairs leading to the double French doors, instead slipping through the side gate and descending the narrow steps to the basement level, the air growing cooler and more shadowy with each step. I fished my key from my pocket and worked the lock, the mechanism creaking open with a groan.

"Mom?" I called out, my voice echoing off the walls of our small two-bedroom apartment, but the only response was silence. I seized the opportunity to indulge in some solo time, settling into my favorite nook, where my trusty chair with worn cushions molded to the contours of my body. I immersed myself in the pages of my current read, devouring the words of feminist thinkers, eager to absorb their ideas and insights. The movement was gaining momentum, and I wanted to be prepared for the intellectual debates and discussions that awaited me at NYU, my mind hungry for knowledge and perspective.

My mom is my best friend and confidante. She had recently found love again, and while I was happy for her, I couldn't help but feel like I was being left behind, a reminder of a past life she was eager to forget.

A few hours later, my mom and her boyfriend returned from their evening out and headed straight to their bedroom, exchanging pleasantries with me about their day. As I prepared to retire for the night, something outside caught my attention through the ground-floor window. I couldn't believe my eyes, it looked like an entire circus was set up across the street in Riverside Park.

I rubbed my eyes, wondering if the fatigue of the day had conjured up a mirage, but as I gazed out the window again, the vision remained. A circus, its black and white wave pattern tents shimmering like dark diamonds in the night. How had I missed this wonderland just hours before?

The urge to rouse my mom and share the discovery was strong, but I was transfixed, my feet rooted to the spot. The circus was eerily still, its silence only adding to the enchantment. Never had I seen such a spectacle, especially not in our neighborhood.

As sleep beckoned, my mind raced with visions of death-defying acrobats, majestic beasts, and thrills beyond my wildest dreams. The promise of adventure hung in the air keeping my imagination awake, leaving me yearning for dawn to arrive.

CHAPTER
TWO

The next morning, I couldn't wait to explore the mysterious circus that had seemingly appeared out of thin air. I quickly got ready and raced to get outside. I was swept up in a sea of people, all eager to experience the circus for themselves. The crowd was massive, and I struggled to make my way to the front, the line snaking around the block.

Just as I was about to reach the entrance, Gary appeared in the crowd, his expression a mix of concern and annoyance. "I knew you'd be here when you didn't answer the door," he said disapprovingly and clearly out of breath from running to find me.

"This place is a rip-off, let's get out of here before we waste all our money." I hesitated, my desire to enter the circus wrestling with Gary's sensible words. But as I gazed longingly at the black and white tents, I reluctantly agreed to leave knowing I was going to need every penny saved for schoolbooks.

As we navigated through the throng of people, a familiar face suddenly appeared before me. It was Eve, the woman I had met at the library just yesterday. She strode towards me with a confident smile wearing go-go boots with a bright mini skirt. I froze, my eyes locked onto hers, as Gary disappeared into the sea of faces. "Hi Nicole," she said, with a cryptic smile. She had a bit of mystery about her.

I returned her greeting, my curiosity piqued by this unexpected encounter. "Are you heading to the circus?" I asked. She nodded, her smile growing wider. "Why don't you join me?" Her eyes glinted with excitement.

I hesitated, my gaze scanning the crowd once more for Gary, but he was nowhere to be found. Eve sensed my hesitation and pulled out a black envelope from her metallic box-purse, the white wax seal gleaming in the morning light. "Don't worry, I have free tickets!" she announced, smiling. My jaw dropped in amazement. "Far out!" I exclaimed. Eve grabbed my hand like we were close friends and said, "Let's go!"

As Eve led me towards the circus entrance, skipping the line, my eyes were drawn to the bold sign that towered above us: "Darlington Circus" it read, in letters that seemed to dance with excitement. The words seemed to pulse with a magic all their own, as if they were beckoning me to enter a world beyond the ordinary. Eve handed me one of the precious tickets.

The line moved quickly, with the entire city flocking to the enormous Circus in Riverside Park. The massive setup stretched as far as the eye could see, causing a traffic jam and drawing a huge crowd. I was in awe, struggling to keep up with Eve as she pulled me along not caring she was cutting the line.

When we reached the front of the line, a solitary door stood with no walls on either side, but security insisted we enter through it. Suddenly, the atmosphere transformed, and it was like nothing I'd ever experienced. The world around us shifted in an instant. It had to be magic if you believe in that sort of thing.

The sweltering summer heat gave way to a refreshing coolness, with occasional gentle breezes rustling my brown shoulder-length hair. I stood enchanted by the circus, surrounded by incredible performers and endless rows of black and white tents. Eve raced ahead, her determination palpable, while I lingered, indulging in the mouthwatering aromas wafting from the food vendors.

As Eve led me down the winding cobblestone path, I couldn't help but gaze in wonder at the enchantment that lay within the circus boundaries. The air was alive with the sweet scent of sugar and spices, and the sound of laughter and music drifted on the breeze.

In the distance, I spotted a majestic weeping willow tree standing tall amidst the vibrant tents, its long, graceful branches swaying gently in the wind. I halted my step, my fascination was growing, for I had never known a willow tree to grow in Riverside Park. Its presence here, amidst the whirlwind of color, seemed almost otherworldly.

I tugged on Eve's hand, trying to slow her down. "Wait, Eve! I want to see the acrobats!" I said, gesturing towards a nearby tent where a troupe of performers were balancing on a high wire. But Eve just laughed and kept pulling me along. "Come on, we have to get to the main event!" she exclaimed eagerly.

As I gazed upward, a tightrope walker appeared above me, suspended in mid-air like a fleck of magic. I released Eve's hand, my fingers unfurling like petals, and stood transfixed, my eyes wide with wonder.

'What is this place?' I said in bewilderment. Eve halted and shook her head at my naivety. 'It's magic!' she declared. With that, she grasped my arm and swept me along with a rush of urgency, as if the very magic of the moment might vanish if we tarried.

I reluctantly followed her, feeling like a child being dragged away from a favorite toy. The circus appeared to be a never-ending spectacle, a mesmerizing maze of delights that seemed to stretch on forever. But that was impossible, I knew Riverside Park had limits, and yet, somehow, the circus had managed to pack an entire world of wonder within its modest boundaries. It was as if the park had been transformed, its ordinary landscape enchanted to accommodate the magic of the circus.

We weaved past vendors selling colorful balloons and sugary treats, and I caught glimpses of fascinating acts. A fire-breather, a contortionist, a juggler expertly juggling flaming torches. But Eve didn't stop until we reached a solid black tent at the very back of the circus. 'We're here!' she announced, pushing open the flap and quickly pulling me inside.

As we entered the tent, I was surprised by its emptiness. 'Hey, what's going on?' feeling a surge of confusion. She had dragged me into an abandoned tent. I was about to turn and leave when I noticed Eve laughing at me, her eyes sparkling with amusement. 'What's going on?' I repeated, feeling uneasy. Eve quickly composed herself, noticing my fear. 'I know you have no idea why I brought you here,' she said calmly, 'but just wait a few more seconds, and he should arrive.' Her voice trailed off as the tent flap swung open, and a tall, handsome man in a top hat and crimson ringmaster suit strode into the doorway.

Instantly, fear gripped me as I realized I was alone with strangers in a mysterious tent. Eve's intentions were unknown, and I felt trapped. But as the ringmaster approached, his eyes locked onto mine.

'Nicole.' Something in his gaze made me feel like he knew me intimately. His piercing sea blue eyes hypnotized me, and I fell into a trance-like state. A sudden, searing pain exploded in my head, and I clutched my skull, overwhelmed. As I struggled to cope with the agony, Eve and the ringmaster rushed to my side, their voices inaudible amidst the torment. Then, as abruptly as it began, the pain ceased, and my memories came flooding back.

"I'm back! I'm back!" I exclaimed, my voice filled with a sense of wonder and realization. Tears streaming down my face, I felt a flood of memories rush back, like a dam breaking. I remembered everything. It was all coming back to me.

I had been reincarnated once again, I remembered the lives I'd lived before, the love I'd known, and my immortal family. Bellamy Darlington, the captivating Ringmaster, was my husband. "Daddy." I cried as memories of our past lives together flashed through my mind like vivid snapshots, each one capturing a moment of our love story.

His eyes, brimming with tears, locked onto mine, and I saw the weight of eighteen years of searching and longing in them. I threw myself into Bellamy's arms, holding him tight as if I'd never let him go. The warmth of his embrace was like coming home.

'Welcome home,' Eve said with a smile. I wrapped my arms around her, holding her close as I hugged her tight. She was more than just my best friend. She was always the one to find me and bring me home.

When I returned to Bellamy, his lips claimed mine in a kiss that was nothing short of enchantment. The world around us melted away as his mouth moved against mine, weaving a spell that quieted the turbulent depths of my soul. The stormy waters of my reincarnated essence stilled.

As I gazed at the faces before me, a sense of awe and profound gratitude washed over me. These people, my family, had stood by me unwaveringly, even when my own memories had abandoned me.

Though my recollections were hazy and fragmented, one truth shone brightly: I was home. In this moment, all else faded into insignificance. The weight of my past lives, the struggles, the triumphs – none of it mattered. All that mattered was the love that surrounded me and the knowledge that I was exactly where I was meant to be.

"Where is she?" A voice boomed from behind, piercing through the tent's canvas. I turned to face the speaker, and my eyes met Velar's emerald gaze. Bellamy released me, and I instinctively ran into Velar's open arms.

He swept me up, twirling me around with a joyous laugh, before setting me down and gazing down at me. His smile illuminated his face, revealing the hint of vampire fangs. 'Look at you!' He exclaimed.

Tears of joy streaming down my face, I gazed at the familiar faces before me. My heart overflowed with emotion. I was finally reunited with my immortal circus family, the people I had loved and lost so many times throughout the centuries.

The curse, cast by a vengeful witch all those years ago, had granted eternal life to everyone in the circus... except me. I was the sole exception, forced to live out my life while everyone around me remained immortal.

The four of us were elated at my return, and I was consumed by emotion. We spent some time catching up, sharing stories, as the circus bustled around us. The smell of kettle corn and sugar wafted through the tent.

But then, a sudden memory pierced my mind like a dagger. "Did you know I was murdered?" I blurted out just as the memory came into my mind. Bellamy and Velar exchanged a weighted glance, their eyes locking in a silent understanding. Velar nodded solemnly, his expression somber.

"We got him." His voice low and reassuring, a gentle promise of justice. Bellamy's eyes filled with pain and regret, his gaze dropping as if the weight of his failure was crushing him. "I'm so sorry I wasn't able to protect you, baby girl," his voice cracking with anguish, the words spilling out like a confession.

As I closed my eyes, the vibrant sights and sounds of the circus blurred around me, and I was transported to a different time, a different life. Nineteen-forty-nine.

I saw myself, younger, with the same brown hair. I saw him, the handsome stranger, with a charming smile and a heart full of deceit. I felt the cold blade slice through my skin, the warmth of my blood spilling onto the sidewalk.

The pain, the fear, the shock, it all came flooding back, as if it had happened yesterday. My mind recoiled in horror as I remembered the life I had lived, the life that had been brutally taken from me.

Tears streamed down my face as I saw the depth of Bellamy's sorrow. "It's not your fault," I comforted him. Velar's eyes narrowed, "Nothing like that will happen to you again," he vowed, but I knew not even a vampire could predict the future.

As we stood there, lost in our emotional reunion, I began to hear the murmur of a crowd gathering outside the tent. I knew it was the circus performers and crew, eagerly waiting for me to emerge and greet them. Bellamy requested that I take my time, and they would wait until I was ready. He's always overprotective of me and I missed that about him. He always cared the most for me during my many lifetimes.

My memories may only have returned when my eyes locked onto Bellamy's, but I was sure that everyone who had seen me arrive with Eve was excited to see me again. With a deep breath, I prepared to face the people I had considered my immortal family, my heart racing with overwhelming excitement.

As I stepped out of the tent, a sea of familiar faces greeted me, their eyes shining with joy and wonder. The circus performers and crew surged forward to greet me. I waved at everyone approaching me, my smile glowing.

I saw Luna, the aerialist, her wings shimmering in the sunlight; Kaid, the fire dancer, gleaming with excitement and smiling; and Ohna, the fortune teller, her eyes sparkling with tears. Anise approached and handed me a bouquet of sunflowers.

The crowd parted, and I saw the rest of the circus family, each face a reminder of a memory, a joke, a shared moment. There was Prudence, a contortionist, her grace and beauty still breathtaking. The Blackwood family was next to greet me. They were a family of witches. I felt like a prodigal daughter, returning home after a long journey.

I'm unsure if you've ever experienced reincarnation, but it's a truly peculiar sensation. It's as if I've been on an extended journey, and upon returning, everything seems eerily familiar. Faces appear unchanged, as if no time has passed at all.

Yet, with each rebirth, I notice subtle changes within myself. One constant remains, though: my first name is always Nicole. Ambrette Blackwood ensured that this detail was woven into the ritual, allowing them to track me down when I die and am reborn in the same year.

Even with the consistent name, Nicole, it often takes them a considerable amount of time to locate me again. The search can be arduous, and the gap between reunions can be extensive. But Ambrette's ritual ensures that the connection remains.

After the warm greetings and hugs, everyone returned to their posts, the bustle of the circus resuming. The performers went back to their acts, the vendors returned to selling their treats, and the crew resumed setting up for the next show.

As Bellamy and I concluded our conversations with my friends, we hastened towards the majestic centerpiece of the circus, a towering weeping willow tree, its branches swaying in the gentle breeze. Our secret portal to the mystical realm of Jubilee beckoned. Just as we drew near, a familiar voice rang out, 'Hey!' I froze, my feet rooted to the spot as Gary emerged from the crowd, anger grew in his eyes.

"I'll handle this,' Bellamy said, his voice firm and protective, as he positioned himself between us. Gary's gaze fixed on me with a mixture of anger and possessiveness. He must have been driven over the edge by seeing me with another man, because he didn't hesitate when he threw a fist at Bellamy. But Bellamy was quick, anticipating the juvenile move, and he caught Gary's fist in a firm grip.

Gary 's eyes widened in confusion as he looked at Bellamy, realizing that he was outmatched. I could see the pain and tension in Gary's face, and I knew I had to intervene. 'I've got this.' I stepped forward to take control of the situation. Bellamy's hands fell away, but not before he gave me a subtle nod of approval.

"What's going on, Nicole?' Gary asked, with confusion and concern, as I pulled him aside, distant from Bellamy's ears. We stood beneath the twinkling lights of the circus, the sound of laughter and music fading into the background.

'Gary, I have something to tell you,' I said hesitating slightly, 'I'm leaving. I've joined the circus.' I paused, unsure of how to reveal the truth without revealing the secrets that I had to keep hidden.

'I was going to tell you.' I trailed off, my eyes darting back to Bellamy, who stood a short distance away, his eyes fixed on us with an unreadable expression.

'That's outrageous!' Gary exclaimed, his voice rising in anger and hurt. 'What about school? And who is that man you were holding hands with, looking all chummy with, isn't he a bit old?' He spat the words out, his eyes filled with tears. I saw the worry and betrayal in his eyes, and my heart shattered into a million pieces. I had never broken someone's heart before, not in this lifetime, anyway.

"I'm sorry, we both knew we were headed for a breakup, didn't we?" I said, my eyes cast downward, feeling a twinge of guilt but also a hint of detachment. I knew I didn't love him the way he loved me, and it was my fault for not ending things sooner.

I looked back at Bellamy who was patiently waiting. When I turned back to Gary, I saw tears streaming down his face. I had never seen him cry before, and it only made my stomach twist in knots. 'I'm sorry,' I meant it, sort of.

As he stared at me like a deer in headlights, The comparison to Bellamy was unavoidable, and I couldn't help but feel a twinge of disappointment in myself. How had I ended up with someone so... ordinary when I'd experienced the extraordinary with Bellamy? The contrast was stark, a harsh reminder of the passion, the excitement, and the sense of belonging I'd felt with Bellamy. *What was I thinking?*

I gave him a sympathetic hug, but as I turned and walked away, my heart was soaring with every step. I tried to rein in my excitement, to slow my pace, as I made my way back to Bellamy. But it was no use, I felt alive, unshackled from the world I once knew.

Gary's departure was just a blur in my peripheral vision. My shoulders relaxed, and I knew I was exactly where I was meant to be. The life I'd been destined for was waiting for me, wrapped in the arms of my eternal husband.

We made our way to the giant weeping willow tree. With Bellamy's hand on my shoulder, I felt the familiar tingle of his magic. This was our secret entrance, hidden in plain sight, and only accessible to those who shared the circus's curse – or blessing.

Bellamy's nod was a subtle yet significant gesture, a silent acknowledgement that I was now free to enter our hidden world. His magic was still radiating in my body. With a gentle nod of his head, I stepped forward.

I reached out, my hand finding the comforting familiarity of the willow tree's trunk, where our initials - 'B' and 'N' are etched into the wood. As I gazed at the weathered carving, I was struck by the harsh realities of time, and that realization made me grasp just how long eighteen years truly was.

The portal magically opened, revealing the spiral stairs that descended into the magical realm of Jubilee. I quickly made my way down the tree's spiral stairs. At the bottom, I paused, gazing out at the whimsical town before me. It was a peculiar feeling, missing a place I had only just remembered.

Bellamy appeared behind me, wrapping his arms around my waist and nuzzling his nose into my neck. "Welcome home, baby girl," I turned to face him, and our lips met in a tender kiss. The familiarity of his touch transported me back to our countless kisses, making Gary's seem almost childish in comparison.

Bellamy, born in fifteen-thirty-six, carried himself with mature, worldly confidence that was both captivating and intimidating. His piercing blue gaze and gentle smile made me feel like I was the only person in the world, and yet, his presence was like a fortress, making me feel untouchable and safe from harm.

From the tree I strolled towards the town square, I couldn't help but absorb every detail, noting the changes since my last life. At first glance, everything seemed unchanged, the Victorian town homes to the left of the square still stood proudly. The charming town square itself looked freshly plucked from the Victorian age, its gardens bursting with vibrant blooms. In the distance, the Emberlynn Forest rose like a verdant jewel, its lush canopy of greens, golds, and crimson hues that seemed to pulse with an inner light. The rolling hills, soft and serene, served as a gentle precursor to the forest's vibrant splendor.

The wind's soft caress brought the essence of the Opal Sea, its salty perfume intertwining with the resinous scent of pine trees. The two fragrances entwined, transporting me to a place where the majestic sea met the ancient forest.

My feet carried me along the cobblestone path, but I veered left, drawn to a clearing that wound through the woods to the right of the square. The soft pine straw crunched beneath my feet, like a plush carpet welcoming me home. I wandered through the dense yet intimate woods, a smile spreading across my face as I caught sight of Casmira waiting for me.

My home, a majestic Gothic Victorian manor, boasts four floors, a steeply pitched gabled roof, and four round towers, all encircled by a wrap-around porch. She's a true marvel, always making my life easier. A gift from Bellamy many years ago.

"Casmira, I'm home!" I announced approaching the gate, Bellamy followed closely behind me. The wrought iron gate swung open, inviting me to enter. Oh, magic! I was beyond happy, my heart overflowing with joy. After living without it for so long, having magic back in my life was stepping into a fantasy novel. I adored my husband and my immortal family, but living with magic was truly living.

The front door burst open with a joyful creak, as if it too were excited for my return. I stepped inside, calling out, "I'm back!" The warm aroma of cinnamon filled the home. Bellamy noticed me taking in the familiar sights and scents, and with a tender smile. "She missed you..., but not as much as I have." I wrapped my arm around his handsome frame, feeling a deep sense of belonging and comfort in his embrace.

I hastily explored every nook of my home, taking in the familiar treasures, old pictures of my past lives lining the hallway, the antique teapot collection in the kitchen, and Salvadore Dali's art adorning the manor walls. The conservatory was a lush oasis, filled with fresh herbs and vibrant flowers. Everything was exactly as I had left it, frozen in time.

I sprinted up to the third floor, where our bedroom awaited. Impeccably arranged like a show house, but it wasn't a show house, it was all mine. Before heading back downstairs, I leapt onto my oversized bed, sinking into its comforting embrace. The mattress at my mom's house was nothing compared to my bed in Casimira. Sleeping on it was like floating on a cloud. I knew I would sleep well tonight.

At that moment, it finally hit me, I was leaving my life behind in NYC. A pang of sadness struck me, knowing I'd miss my mom, but I was happy for her new relationship, and I knew we'd stay in touch. Most of my past lives when Bellamy would find me again, I would keep in touch with my family from that life, except for when I grew up in an orphanage.

As I left the bedroom, I spotted Bellamy emerging from our playroom and quickly closing the door behind him. "What were you up to in there?" I asked, curiosity piqued. He flashed a sly smile, "I have a surprise for you later." I smiled, anticipating something naughty, and quickly made my way downstairs before Bellamy could change his mind.

He playfully spanked my ass as I passed by. *God, I missed him.* No one in this life had done that before, and it felt exhilarating to have him as my Dominant, knowing he could bring out this side of me.

As we reached the bottom of the stairs, a knock at the door broke the silence. Bellamy and I walked together to answer it, and when I opened the door, Miss Poppet stood before us, beaming with a warm smile and an elephant ear.

I gave her a big hug. "Welcome back, my dear! I've missed you so much!" I couldn't fully grasp her emotions, but I knew I had missed her too, despite only remembering her today. It was a strange, disorienting feeling, adapting to this life, where memories and emotions blurred the lines between past and present.

After a brief visit, Miss Poppet returned to her bakeshop in the town square. As I followed her out the front door, I gazed through the trees and noticed some performers and crew members returning home after a long day at the circus. Suddenly, I remembered that I needed to say goodbye to my mom before leaving with the circus.

Bellamy, as if reading my mind, said softly, "Go ahead, I'll close up the circus. When you return, we can jump." I nodded in appreciation and hastily headed towards the door. Just as I was about to depart, Bellamy's strong hand grasped my arm, pulling me back into his embrace. "Please hurry baby girl, I don't want to miss you a second more."

As the sole wielder of magical powers, Bellamy would conjure his extraordinary abilities to transport us through time and space, effortlessly 'jumping' us from one town to the next. With a flick of his wrist and a surge of mystical energy, we would vanish into thin air, only to reappear in a new location, ready to mesmerize audiences with our enchanting wonders. Our travels were a symphony of magic and mystery, as Bellamy's powers propelled us forward, leaving a trail of awe and wonder in our wake.

When I re-emerged at the circus, I noticed that most of the guests and performers had departed, leaving only the crew and a single tent still buzzing with activity for the finale performance. Just as I reached the exit gate, Eve rushed over to me, looking stunning in a shimmering outfit and perfectly applied makeup.

It was hard to believe that just this morning, she was a complete stranger to me. The whirlwind of emotions was always overwhelming and I'm not sure I'll ever get used to it. "Where are you going?" Concern etched on her face. I paused and replied, "I'm going to say goodbye to my mom. Don't worry, I'll be back." She nodded understandingly, and I headed out of the circus gate.

Exiting the circus was like being slapped in the face by a wave of hot, humid air. The sticky warmth enveloped me, making my skin prickle with sweat. Luckily, I didn't have far to walk, or the oppressive heat might have been overwhelming.

As I crossed Riverside Drive, I couldn't help but gaze back at the circus, my heart still aglow with wonder. It was surreal to think that this circus, full of magic and marvels, was here for me. I felt a deep sense of enchantment and gratitude. With a thoughtful sigh, I stepped into my apartment building, my mind practicing the conversation I would have with my mother.

My mom sat alone on the couch, watching the Andy Griffith Show. As I entered, she asked, "How was the circus?" Knowing exactly that's where I had spent the day. I tried to contain my excitement, saying, "It was amazing," before finally asking, "Can we talk?"

She turned off the TV and asked, "What's going on?" I took a seat and began to explain, "I got a job." I paused, and she smiled, prompting me to continue. "I'll be traveling with the circus; they hired me." My mom looked flabbergasted. "What do you mean? What will you do in a circus?" I hesitated, collecting my thoughts before further explaining my new role.

Just as I was about to reveal more about my plan, a knock at the door interrupted us. Before I could say another word, my mom got up to answer it. For a brief moment, I wondered if it might be Bellamy, but to my surprise, it was Gary standing in the doorway. My heart sank as my mom welcomed him in, oblivious to the turmoil brewing inside me.

"What are you doing here?" I asked him, my tone laced with annoyance at his unexpected visit, especially after our breakup earlier. My mom looked perplexed by my question and turned to me, "Did you tell him you're joining the circus?" I nodded, and before I could respond further, Gary interjected, "Did she tell you about her new boyfriend, too?" His words hung in the air, and I could sense my mom's confusion deepening.

The two of them stood staring at me, awaiting answers. "Why don't you take a seat?" I suggested to my mom, but they both sat down, their eyes fixed on me. I took a deep breath and continued, "I'm joining the circus, and we leave tonight, so I just came to say goodbye." I could sense their shock and confusion.

I knew I couldn't reveal the truth about my reincarnation or the immortal circus. They would think I was crazy and have me committed to a mental hospital. So, I opted for a more believable explanation. "I was at the circus earlier today, and they were holding auditions. They hired me on the spot," I said, trying to sound convincing. It was a lie, but it could have happened, maybe. *I hoped they would believe it.*

"Well, I knew you were too good for this city." My mom said, her words surprising me with their warmth and encouragement. It was a rare display of support from her, and I felt a weight lift off of my shoulders.

She continued, "I am proud of you, Nicole. I know you are going to do great things in this world." Gary 's reaction was utter bewilderment; he sat there, speechless, his eyes wide with confusion. I hugged my mom tightly, savoring this moment of acceptance and pride.

Quickly, my mom began packing a bag for me, pulling out her fancy suitcase to carefully pack my clothing. I didn't have the heart to tell her that I wouldn't need any of it, so I let her continue, filling the suitcase with my belongings. I could sense her excitement for me, but also her sadness at my leaving. I reassured her repeatedly, "I'll keep in touch, Mom. I promise." She smiled, trying to hide her tears. I hugged her again, taking my time, knowing that this goodbye was different from any other.

Gary decided to walk me out, but we hadn't spoken much, and I didn't really want to talk to him. I just wanted to quickly get back to the circus. He insisted on carrying my suitcase, but once we were on the street, I reached for it. "No, I got it," he said.

I wanted him to leave. I didn't want him to walk me to the circus, knowing that no one could enter once we were ready to jump. "I'll walk you over there," He insisted, and so we crossed the street to the circus front gate.

I reached for my case again, and this time, he handed it over. "Thank you," I said, but before I could enter, he grabbed my arm, halting my step. "I don't want you to go; you belong here."

I offered Gary a gentle smile and said, 'I wish you all the best in your life.' But my words seemed to fall flat, and his expression darkened with anger. He tightened his grip on my arm, his fingers digging in possessively.

'You're just going to leave?' he growled, his voice low and accusatory. When I nodded, he snatched my suitcase back, his eyes flashing with desperation. 'Stay, please,' he begged, his voice cracking. 'Let's talk about this. Don't just walk away."

"Gary, I need to go; they're waiting for me," trying to reason with him. But he rolled his eyes and sneered, "You only got this job because that guy just wants to sleep with you!" I didn't get angry, but I was annoyed and done explaining.

"Let go," I said in a firm voice, but Gary, using his strength, held on tight to my suitcase. Then I remembered that I didn't even need anything in my suitcase anyway, so I let it go and walked through the circus gate. Leaving Gary with his mouth hanging open in shock.

The circus was empty now, everyone had departed, and I walked towards the weeping willow tree. In the distance, I heard Gary 's voice behind me and I suddenly stopped. "You can't be in here!" I said, irritated. Gary retorted, "Noone is even here, looks like they didn't wait for you."

He gazed around admiring the empty circus. "Maybe they'll hire me too." He said. *Fat chance!* He was so arrogant, acting like he could simply work here? I turned back, trying to escort him outside the gate, but he was defiant.

Just then, Velar appeared startling both of us. "What's going on here?" he asked in a firm authoritative voice. Velar hid his fangs from Gary, and I felt a bit of relief seeing that he was there to intervene.

"None of your business," Gary snapped at Velar. Without wasting any time Velar simply looked him straight in the eyes, locking him into a trance. "It's time for you to leave now," he commanded as he slowly took the suitcase out of Gary's hand.

I realized that Velar was using his mind control powers on Gary. Without saying another word, he turned and walked out of the circus. I remained silent until he was out of sight.

"Are you ready Nic?" Velar asked, smiling with his fangs showing. "I'm ready!" I replied, and the two of us headed home.

CHAPTER
THREE

When we returned to Jubilee, Bellamy had transformed the enchanted sky to a breathtaking nighttime canvas, with stars shining brightly above. "I'm so happy you are back." Velar said, his emerald eyes locking onto mine as he paused mid-step. "It feels terribly different when you aren't here." I sensed a deep longing in his words, a desire to connect beyond surface-level pleasantries.

I retraced my steps towards him, feeling an inexplicable pull towards him, he is one of my oldest and closest friends. When I was close enough, I looked up to meet his gaze and said, "I can't imagine honestly."

Velar's gaze held mine, his expression softening. "So, you and Bellamy are still so in love... after every lifetime." I waited for the punchline, but it never came. *Was he asking me or telling me?* I smiled, "Yes, I love him just as I always have."

Velar's response was a warm smile, his fangs gleaming in the light. "It's a beautiful thing." I took his arm, and we continued our walk. As we strolled back to Casmira, I admired the celestial display. Through the trees, I saw the lights of my home glowing, indicating a warm welcome from my closest friends inside.

Pausing at the front gate, I gathered myself together. Velar noticed my hesitation and said, 'Eighteen years has been too long without you.' I struggled to comprehend the passage of time, my mind reeling as it often did since returning to this life. We stood at the gate until I was ready, and then it magically swung open.

'Come on, you got this,' he encouraged, nudging me forward. A fierce gust of wind from Velar's direction caught me off guard, sending me stumbling forward as I fought to regain my balance. Meanwhile, he darted ahead with a swift sprint, no doubt to announce my arrival to everyone.

I walked at my usual pace up to the front door and, upon opening it, was greeted by my closest friends, all beaming with joy. As the wine flowed, their cheers of 'Nicole!' echoed through the room, warm and jubilant. I smiled, humbled by the outpouring of love, as I made my way through the crowd, embracing each dear friend in turn.

Bellamy rushed to my side, noticing the crowd surrounding me, and quickly took my hand, 'Time to jump!' Bellamy exclaimed, his eyes sparkling with excitement. He took my hand, and together we stepped outside onto the wraparound porch. With a sweep of his arms towards the sky, a vibrant energy pulsed through the air, felt by all. And within seconds, Darlington Circus vanished from NYC, transported to a new and wondrous location elsewhere in the world. Cheers erupted from inside the house.

Afterwards, Bellamy led me to the kitchen where a glass of wine awaited me. Eve and Anise approached, their faces beaming with excitement. "We have so much to catch up on!" Anise exclaimed, and I knew she was right. But before the conversation could begin, Bellamy intervened, sensing my overwhelm. "In time," he said with a gentle smile. The truth was, "overwhelming" didn't even begin to describe the sensation of being bombarded with questions and eager faces.

I was thrilled to see everyone again, but my mind reeled from the sudden onslaught of attention. Everyone wanted to know about my current life - who I was, how I liked NYC, and more. Bellamy seemed to read my thoughts and began expertly escorting everyone out of the house, giving me the reprieve I so desperately needed.

When the last person bid me farewell, I was left with my closest companions - Bellamy, Eve, and Velar. Together, the four of us had always been the driving force behind the Circus and Jubilee. Now that I was back, I couldn't wait to dive in again and be an aerialist, maybe even try something new this time around. My new life was full of endless possibilities, and I felt a sense of excitement and renewal.

We settled into the cozy living room, the crackling fire casting a warm glow on our faces. Velar, Bellamy, Eve, and I had spent the evening catching up, sharing stories and laughter. Eve and I sipped on our favorite vintage, while the men indulged in fine scotch. Casmira's magic ensured that our glasses were always full, refilling after each sip I took. I had never been this drunk before, in this life anyway, and my friends found it absolutely hilarious to watch as I slurred my words.

Velar and Eve couldn't contain their laughter, joking that I was a "lightweight." Velar's guffaws filled the air, while Eve playfully suggested "We need to get you drunk more often!" But Bellamy stepped in, calming the situation with a gentle

"Now, now, play nice." He sat beside me, making sure I was steady, and eventually offered me a special potion to help me sober up.

As the night wore on, our conversations grew more animated, our jokes more ridiculous. After the magical drink I was feeling like myself again and could enjoy the conversations. But then, the mood shifted, and we found ourselves reminiscing about the past.

'Do you remember being murdered?' Eve asked, her eyes sparkling with curiosity. I nodded tentatively, my mind still foggy, but Bellamy recounted the story again to help jog my memory.

"Walt was his name. He had always been fascinated by the circus and desperately wanted to join. He would constantly show up, trying to impress us with his skills. But I of course had to keep sending him away, I couldn't take the chance of him finding out our secret."

We listened intently to Bellamy's words. He continued, "His obsession grew, and one day, he followed you when you left the circus and entered the mortal world. Driven by anger and resentment towards me, he killed you, Nic. He took your life because I denied him the one thing he wanted most, to be part of our circus." Bellamy said, sounding defeated.

"But we caught him," Velar said, his voice firm. 'We made sure he paid for what he did.' I nodded, a sense of closure washing over me.

'Yes, you did. And I'm grateful for that.' Bellamy said to Velar. I felt a shiver run down my spine, but it wasn't fear - it was relief. Relief that my friends had avenged my death, and that I was back now. 'Thank you,' I said. 'Thank you for taking care of me, even in death.'

Before anyone could say a word, Bellamy declared, 'This is exactly why we need a new rule.' I playfully rolled my eyes, knowing my husband's love for rules. 'From now on,' he continued, 'you're not to leave the circus unless you're accompanied by someone I approve of.' I nodded in agreement, thinking it was an easy enough rule to follow, especially since I had no desire to leave Jubilee or the circus anyway.

As the night wore on, Bellamy's subtle maneuvers became more pronounced. With a subtle nod, Bellamy dismissed Eve and Velar, his intentions clear. He wanted me all to himself.

With a discreet smile, he ushered them out the door, and before I knew it, we were alone, the silence between us thick with anticipation. Eighteen years had passed since I last saw my love, and I knew he had been eagerly awaiting my return. I was well aware of his desires, but I chose to wait for him to say the word.

With a gentle yet fiery touch, he grasped my chin, tilting my face upwards, and claimed my lips with a passionate kiss. As our mouths entwined, his magic surged through me, setting my soul ablaze and making every cell in my body hum with delight.

"I need you baby girl," he said as gently pulled away. I smiled knowingly. He pulled me up the stairs, hand in hand. I expected him to lead me to the playroom, but instead, he guided me into our bedroom. Noticing my surprise he teased, 'In due time, my love. For now, I want you in our bed,' his words dripping with desire.

I was eager and impatient to make love with Bellamy. Every time we reunited, our connection only grew stronger. Each intimate encounter fueled our passion, leaving me feeling more deeply connected to him than ever before.

As I stood beside our bed, Bellamy flicked his wrist, and in an instant, my clothes fluttered to the floor, leaving me standing in only my lace bra and panties. He strode towards me with a wicked grin, his own clothes vanishing off of his skin, so that by the time he reached me, he was completely naked. I gazed in awe at his chiseled, hard body. My eyes roaming over his perfect massive form as he drew closer to me.

He swept me up in his arms and gently laid me on the bed, his movements swift and passionate. He then quickly positioned himself above me, his body pressing down on mine in a gentle yet intimate embrace. As he began to kiss me softly, his weight on me sparked a thrill of arousal, and I felt my desire for him grow with each tender touch.

Slowly he traversed my body, his lips and tongue leaving a trail of kisses and gentle licks in their wake. He was like a wild animal tasting and teasing its prey. As Bellamy's fingers traced gentle patterns on my skin, I felt a deep sense of connection and trust.

His fingers found me, and he inserted them slowly being very gentle. I moaned and he whispered with warmth and affection, "Good girl." My heart raced with excitement, and I wanted him. He must have read my mind, or he also wanted the same thing because he swiftly mounted on top of me.

With a tender touch, he reached out and brushed a strand of hair behind my ear, his eyes locked on mine with a loving gaze. The air was filled with a sweet sense of intimacy, and I felt my soul stirring with emotion. As my eyes were locked onto his seductive blue eyes, he pushed himself inside me.

My breath escaped me in a soft whoosh, leaving my mouth agape. He paused briefly and I watched as his enchanting aura spiraled around him and I felt the magic vibrating inside my entire body. Every breath felt like a sigh of contentment, and every moment felt like a surrender to pure bliss. A sense of euphoria that was both exhilarating and surreal.

How could I ever forget how amazing our sex was? Bellamy's love was a slow-burning fire that consumed me, body and soul. He took his time, exploring every inch of me, and made love to me with a tenderness that left me weak. Every touch was a declaration of his devotion. He was gentle, yet passionate, and I felt like I was melting into every position he put me in.

Our sex life was always exhilarating. I savored every moment of our intimate connection, knowing that soon Bellamy would want to spice things up and explore my desires and boundaries in the playroom. I was thrilled to see where our passion would take us next. Reaching new limits each lifetime.

In a whirlwind of ecstasy, I reached climax after climax, each one surpassing the previous in intensity and bliss. Just when I thought it couldn't possibly get any better, Bellamy would take me to new heights, pushing my mortal body to its max and I would willingly surrender. And when I could take no more, he gently laid me down to rest, my body and soul satiated. He left me slipping into a deep and dreamless sleep.

The next morning, I woke up feeling dreamy and disoriented, still basking in the afterglow of our wonderful night together. It took me a moment to shake off the sleep and fully awaken. It wasn't a surprise Bellamy wasn't next to me, he was always busy doing something.

A fresh cup of coffee appeared on the bedside table. "Thank you, Casmira," I said before I took my first sip. I savored the delicious smooth taste and quickly realized that it was charmed. In seconds I was out of bed full of energy and ready to start the day.

I wrapped myself in my plush robe and descended the stairs, the aroma of freshly baked pastries wafted through the air, teasing my senses and stirring my appetite. I was eager to indulge in the culinary delights that awaited me. But my stomach's growl was silenced by the sound of the front door opening, and I turned to see Bellamy walk inside, his body glistening with droplets of water from his morning swim in the Opal Sea.

He was a remarkable sight, his dark hair slicked back, revealing the chiseled features of his face. With just a towel wrapped around his waist leaving little to the imagination, he flashed me a radiant smile.

Despite being bound to this enigmatic man for centuries, his presence still had the power to unravel me. Every glance, every whisper, every gentle touch sent shivers coursing through my veins. The butterflies in my stomach danced with reckless abandon.

Without a care for his wet state, he enveloped me in a passionate embrace, burying his face in my neck and inhaling deeply. The scent of the sea on his skin was intoxicating, and I felt my senses come alive as I breathed it in.

"Good morning, my dear," he whispered. "I'm so thrilled you're back. "The mere sound of his British accent was enough to send me into a delightful tailspin. The smooth, velvety voice left me weak in the knees and utterly bewitched.

'Let's start the day together,' he whispered, his warm breath dancing across my ear. 'We have so much to catch up on, and I want to savor every moment with you.' His words were like honey.

I nodded eagerly, my heart racing with excitement. He took my hand, his fingers intertwined with mine, and led me to the kitchen, the scent of freshly brewed coffee and chocolate croissants filling our noses.

"Ah, perfect timing," Bellamy said with a chuckle, as he pulled out a chair for me at the table. "I had the chef prepare your favorite breakfast." I laughed as I sat down at the table ready to devour the most delicious croissant in the world. Knowing the chef he was referring to was just Casmira's magic.

After I finished my breakfast, Bellamy revealed, "I have a surprise for you!" I was intrigued because I absolutely love surprises. I hastily rose from my seat, eager to get ready. However, Bellamy's gentle grasp on my hand halted me in my tracks, and he inquired with a playful smile, "Where do you think you're going?"

I instinctively knew his desire and paused, turning to face him. With a flick of his wrist, Bellamy's magic vibrated through me, adorning me in a stunning black and white dress that mirrored the circus tents I had designed years ago. The fabric seemed to shimmer and swirl around me, as if infused with the essence of the big top.

Next, Bellamy's magic danced through my brown hair, releasing it from its confines and crafting soft, bouncy curls that framed my face. I felt transformed. "Shall we?" Bellamy asked, offering his arm with a gallant smile. I accepted, and together we stepped into the radiant sunlight, ready to embrace the wonders of my first full day back home.

We stepped out of Casmira into a beautiful day. The sun shone brightly, and the temperature was a perfect seventy degrees. I couldn't help but notice the extra sparkle in the air, which I knew was due to Bellamy's joy at my return. As we made our way through the tree clearing, I saw Jubilee in all its vibrant glory. The town square was bustling with performers and crew members scurrying about.

"Isn't the circus opening today?" I asked, realizing everyone should be at the circus already. Bellamy smiled and said, "No baby, Today, we'll relax and get ready for tonight." I had almost forgotten about the ritual, but Bellamy's casual mention of it made me remember. I knew he was aware of my discomfort with the tradition, which made his nonchalant reference to it understandable.

Samsara was a ritual we performed every time I returned, a ritual that allowed me to reincarnate every time I died. A knot formed in my stomach as I realized that soon I would once again be having sex in front of everyone in Jubilee.

I forced a smile to hide my unease, but Bellamy read my expression and quickly reassured me, 'You'll be fine,' his voice calm. I nodded, trying to believe him. I had done the Samsara ritual many times before, but I still hated it. The memories of my previous experiences were hazy, but I remembered the intensity, the rush of emotions, and the transformative power of the ritual.

Just as I was soaking up the vibrant atmosphere, Clove approached us with Orlow, my beloved pet elephant, by his side. My excitement overflowed, and I couldn't help but jump up and down, eager to greet them.

The magnificent beast, a beautiful African elephant, we had saved years ago from a horrible circus that was cruel to their animals. That is the reason he only has one of his tusks. As he approached me, he instantly picked me up with his trunk and lifted me high into the air. I petted and hugged him, feeling a deep affection for this gentle giant.

As Clove handed something to Bellamy, he nodded in thanks. But before I could wonder what was being exchanged, Bellmay turned to me with a mischievous glint in his eye. 'Ready to explore Jubilee?' He asked. I knew exactly what he meant. My heart swelled as I stepped closer to the majestic elephant, his trunk curling around me like a gentle embrace.

With a graceful lift, he hoisted me onto his back, and I settled in, hiking up my dress to straddle him comfortably. Bellamy followed suit and settled in behind me. With a soft rumble, Orlow began to move, his gait smooth and rhythmic, carrying us into the heart of Jubilee.

As we rode through the town square on Orlow's back, we were greeted by a sea of smiling faces. Everyone waved or called out a warm welcome, and I felt a sense of joy and belonging wash over me. 'Mrs. Darlington!' I heard repeatedly, the name echoing through the square. It was a bit strange to hear my name once again, I have been so used to Nicole Sullivan from this lifetime.

Bellamy smiled and waved alongside me, his eyes shining with happiness as we made our way through the crowd. Orlow, sensing our pleasure, moved with a gentle grace, his trunk swaying in time with the cheers and greetings. He was proud to be carrying me, his steady stride and raised head exuding a quiet confidence.

After the town square, we made our way to the gardens, where Bellamy picked me some beautiful flowers, his hand outstretched. The people working in the gardens came to welcome us and Orlow, and they fed him some fresh hay and juicy apples, which he eagerly devoured.

As we bid farewell to the gardeners, we meandered towards the town homes nestled east of the town square. Eve emerged from her cozy abode, her eyes sparkling with warmth as she greeted us. Our conversation was brief, however, as she was bound for a rehearsal with a group of fellow performers. I watched her hurry off, her enthusiasm infectious, and felt my own excitement stir. The thrill of aerialist performance beckoned me once more, and I couldn't wait to soar through the air again.

As we arrived at the Opal Sea, Orlow came to a gentle stop, and Bellamy and I dismounted, eager to explore the shimmering waters. We led Orlow to a shady thicket, where he settled in, contentedly swishing his trunk.

Meanwhile, Bellamy and I wandered towards the sea's edge. I kicked off my shoe and hiked up my dress, the warm sand squishing between my toes and stepped into the water, instantly feeling the tingling sensation of magic. I couldn't stop smiling.

Bellamy glanced around, ensuring we were alone, and with a mischievous flick of his wrist, my clothes vanished. I gasped, covering myself, and exclaimed, 'Daddy!' Bellamy's chuckles echoed through the air as he admired my form. Even Orlow turned his head, embarrassed.

Finally, once Bellamy's laughter subsided, he dressed me in a sleek thong bikini, a choice I wouldn't have made for myself, but I was happy to see Bellamy enjoying himself. Pleasing him brought me joy, even if the outfit wasn't my usual style. With a playful sigh, I surrendered to Bellamy's mischief, knowing resistance was futile.

As I waded deep into the Opal Sea, the warm water enveloped me like a silken embrace, and I let go of all remaining hesitation. As I floated effortlessly, the water supporting me with gentle buoyancy, I felt a sea nymph's freedom.

My hair flowed like seaweed, and my skin shimmered with a soft, pearlescent glow. I closed my eyes, allowing the water's soothing melody to lull me into a state of serenity. With my eyes closed I felt Bellamy's hands brush against mine, and I smiled, knowing he was beside me, sharing in the magic of this world.

As we floated in the Opal Sea, Bellamy's gaze ignited a fire within me. His eyes burned with a passion that seared my skin, making my heart race and my senses tingle. I felt the weight of his desire, the air thick with tension as our bodies seemed to gravitate towards each other. I knew what he wanted, it was the same thing I craved - his touch, his love, his everything.

We drifted closer, our bodies swaying to the rhythm of the waves. Bellamy's lips met mine, his kiss gentle yet passionate, like the ebb and flow of the tide. I felt myself melting into him, our love merging like the sea and sky at the horizon. The water cradled us, a soothing embrace, as we lost ourselves in each other's arms.

When we emerged from the Opal Sea, Bellamy took my hand, and we strolled along the shore, the warm sand beneath our feet. The sun began to set, casting a golden glow across the enchanted sky. Bellamy wrapped his arms around me, pulling me close. "I love you," my voice barely audible over the sound of the waves. "I love you too," Bellamy replied, his lips brushing against my ear. "In every way."

Bellamy's words, "I love you in every way," held a deeper meaning, for he had loved me across countless lifetimes. In every reincarnation, he had found me, and his devotion had remained unwavering. I had been older, younger, and everything in between, yet his love had remained constant.

Through every iteration of life, death, and rebirth, his love had endured, a flame that burned bright and true. And in this life, he stood before me, his eyes shining with the love of centuries.

Before we left, I made Bellamy dress me in something other than my bikini. With a flick of his wrist and a playful roll of his eyes, he effortlessly transformed my appearance once again. The sleek thong bikini vanished, replaced by the familiar black and white dress, its fabric rustling softly as it settled on me. The only thing missing was a bra and I knew it was intentional. *Horney scoundrel.*

Bellamy and I mounted Orlow, continuing our journey to the Emberlynn Forest. We rode in comfortable silence, the only sound being Orlow's gentle hum and the soft rustle of leaves beneath his feet. Suddenly, a figure emerged from the forest. Velar, his piercing emerald eyes and muscular build unmistakable even in the fading light.

He walked alongside us, his long strides matching Orlow's pace, as we approached the Blackwood's cottage. The thatched roof and twinkling windows welcomed us. Velar's massive, tattooed arms enveloped me as he helped me down from Orlow's back, his gentle yet firm grasp making the descent feel effortless.

Clove, the youngest Blackwood witch, burst out of the cottage with a joyful energy, a fresh bundle of hay cradled in his arms. "Hey, Orlow. Thatta, boy!" he exclaimed, patting his leathery skin. He fed Orlow some hay, watching as the elephant's eyes lit up with delight. Then, with a gentle pat on the trunk, Clove led Orlow to the cozy barn out back, its massive door adorned with soft lanterns and fragrant with the scent of dried herbs.

As we bid Clove farewell, Velar accompanied us on our stroll back to Casmira. Along the way, the vibrant atmosphere of Samsara preparations unfolded before us. The townspeople scurried about, setting up seating around the stage with eager anticipation.

The knowing grins on the faces of the townspeople, their eyes glinting with excitement, only added to my nerves. A towering woodpile loomed before the stage. My mind started to drift to a past Samsara, when there were just a few townspeople and now it seemed like everyone in Jubilee was going to be there.

Shattering my daydream, I hear, "Are you ready for tonight, Nic?" Velar teased, knowing I was not. Bellamy confidently interjected, "She will be great." His reassuring perfect smile and Velar's nod of encouragement calmed my jitters.

As we returned to Casmira, Eve's timely arrival coincided with ours, and I knew she was there to help me prepare for the ritual. Upon entering the house, the aroma of roasted duck wafted through the air, making my stomach growl. We gathered in the dining room, and each took a seat, three delicious dishes appeared in front of us.

The duck was cooked to perfection, and I savored each bite, losing myself in the flavors. I couldn't get enough roasted potatoes. Eve's playful comment, "Looks like you missed Casmira's cooking," brought me back to the present, and I smiled, feeling grateful for the warmth and camaraderie. Velar's laughter brought my gaze to his blood-stained lips, a stark reminder that his thirst was quenched by a different kind of sustenance. Unlike the rest of us, Velar was presented with his signature crimson beverage, which he promptly devoured in one swift gulp. As soon as he set the glass down, I watched in endless amusement as it miraculously refilled itself.

After dinner, Eve and I retreated upstairs, our wine goblets in hand, to prepare for the ritual. Bellamy's gentle kiss on my forehead lingered. I knew that the next time I would lay eyes on him would be at the altar, surrounded by the trappings of the ritual. I felt a bit excited when I remembered that Bellamy had left a special outfit for me to wear tonight.

As I entered my bedroom, I saw a stunning black outfit laid out for me. The black lingerie was exquisite, with intricate lace and delicate straps that were classy and sexy. Bellamy's note accompanied the outfit, his handwriting elegant as always.

Baby girl -I'll be patiently waiting for you at the altar, just as I always have, and I always will, until time loses all meaning. -Daddy

Bellamy's note calmed my frazzled nerves, a poignant reminder of the unyielding love we share. Despite the trials we've faced, our love has remained a constant. As we sat there, sipping our wine, the sound of Bellamy and Velar's departure echoed through the house, signaling that the time was drawing near. I took a deep breath and downed my goblet, hoping the wine would help me forget my mortal nerves.

I slipped into the lingerie, the soft fabric caressing my skin as I admired my reflection in the mirror. I gasped in delight, feeling like a true seductress. The fabric hugged my curves in all the right places, and the matte color seemed to accentuate my pale skin.

Eve launched into a story about my time away, filling me in on all the details I had missed. But my mind wandered, consumed by anxiety and nerves. I couldn't shake off the feeling of unease, despite Eve's attempts to distract me. It was as if she had forgotten that I wasn't like her anymore.

As an eighteen-year-old mortal, I felt the weight of my fragile existence. Despite having lived many lives, I will always unfortunately be mortal. My mind wandered back to all the times

I had died, all the lives I had lived. Eve's story trailed off as she noticed my distant gaze, my mind a thousand miles away.

She gently took my hand, her touch warm and reassuring. "You've got this," her voice soft and encouraging. Just then, the sound of drums echoed through the air, the beat pulsing like a heartbeat. It was time. I felt a surge of adrenaline mixed with fear. I took a deep breath, preparing myself for what was to come.

Together, we walked towards the hills, the drums' insistent rhythm calling to us like a siren's song. Before we reached the clearing, Eve pulled out a black feathered mask and gently turned me around, tying it securely behind my head. The mask seemed to transform me, imbuing me with a sense of power and mystery. Now, I was ready to brave the sea of revelers. As we emerged from the trees, I saw the townspeople of Jubilee gathered before us, their faces eager and expectant. They parted to let us through, their eyes fixed on me.

Eve escorted me to the stage where Bellamy stood tall, his piercing eyes visible behind a black ram horn mask that seemed to hold secrets of its own. Beside him stood the enigmatic Ambrette Blackwood, her presence radiating an aura of mystique and power. As the leader of the ritual, her eyes gleamed with a deep understanding of the ancient arts, and her very being seemed to command respect. The mask that concealed Ambrette's face was a labyrinth of black lace and gleaming silver threads, its beauty both captivating and unsettling.

As the drums slowed their relentless pace, the beats grew more deliberate and ominous. Flames from a giant bonfire grew to life, casting flickering shadows on the surrounding faces. As I gazed out into the crowd, I saw that many of the townspeople had already begun to embrace the ritual's sensual energy.

Some wore lingerie or nothing at all, their bodies swaying to the rhythm of the drums. Others had already succumbed to their desires.

Bellamy pulled me close, taking my hand in his. With a gentle yet confident gesture, he raised our arms towards the sky, and the crowd's enthusiasm ignited like wildfire. Cheers and applause erupted, the air electric with anticipation.

Ambrette's nod was the spark that set the ritual ablaze, and as our arms reached for the heavens, the drums pulsed with renewed fervor, the flames danced higher, and the night itself seemed to vibrate with ancient power.

As I stood in front of the crowd, Bellamy's hands moved with reverence as he gently removed my lingerie. Slowly taking his time for the crowd. *Always a showman.* Once I was standing naked for all to see, Bellamy removed his clothing, leaving only his horned mask to match me.

With ease, he lifted me onto the altar, my body surrendering to the moment. The world narrowed to the warmth of the fire, the beat of the drums. His piercing blue gaze swept across my bare skin, drinking in the sight of me sprawled out on the altar like a sacrifice to the gods. His eyes lingered on the curves of my body, as I lay exposed and vulnerable before him.

His fingers danced across my skin, slowly making his way inside me feeling my wetness. I instinctively parted my legs, inviting him closer. I felt his hardness against me, my body trembling with anticipation. Slowly he pushed himself inside, taking away my breath. I let out a moan and he smiled arrogantly.

He gently turned me onto my hands and knees, positioning himself behind me. As I gazed out at the crowd, I saw a sea of entranced faces, their bodies intertwined in sensual embraces, their lips locked in fervent kisses. The air was filled with passion and desire, and I felt myself becoming one with the ritual.

The drums pulsed through the crowd, bodies swaying in time like a chorus of reckless abandon. I felt Bellamy's warm hands on my skin, his hot breath on my neck, and the world spun around me in a blur of pleasure and excess. The night wore on, and the lines between reality and fantasy blurred, leaving only the thrum of the music and the rush of forbidden delights.

Before I knew it, the ritual had reached its climax, and Bellamy had reached his own, his body shuddering with release as he whispered, "baby girl." I felt his warmth spread through me, leaving him breathless and spent.

As the afterglow dissipated, I hastily wrapped myself in a robe, suddenly aware of the gaze of the crowd upon me. Glancing out into the sea of faces, the ritual had descended into a frenzied orgy, with bodies entwined in every direction. The air was heavy with desire, and the sounds of pleasure.

As we emerged from the ritual, the crowd cheered. Bellamy turned to Ambrette, his eyes shining with gratitude, and said his thanks, a gesture he repeated every time we performed the ritual. Ambrette nodded and Mesidor walked up to help his wife off of the stage.

I felt a wave of relief wash over me, knowing that the ordeal was finally behind me. And yet, even as I basked in the glow of completion. I would return, reincarnated and reborn, my soul bound to this cycle, forever entwined with the fate of my beloved immortal family.

Bellamy and I slipped through the crowd, our bodies weaving together as we made our escape into the night. The revelers parted like a sea, their faces flushed with pleasure and their eyes gleaming with a wild, untamed energy.

We didn't look back, our hearts pounding as we vanished into the darkness, bound for the sanctuary of Casmira. As we disappeared from view, I raised my hand in a silent farewell, the gesture mirrored by Bellamy. The crowd surged forward, their cheers and laughter echoing through the night air as they continued their uninhibited celebration.

When we arrived home, the sounds of the ritual still lingered in the air. Bellamy led me to the playroom, his eyes sparkling with excitement. 'Are you ready for your surprise?' he asked, his voice full of anticipation. I nodded eagerly, my curiosity piqued. Inside the room, a mysterious box sat on the bed, waiting to be opened. I approached it with a mix of excitement and nerves, wondering what Bellamy had in store for me.

I opened the box slowly to reveal a cordless massager, the latest craze. I saw this sex toy advertised in one of my mother's magazines. I felt my face instantly blush. Bellamy's fingers wrapped around mine, his touch warm and reassuring as he gently took the toy from my trembling hands.

His voice was low and soothing, a gentle command that sent shivers down my spine. 'Lie down,' he whispered, his breath caressing my ear. I obeyed, my body surrendering to his guidance as I reclined on the soft surface, my heart racing with anticipation.

Oh, dear God! I've never experienced such intense pleasure in my life. I had no idea it could be this incredible. My moans grew louder teetering on the edge of screams of ecstasy. Bellamy expertly positions the massager, and I pleaded with him to continue, my body craving more. My orgasm was a tidal wave of pure bliss. *Best invention ever!*

CHAPTER
FOUR

The next day, I awoke to the savory aromas of sizzling meats and freshly baked bread wafting from the kitchen, signaling a grand feast in Jubilee. The air was filled with the tantalizing smells of roasting vegetables, herbs, and spices, teasing my senses.

The day after the Samsara Ritual, we gathered outside in the lush meadow next to Casmira to celebrate my rebirth. Soon long tables will be stretched across the green, laden with an endless array of dishes that Casmira had prepared for the entire town of Jubilee.

As I lay there, I heard the sound of footsteps and muffled voices coming from below me. Downstairs, I heard Velar and Eve's infectious laughter echoing through the manor. I turned to rouse Bellamy, but he was already up and out of bed.

Before heading downstairs, I stepped out my French doors onto my balcony and breathed in the crisp morning air. As I gazed out through the trees, I could see the townspeople stirring to life. The sun cast a warm glow over the scene, illuminating the misty vapor rising from the rooftops and the gentle bustle of activity in the square. It was as if the whole town was slowly awakening from a peaceful slumber, and I felt connected to this vibrant community.

As I descended the stairs, Bellamy greeted me at the bottom with a big smile and a warm mug of black coffee. "Good morning, my beautiful girl," he said. I returned his smile and took his offered arm as he escorted me into the kitchen. Velar and Eve were sitting at the table, their mischievous grins hinting at memories of the previous night's escapade. "Good morning," I said, taking in the cozy scene and the tantalizing aromas of freshly baked pastries.

"Are you ready for the day?" Eve asked, her eyes sparkling with excitement. I nodded eagerly, my stomach growling in anticipation. "Of course! A giant feast just for me!" Velar laughed, but the truth was I couldn't wait to indulge in Casmira's culinary delights. The magical food was always a treat, and I loved to eat my fill.

After I finished my coffee, Bellamy instructed. "Time to get ready, I've picked out your outfit. It's waiting for you." With that, Eve and I dashed up the stairs. As I entered my room, my eyes landed on a stunning brand-new red dress, hanging in midair.

The sight of it brought back memories of a few months ago, when I had spotted it in Bloomingdales while shopping with my mom. I had fallen in love with its beautiful sexy shade and intricate details but the price tag made me say fuhgeddaboudit. Yet, here it was, mine to wear.

"Bellamy just had to get it for you," Eve's voice filled with a knowing smile as she stood behind me. I realized that Bellamy had been watching and observing my life for a while now, studying me as I navigated my way through this new life. It was as if he had been waiting for the perfect moment to reveal this special gift, and now that it was here, I felt a sense of gratitude.

Once I was ready, I descended the stairs in my stunning new red dress. Bellamy welcomed me with a warm smile and exclaimed, "Always stunning!" I smiled back feeling his compliment. Bellamy took my hand to escort me out of the house. "I'm utterly spellbound by you every day." His words made me blush.

As we emerged from Casmira, the four of us stepped into a sea of expectant faces. The gathered guests parted, allowing us to take our designated positions. Bellamy and I sat at the head of a beautifully adorned table, our eyes locking in a silent understanding as we faced each other from opposite ends. Velar and Eve, meanwhile, took their places at the other tables, their presence radiating an air of quiet confidence.

Bellamy rose to his feet, his eyes aglow with warmth and gratitude. His voice, filled with emotion, captivated the attention of all. 'Thank you, dear friends, for joining us in this joyous celebration,' his words dripped with sincerity. 'Last night, the ritual was a resounding success, and my darling wife, Nicole, will reincarnate once again. He paused, his gaze sweeping to mine, before concluding with a triumphant flourish, 'To Nicole, I will always find you and bring you home.' The assembly erupted into a chorus of cheers and applause

As he finished, the windows of Casmira burst open, and a flurry of dishes, plates, silverware, and napkins flew out, carefully placing themselves in front of each guest. The tables were soon piled high with an array of delectable dishes. With eager anticipation, everyone dug into the feast.

As I engaged in conversation with the people sitting at my end of the table, I found myself nestled between two of the most talented contortionists, Millicent to my right and Eudora to my left. We chatted about their acts, and I was fascinated to hear about the new performances they had added since I last saw them perform.

Further down the table, the Bally twins, Pixie and Poppy, waved at me with infectious enthusiasm. We call them the giggle mugs. Those sweet smiling girls were always up to something mischievous, and I couldn't help but smile as I wondered if they had planned any surprises for today.

Henry and Anise sat further down, and it was heartwarming to see them together. It was clear that their friendship had blossomed into something more. It made my heart swell with happiness. I remember when they first met. Anise had been working at the circus, and Velar brought Henry, who is also a vampire, here for sanctuary. Anise lives in a townhome next to Eve, while Henry resides in the Emberlynn Forest not far from the Blackwood's cottage.

After I was stuffed full of the delicious food, I sat back and listened to the stories and camaraderie between my immortal friends. They had shared tales of the circus acts, the places they had been, and all the excitement I had missed. From death-defying acrobatic feats to mesmerizing illusions, they recaptured the thrill of their performances. They spoke of the mystical creatures they had encountered in the forest, and the magical experiences they had.

As we shared stories, I couldn't help but think about the circus and its secrets. The immortals, our hidden world, magic, and the tales of experiences all swirled together in my mind. Bellamy's voice echoed through the sky through invisible speakers, causing us to stop talking. He thanked everyone and announced that we would be opening the circus tomorrow. I couldn't wait, it would be my first day back and I was ready.

A buzz of excitement rippled through the group as we all started chattering about the upcoming acts and performances. As the night wore on, we all began to disperse, eager to get some rest before the big day ahead. I gazed up at the starry sky, feeling a sense of anticipation. Tomorrow, the circus will come alive, and I will be a part of it once again.

As most of the crowd dispersed, Anise, Eve and I walked towards the front steps of Casmira. Bellamy jumped us to a new destination somewhere in the world and I felt the familiar vibration coursing through the air as we settled wherever we had landed.

Our conversation was shattered by a deafening KABOOM! A sudden, jarring explosion erupted, its deafening blast thundering above us like a clap of doom. The sound was so intense that it seemed to shake the very foundations of our existence, yet its source remained eerily, ominously invisible.

The sound seemed to emanate from everywhere and nowhere at once, leaving us bewildered and disoriented. We scanned the darkness, our eyes straining to pinpoint the origin of the disturbance, but whatever it was, was hidden from our sight.

I immediately turned to Bellamy, expecting answers, but his expression was just as perplexed as the rest of us. The air was thick with tension as we stood there, frozen, listening, waiting for some indication of what was happening. Bellamy's voice broke the silence, his tone firm and commanding. "Henry, Velar, come with me to check on the circus." Briar stepped forward, volunteering to join the group and we watched as they headed towards the entrance.

I invited Eve and Anise inside to wait for their return. *What was happening? What had caused that unearthly noise?* I couldn't shake off the feeling that something was wrong.

The three of us sat down in the cozy living room. A warm glow spread through the air as a fire crackled to life, casting a golden light on the surroundings. The flames danced and flickered, warmth that seemed to embrace everything in their vicinity. I knew Casmira had read my mind and was trying to help settle all of our nerves. I kept looking at the door, expecting it to burst open at any moment.

"Shall I pour you some wine or tea, ladies?" I asked, attempting to ease the tension in the air. "What do you think it was?" Anise asked, her brow furrowed in concern. "I've never heard anything like it before," Eve added, with a hint of unease.

I poured two glasses of wine and handed them to Anise and Eve, hoping the gesture would help soothe their minds. "I'm not sure what that was," I admitted, "but I'm sure Bellamy and the others will figure it out. Let's just relax and wait for them to come back."

As the minutes dragged on, my restlessness grew. I began pacing back and forth, my footsteps echoing through the eerie silence. Eve's calm demeanor faltered for a moment as she watched me wear a path on the wood floor.

'It's going to be okay,' she said softly, trying to reassure me. 'We probably just landed somewhere that has construction going on.' Anise's eyes widened with fear, her gaze darting nervously back and forth between Eve and I. Eve placed a comforting hand on her arm. 'They will be back soon,' she said with conviction. 'And I'm sure he'll jump us to a new location.'

I nodded in agreement, but my curiosity got the better of me. 'I'll be back,' I said, already heading towards the door. 'I'm going to wait for them at the entrance.' Anise sprang from her chair, her eyes wide with concern. 'Are you sure?' Her voice was laced with hesitation. Eve's expression turned resolute. 'We'll all go with you.' Anise nodded, and the three of us set off together, our footsteps echoing as we ventured out of Casmira.

The night air was alive with the magic of Jubilee, the stars twinkling like diamonds scattered across the velvet sky. As we wandered through the wooded path, I couldn't help but gaze up in wonder. The trees parted, and the town square came into view, many windows still aglow with soft light. I'm sure they were all waiting to find out what the explosion was all about.

We reached the ancient weeping willow, our portal to the real world. Eve, Anise, and I exchanged a cautious glance before peeking inside. The hollowed trunk was silent, the only sound was our own ragged breathing. We lingered at the base of the spiral stairs listening in stillness.

I began to ascend the spiral stairs, but Eve's grip on my arm halted me abruptly. 'No way,' she said urgently, her eyes wide with concern. I turned back to face her, my voice reassuring. 'I'm just going to take a look.' Eve's expression turned fierce. 'Hell no, Bellamy will kill me if I let you go up there.' I tried to placate her. 'I won't leave the tree, I'm just going to take a peak.

Eve's grip relaxed, and she released my arm, her eyes still filled with worry. I took a deep breath and continued up the spiral stairs. As I ascended, the silence grew thicker, and the air seemed to vibrate with secrets. I reached the top and peered out of the tree's portal.

The vacant circus looked as it always did. I scanned around the circus, not leaving the tree like I promised. I took my time scanning around the familiar circus. I could see most of the grounds, but nothing seemed out of place. Yet, the four men were nowhere to be seen.

'What do you see?' Anise yelled up from the base of the stairs, her voice echoing through the stillness. I peered down at her and Eve, their faces tilted upwards in anticipation. 'Nothing!' I shouted back down, my voice carrying across the deserted circus grounds. The silence seemed to swallow my words whole, leaving only an unsettling stillness in its wake.

I took another sweeping glance over the deserted circus, my eyes straining to detect even the slightest hint of movement. Just as I was about to retreat down the stairs, Anise and Eve reached the top, their faces set with determination. Eve stepped out into the circus, her gaze scanning the empty grounds with a mix of curiosity and trepidation.

Anise and I exchanged a hesitant glance before slowly following her lead. We ventured out cautiously, our footsteps quiet on the cobblestone. We didn't go far from the tree in case we needed a swift retreat.

Eve and Anise urged me to return to the tree, but I refused to leave. We compromised, deciding to approach the circus's front gate together, hoping to find Bellamy, Velar, Henry, and Briar. We moved cautiously, our senses heightened as we stuck close together.

Just as we approached the entrance, a faint, ''Ooooooooooooo'' whisper seemed to caress our ears, carried by an unsettling wind from behind us. We spun around, our hearts racing, as a dark shadow darted through one of the tents with an unnerving swiftness.

We stood frozen, our eyes locked on the tent, before turning to each other with a mix of fear and confusion. 'What was that?' I whispered to Eve, my voice trembling slightly. Anise's eyes were wide with concern as she asked, 'Could it be one of the men?' Eve's gaze lingered on the tent, her expression unreadable, before she replied, 'No, it's not them.'

A moment later, the faint 'Ooooooo-oooo' sound echoed again, sending shivers down our spines. This time, it seemed to come from all directions, and we couldn't pinpoint its origin. All the hair on my body rose as I whispered urgently to the girls, 'Get back to the tree – now.'

We began walking slowly back towards the tree. However, our apprehension quickly turned to fear as another shadowy figure appeared on the canvas, sending my heart racing. It was bigger than before. We froze, our eyes fixed on the spot where the shadow was, then as quickly as it appeared it vanished.

Without a word, we suddenly exploded into a blind, panicked sprint, our legs flailing wildly as we desperately clawed at the air, fleeing from the unseen horror that lurked behind. Our feet pounded the ground in a frantic, stuttering rhythm. We ran with abandon, our breaths coming in short, shrieking gasps, our eyes bulging with sheer terror.

Just as the willow tree's branches came into view, dark silhouettes emerged from the left. We all let out primal, blood-curdling screams, our voices shredding the night air like razor-sharp claws. Anise's terror was so all-consuming that her legs turned to jelly, and she crumpled to the ground. 'It's okay, it's okay!' Eve yelled, her words struggling to penetrate the fog of fear that had consumed us.

As my screams finally subsided, I realized that the shadows were just the men - Bellamy, Velar, Henry, and Briar. A wave of relief washed over me, but it was short-lived. Bellamy's urgent bark, 'Get back to Jubilee, now!' sent us all scrambling. We didn't need to be told twice. Henry swiftly helped Anise to her feet, and we took off in a sprint, our feet pounding the ground in unison.

We didn't dare stop until we reached the safety of Jubilee. Without hesitation, Bellamy raised his arms to the sky to jump us out of here. The vibrations felt distinct this time, like a subtle hum beneath our feet. I watched intently as Bellamy focused all his energy on launching us out of here. His face contorted with effort, he channeled an immense amount of magic, his hands trembling with the strain.

With a radiant burst of energy, he launched us into the unknown, shattering the haunted place's hold on us. But as we broke free, Bellamy's strength faltered, his body crashing to the ground, drained from the colossal magical exertion.

I rushed to Bellamy's side, relief washing over me as I helped him up. Despite knowing he was immortal, I couldn't shake off the concern that had driven me to his aid. His eyes sunken but triumphant, knowing he'd successfully transported us to safety.

Henry and Velar were engaged in a hushed conversation, trying to make sense of the inexplicable phenomenon we had just witnessed. I had lived through many lives, but nothing had ever terrified me as much as what we had just seen. The unknown entity or event had left us all shaken, and I couldn't help but wonder what it was.

Bellamy's reassuring words, 'We're far away from whatever it was,' brought a wave of relief washing over us. I was grateful that we had escaped the haunted place in time. The exhaustion of the day caught up with us, and we knew we had a big day ahead, running the circus. We decided to call it a night, looking forward to a well-deserved rest and a brighter tomorrow.

Briar headed home to his wife Ada, who was probably worried about him, knowing her. Henry walked Anise to her townhouse, while Velar and Eve walked Bellamy and I home to Casmira. Along the way, we chatted incessantly about what could have been, our minds still reeling from the mysterious encounter.

'My magic has never put us in harm's way before. That was quite unusual, I must admit.' Bellamy said. He seemed puzzled and concerned, as if his magic had behaved unpredictably.

"How many shadows did you see?" Eve asked Bellmay and Velar. Bellamy stopped walking abruptly, causing us all to halt.

"Shadows?" he repeated, confusion etched on his face. Velar chimed in, "We didn't see any shadows, but we heard eerie sounds outside the circus."

Bellmay's expression turned worried, and he nodded in agreement. "When we walked outside the circus, I knew we were in a horrible place. I could just feel the bad energy." He said putting his arm around me. "Where did you jump us to?" Velar asked. "I don't know exactly, we were somewhere in the Armenian Highlands of eastern Turkey."

The air was heavy with unease, and although everyone else seemed relieved, Bellamy's expression remained troubled. He simply resumed walking towards Casmira, his eyes fixed on some distant point.

We all trailed behind him, but he seemed lost in his own thoughts, his mind a thousand miles away. When Velar and Eve bid us farewell and headed off into the night, Bellamy didn't even acknowledge their departure, instead he walked inside Casmira. I wished Velar and Eve a good night, my eyes lingering on their receding figures as they disappeared into the woods, wondering what was weighing on Bellamy's mind.

When I went inside, I didn't see Bellamy anywhere. 'Daddy?' I called out, but there was only silence. I searched the downstairs area before heading up to the third floor. As I reached the halfway point, I heard the sound of running water coming from our bathroom.

I cautiously walked in and saw Bellamy showering. At first, I just observed from the doorway, but then I realized he was standing still, letting the water fall on his head, lost in thought. The steam was starting to cover the glass, so I walked closer to maybe get his attention. His eyes seemed a thousand miles away, and I knew he was still thinking about the shadows.

"Everything ok?" I asked, watching Bellamy with concern. He looked up, startled, and our eyes met. Instantly, he was out of his trance-like state. A warm smile spread across his face. "Sorry, baby girl. I was just thinking about where we had landed." He stepped out of the shower, the water turning off on its own. His expression was reassuring. "It's nothing to worry about."

As Bellamy emerged from the water, I couldn't help but notice the way the droplets clung to his chiseled physique, accentuating his lean muscles. The water seemed to hesitate, as if reluctant to leave his skin, before evaporating instantly upon reaching the floor. Bellamy's eyes met mine, and for a moment, he allowed me to take in the sight of him, his gaze almost daring me to look my fill. Then, with a hint of a smile, he wrapped a towel around his waist, the gesture both practical and provocative.

Slowly he walked over to me, his eyes locked on mine and gently kissed me on the forehead. 'Not tonight, baby girl,' he whispered with a knowing smile, aware of my desire for him. I knew he must still be deeply preoccupied with his thoughts, as it was rare for him to resist my advances.

After my shower, I slipped into our oversized bed. Its softness cradling me in comfort and instantly made me feel drowsy. Bellamy's arms wrapped around me, pulling me close, and I snuggled deeper, resting my head on his chest. As I drifted off to sleep, I sensed that Bellamy was still lost in thought, as I nestled deeper into his warm embrace.

CHAPTER

FIVE

The next morning, Bellamy swept into our room, a dazzling smile on his face. He carried a tray laden with a mouthwatering breakfast spread in his hands. The smell of crispy bacon, freshly baked croissants, and freshly squeezed orange juice filled the air.

'Good morning, baby,' his eyes sparkling with warmth. His worries from last night had seemed to have vanished. For a moment, I considered asking about his mood change, but the sight of the delicious food and his charming smile made me hesitate. Instead, I expressed my gratitude, 'Thank you Daddy, this looks incredible!

As I indulged in the breakfast spread, my mind briefly wandered to my mother in this lifetime, wondering about her and her boyfriend back in NYC. Our usual breakfast routine consisted of coco puffs cereal, a stark contrast to this indulgent spread. For a fleeting moment, I felt a pang of guilt before shaking it off and savoring the delicious food.

"We have a big day today," Bellamy said, his eyes sparkling with enthusiasm as he watched me savor the flaky croissant. I couldn't help but feel a thrill of excitement, knowing I was heading back to the circus. Although I wouldn't be performing just yet, I was eager to start training again.

As an aerialist, like Eve, I had always loved the rush of flying through the sky, the wind in my hair, and the audience's gasps of wonder below. I couldn't wait to get back into the swing of things, literally!

I quickly finished my breakfast and got ready, but I found myself lingering in my closet, nostalgically gazing at my clothes from past lifetimes. Bellamy sensed my hesitation and swooped in with his magic to help speed up my progress.

His magic styled my hair, and before I knew it, he had dressed me in a stunning black and white shimmering leotard that sparkled like the stars in Jubilee. I smiled, recognizing his subtle hint to hurry up.

Together, we joined the crowd heading up to the circus, the excitement building as we approached the entrance. As we reached the top, Briar remarked to Bellamy, "Lots of lot lice," his tone laced with a hint of annoyance.

But I knew the real reason for the line outside of the gate, people adored Darlington Circus, and crowds always lined up eagerly to get inside. Unfortunately, immortals had little patience for mortal pace, but as a mortal myself, I understood the excitement and anticipation that came with waiting to experience a show or event.

Bellamy led me to the backyard, a secluded area off-limits to guests, where Anise and Eve were waiting. This was my usual practice spot, where Velar would typically assist me, but he was busy preparing for his strongman act. As the Ringmaster, Bellamy gave me a lingering kiss before heading off to open the circus and prepare for his own performances in the Big Top.

Anise, having some time before her act, helped me get back into the swing of things. My mind remembered the movements, but my body needed to rebuild its strength and muscle to climb the silks and ropes again. It was a physical challenge, but one I was ready for.

As the crowd began to arrive, their eyes wide with excitement. I couldn't help but beam with delight as I watched their faces transform with amazement. The soft gasps and murmurs of amazement only added to the enchantment.

As they gazed upon the spectacle before them, their faces sparkled, the children were always my favorite reactions to see. Seeing the wonder of the circus for the first time. I felt my heart swell with happiness, knowing I was a part of creating this whimsical experience.

Around lunchtime, I started feeling peckish and decided to take a break from training to find a snack. I knew exactly where I wanted to go. I joined the line at the elephant ear stand, and my eyes landed on the stand's owner, her signature white hair styled to perfection. She beamed at me, and before I even had to ask, she handed me a freshly fried hot elephant ear, the aroma of fried dough and sugar wafting up to tease me.

We chatted for a bit, and then I took my treat and wandered off to explore the circus, the sweet scent of sugar and spices trailing behind me. I strolled past the jugglers, their clubs flying through the air, and the contortionist, their bodies bending in impossible ways. The sound of laughter and music filled the air, and I felt carefree, taking in the wonders of the circus.

As I ventured into the Big Top, a sense of wonder enveloped me, like a child beholding a marvel for the first time. The big top's majestic canvas seemed to stretch up to the heavens, its every flutter and sway mesmerizing. I had anticipated Bellamy's performance, but Briar stood in Bellamy's place as the Ringmaster, his booming voice commanding attention. I searched the crowd for Bellamy, but he was nowhere to be seen. *Where had he gone?*

I didn't stay for the show; instead, I sought out Bellamy. I knew where Eve would be, so I headed to watch her perform on the aerial ropes. When she finished, she saw me and hurried over before her next act. "Do you know where Bellamy is?" I asked. "He's in the Big Top." She answered me like I had two heads. Before she could run off, I corrected her, "No, he's not. Briar is filling in for him." Eve's eyebrows narrowed, "Let's find Velar."

As we navigated through the crowds, the circus's vibrant energy surrounded us. Performers juggled fire, acrobats soared through the air, and clowns entertained with antics, the usual amazing circus.

Yet, despite the joy and laughter surrounding us, a nagging sense of unease settled in the pit of my stomach. I scanned the faces around me, searching for any sign of Velar. The music and applause created a cacophony that made my skin prickle. I leaned in closer to my companion, my voice barely audible over the din. 'Do you feel that? Something's not quite right.' My eyes searched for any clue that might explain the growing sense of discomfort.

I've learned to trust my intuition over countless lifetimes, and it only grows stronger with each passing life. I could sense that Eve felt it too, as she didn't hesitate to skip her next performance without a second thought. Eudora seamlessly took her place, without question.

As we navigated through the bustling circus grounds, my unease grew. The air seemed to vibrate with an undercurrent of tension, like the moment before a storm breaks. I quickened my pace, my heart pounding in anticipation.

The sky above transformed, dark clouds gathering as a storm approached. But this was no ordinary sky; it was enchanted by Bellamy. *What was he doing?* I thought to myself.

In an instant, a fierce gust of wind erupted, catching us off guard. Balloons burst free from the vendors' grasp, soaring into the air like colorful birds set flight. The crowd erupted into chaos, people scrambling for cover as the wind whipped through the circus grounds. The gusts grew stronger, threatening to knock us off balance. The wind howled around us, a deafening roar that made communication impossible.

As we battled our way towards the backyard in search of Velar, a commotion erupted at a nearby fairy floss stand. The fluffy confection began to balloon out of control, swelling at an exponential rate as it burst its sugary bonds.

At first, the spectacle seemed almost absurd, like a cartoon coming to life. But as the cotton candy continued its relentless expansion, we sprang into action. Velar quickly freed the trapped guests, but the sticky mess only grew, spreading across the cobblestone. Despite our efforts, it just kept growing.

"We need Bellamy," Eve shouted, her voice laced with concern. More crew members and performers arrived to help contain the chaos, keeping the crowd at a safe distance while Eve and I continued our quest to find Velar and Bellamy.

As we sprinted towards the backyard, screams erupted, and we stopped to watch in horror as one of the massive tents collapsed, trapping the guests inside. Eve and I rushed to help.

One of the grandstands fell right on top of a young girl, luckily, she was alive, but she needed help. Her legs were pinned.

I screamed for Eve, and together, we tried to lift it, but it was too heavy. Velar appeared and hurled the pole off of her. A second later Millicent was there to help guide her to her parents and seek medical attention. More of the circus troupe were there helping everyone to safety. I was proud.

As the chaos subsided and the wind finally died, Bellamy's voice announced the circus's closure. What was left of the crowd began to disperse towards the exit. All the performers and crew stayed to help reassemble things. The massive tent would be something Bellamy would have to use his magic to fix.

Once most things were finished, everyone headed back to Jubilee. I was about to follow suit when Bellamy appeared, coming from outside the circus. *What was he doing outside?*

Bellamy's eyes gleamed with shock and confusion as he beheld the chaotic circus. With a swift gesture, he unleashed his magic. With a flick of his wrist the sky cleared to a beautiful day. He waved a hand at the fairy floss mess, and it instantly disappeared into the cobblestone. He pointed his finger at the collapsed tent, and it sprang back to life, rising majestically into the air.

In an instant, all was well once more.

Velar saw Bellamy and came running over, 'What happened to the sky?' Concern etched on his face. 'What was that?' Eve added, her eyes wide with worry. I turned to Bellamy, 'Why were you outside the circus?' I asked, curiosity getting the better of me.

Performers and crew members started to gather around, sensing something was amiss. Bellamy raised his hand, silencing us and our questions, and swiftly instructed, 'Let's get everyone to Jubilee and jump out of here!' Without hesitation, everyone headed to Jubilee.

Bellamy was the last to appear from the willow tree, his arms raised to the sky, and again it seemed to take all of his energy and magic to jump us out of there. Before we walked back to Casmira, I needed to understand what was happening.

"What's going on?" I asked Bellamy, taking his hand. He looked at me, then at Eve and Velar, and then back at me, his expression serious, more serious than I had ever seen him. He scanned our surroundings to make sure no one could hear us.

'I was about to go on stage when I heard my name being called,' Bellamy began, his eyes clouding over with a mix of confusion and unease. 'It was the strangest thing, the voice didn't sound human. I searched for the source, but it seemed to move further away, drawing me outside the circus.'

He paused, his gaze intense. 'What do you mean something was calling you?' I pressed, noticing he'd said 'something' instead of 'someone'. Bellamy's expression turned grim. 'I don't know what it was, but when I stepped outside the circus gate, I felt that same awful feeling I had yesterday. It was something from another world,' he said, his voice low and serious.

A shiver coursed down my spine as I asked, 'What are we going to do about it? Do you think we've lost...whatever that was?' The questions tumbled out of my mouth in a frantic rush. I knew Bellamy didn't have the answers, but I couldn't help myself, the questions spilled out like blood from a wound.

Once back at Casmira the four of us discussed the possibility that Bellamy's magic was the cause. Suddenly, a knock on the door interrupted our conversation. We all walked out to see who it was. When Bellamy opened the door, Mesidor and Ambrette Blackwood stood before us.

The Blackwood's, renowned for their wisdom and leadership, are the most respected witches in the Emberlynn Forest. Their coven looks up to them for guidance, and their son Clove, a skilled young witch, is no exception.

Mesidor was a much older man then Ambrette and with the curse it kept them looking this way permanently. She was a beautiful woman that gleamed with an aura of peace around her. She was nothing like her wicked sister.

"May we come in, Mr. Darlington?" they asked. "Of course," Bellamy replied, ushering them in. I motioned for them to sit in the living room. As we walked in, the fireplace came to life making the common room warm and cozy.

"What can we do for you?" Bellamy asked once they took their seats. Mesidor's expression turned serious. "I believe the circus is being haunted," he said matter of fact.

"Why do you think that?" Bellamy asked, his brow furrowed in concern. Mesidor explained, "The other night, after the feast, after we heard the explosion Ambrette came home and felt an eerie energy." He turned to his wife, allowing her to continue the story. Ambrette's expression turned solemn.

"The energy was really bad. As soon as we landed, I knew it was evil. And I know evil." Her voice cracked with sorrow, and we all knew why - her sister was the one who had cursed us long ago. Ambrette continued, "I felt something dark, something wicked and after today's events, I know it's connected." Mesidor chimed in, "But who knows by what?"

Everyone listened intently, eager to understand the mystery. "What do you suppose we do?" Bellamy asked, looking at the Blackwood's.

"Can you investigate the location where we picked up the uh... the shadows?" Mesidor and Ambrette nodded in agreement. "We'll look into it right away," Mesidor said.

"And we suggest not opening the circus again tomorrow, in case the same thing happens." Ambrette said. They headed towards the door and Bellamy, and I followed them out onto the front porch. Bellamy reassured them that the circus will be closed tomorrow.

When we walked back inside to join Velar and Eve and the sudden realization that the circus is haunted finally hit me. I was just relieved that it was only the circus and not Jubilee itself. That would be truly terrifying.

Shortly after the Blackwood's' visit, Bellamy made an announcement all over the town from the Emberlynn Forest to the opal sea, the Townsquare and everywhere between, that the circus would remain closed until further notice, and everyone was to stay in Jubilee until further notice.

That night, I don't think I slept a wink. Bellamy seemed to toss and turn as well. I couldn't stop thinking about the shadows. *What they were, what they could be, and why they'd come to the circus of all places.*

As I emerged from slumber the next morning, a brisk chill filled the air. The sun was on the cusp of rising, casting a pale light over the room. I heard Bellamy's voice drifting from the fourth-floor balcony, where he was conversing with someone in hushed tones.'

Casmira, I'm cold!' I called out, my voice carrying across the distance. The light flickered in response, indicating she was aware of my presence, but the temperature remained unchanged. I hastily put on a robe and made my way up to the balcony to investigate who Bellamy was speaking with.

As I emerged onto the balcony, I saw Bellamy slam his fist on the table, making the newspaper flutter to the ground. "Haunted Circus?" he growled, his face red with rage. "They're having a field day with this!"

Velar scoffed, his expression unimpressed. "Oh, the press loves a good headline. It'll pass." But Bellamy was having none of it. "It won't pass! This is exactly what we don't need. We can't afford to draw attention to ourselves, especially now."

He paced back and forth, his anger palpable. "We need to keep a low profile, not have our names splashed across the front page. This is a bloody nightmare."

Velar sighed, his eyes rolling heavenward. "Calm down, Bell. It's just a newspaper article. It's not the end of the world."

"Just a newspaper article? You know as well as I do that this kind of publicity can be disastrous, especially for us."

As I approached, I slowed my pace, intrigued by their conversation. Bellamy and Velar turned to face me, their expressions welcoming. "Good morning, baby girl" his warm smile beckoning me closer. He waved me over.

Bellamy noticed the bags under my eyes and said, 'There's nothing for you to worry about, love.' His magical kiss refreshed my face, and when I caught a glimpse of myself in a mirror, I didn't feel how I looked.

How could I not worry? Was he crazy to think I wouldn't worry?

'What are you two doing up so early?' I asked, concerned. Velar looked at Bellamy, seeming to wait for him to explain, as if I needed to be shielded from the conversation.

'Velar arrived early because there were disturbances in the town square and some of the townhomes last night,' Bellamy said, his gaze holding mine. 'Disturbances?' I repeated, my brow rising in concern. 'Here in Jubilee?' Bellamy's expression turned serious, his eyes locking onto mine. 'Yes, unfortunately.'

Bellamy's grip on my hand was tight as he led me to an empty seat at the table next to Velar. "Sit and have some tea," his voice low and serious. I felt a shiver run down my spine as I took my seat.

'So, what happened?' I asked. Bellamy's eyes locked onto mine, his expression grim. 'Anise's townhome was attacked last night.' I gasped, my hands flying to my mouth. 'Is she ok? I mean I know she is immortal right?'

Bellamy's nod was curt. 'She's alive, but...' He paused, his eyes looking down before finding mine again. 'She's traumatized. Whatever happened, it left her shaken to the core.'

'What do you mean?' My mind racing with worst-case scenarios. Bellamy's voice dropped to a whisper. 'It was so bad that she wants to leave the circus.' My eyes widened in disbelief. I needed to talk to her.

"Can I see her?" I asked "unfortunately no, she is petrified and the only person she is speaking with is Miss Poppet, apparently, she won't even let Henry near her. "That's why we have to get to the bottom of this right away," Bellamy said, sounding determined.

We all turned around to see Eve burst through the door to the balcony, her sudden entrance making us jump. 'Everyone's leaving!' Her eyes wide with urgency.

Through the trees we could see lots of movement in the town square. Bellamy and Velar quickly stood up, their faces firm with resolve.

'Where do they think they're going to go?' Bellamy inquired. I remembered that Eve's house was right next to Anise's, and my mind raced with questions. 'Eve, did you see anything last night?' Eve nodded, her expression grim. 'I can't even explain what I saw,' her voice trembling, making a chill run down my back.

Just then, the wind blew and started to howl around us. We all looked at Bellamy, but he shook his head. 'It's not me,' The wind began to pick up even more. 'Get inside!' Velar yelled, already heading for the door. 'What's the plan, Bell?' Velar yelled over his shoulder. As he descended the stairs. Above, the air trembled with the deep rumble of thunder.

Once downstairs, Bellamy instructed Velar, 'You come with me.' He turned to Eve and me, his expression serious. 'You two stay here until I get back.' Velar opened the front door, and a blast of air whooshed in, causing Eve and I's hair to go wild.

'Don't open the door for anyone, I mean anyone!' Bellamy yelled back over his shoulder before disappearing into the storm. 'Wait for me to get back!

As Eve and I huddled inside Casmira's walls, the wind grew stronger, its howling intensifying outside. The trees beyond the window whipped about with fierce abandon, their branches flailing like wild arms. Casmira creaked and groaned, her old wooden bones protesting the wind's relentless assault. Despite the turmoil, the house stood firm.

Just as the wind's howling began to subside, the rain unleashed its fury, pounding the roof like a thousand angry fists. Eve and I stepped out onto the wraparound porch, our eyes fixed on Jubilee as the rain lashed down with a sinister intensity. Within minutes, the meadow beside my house began to flood.

As the rain continued to pour down, I couldn't shake off the worry that it might last for hours. The water was rising rapidly, flooding the pathway that Bellamy and Velar needed to take to get back.

With each passing minute, the storm was becoming increasingly worse, threatening to engulf the only path to Casmira. I feared that if the rain didn't let up soon, the flooding would make it impossible for them to return even with magic.

As Eve and I settled back inside, we huddled by the fire, listening to the storm's fury. The thunder boomed loudly, and the lightning flashed in rapid succession, casting eerie shadows on the walls. Casmira, sensing our unease, prepared a soothing tea that seemed to calm our frazzled nerves. As we sipped our tea, Eve began to recount the events of the previous night, her voice trembling slightly.

"I can't even describe what I saw," Eve started, "but it was terrifying. I heard screams coming from Anise's place, and I jumped out of bed. When I ran to her townhouse, the door was wide open. I didn't know if she was inside or outside."

I listened intently as Eve continued, "I called out for Anise, but as I did, a giant dark shadow swooped towards me. It passed right through me, and when I opened my eyes, it had vanished. I rushed inside to find Anise."

Eve's voice trembled as she continued, "Anise was paralyzed with fear, even when she saw me, she screamed as if I was the one attacking her. It was horrifying." I couldn't understand why Anise would be scared of Eve.

"Henry came over after Miss Poppet was already calming her down, but as soon as she saw him, she started to panic and scream like she was scared of him too."

Eve's expression turned grave, "That's when Miss Poppet suggested taking Anise to a doctor, in the outside world." Eve shook her head in disagreement.

I started to say, 'Well, that's not a bad thing,' but Eve interrupted me, her voice laced with concern. 'We can't have anyone find out about us. If people know we're immortal, what do you think they would do to us?' She paused, looking defeated.

"I tried to get them to stay, but Miss Poppet thought it was best." Eve's gaze dropped to her feet, 'If they find out about Anise, they could keep her or get the government involved? She doesn't even have a valid ID! Honestly, I don't know what they were thinking."

I understood Eve's concern; it was a huge deal to keep their immortality a secret, and I couldn't fathom why Miss Poppet would think it's best to leave Jubilee. I looked at Eve, seeing the worry etched on her face, and knew I had to reassure her. 'We'll figure this out, Eve. We always do."

As the minutes ticked by like hours, Bellamy and Velar's absence grew more unsettling. Eve and I exchanged nervous glances, our anxiety simmering like a pot about to boil over. The rain outside intensified, drumming a menacing beat against the windows like a predator clawing at the door. Every creak of the old house made us jump, our hearts racing with anticipation. And then, a knock at the door shattered the tension.

I leapt to my feet, but Eve's iron grip on my arm froze me in place. Her eyes locked onto mine, wide with warning. "Remember what Bellamy said?" she whispered urgently.

"Don't open the door for anyone." But the knocking persisted, growing louder and more insistent. It was as if something on the other side of the door knew we were in here, waiting... and it would stop at nothing to get in.

CHAPTER

SIX

Eve and I exchanged nervous whispers as we tiptoed away from the windows, our hearts racing with every creak of the floorboards. We made our way to a nook in the kitchen with our senses on high alert. I knew we could try to see who was at the door from this vantage, but when we looked out, there was no one in sight.

We were about to head back to the main room when I heard my name being called. "Nicole..." The voice was soft and tentative, but it sent shivers down my spine. I slowly approached the window, my eyes scanning the ground below, but I couldn't see anyone.

Then, we heard it again, louder this time. "Nicole!" It sounded like Miss Poppet's voice. I went to answer her, but Eve grabbed my arm stopping me in my tracks. "Don't open the door!" Confusion and fear took over as I tried to process what was happening.

The knocking grew louder and more insistent, sending my terror soaring. Whatever was on the other side of the door was probably the same thing that attacked Anise. Eve and I fled to the back of Casmira, desperate to hide in the conservatory.

"Where can we go if it breaks in?" Eve whispered. "It's okay, Casmira won't let anything in," I tried to reassure Eve, but my words were hollow.

As soon as I spoke, a window shattered behind us, making us both jump. We took off running towards the front door, Eve right behind me. I quickly flung open the door and we both escaped screaming the whole time.

I didn't dare look back, fearing what I might see. Instead, I sprinted through the flooded woods, the pouring rain stinging my face. My heart raced with terror as I struggled to navigate the slippery, muddy terrain. Eve was beside me now, and together we ran wildly, our feet squelching in the mud as we desperately tried to reach the square.

Bellamy and Velar saw us through the clearing and rushed towards us. Half the town was watching us sprint towards them, their faces filled with fear and confusion. "What's wrong?" Bellamy asked, concern etched on his face, as he reached us.

I collapsed onto the ground, gasping for air, while Eve tried to explain. "Something...it came...and the window..." Her words were a jumbled mess, but Bellamy seemed to understand. He instructed us to stay with the townspeople while he went to investigate. I pleaded with him not to go, but he reassured me that his magic would keep him safe.

Bellamy was able to halt the storm, but the clouds lingered, casting a dark and dreary shadow over the town. As I caught my breath, I turned to Velar and asked, "What's everyone doing?" Velar's expression was grim. "They want to leave," he replied, his voice low and serious. I looked around at my immortal friends, their faces etched with terror.

I understood their desire to flee, but the thought of them leaving filled me with dread. "Where would they all go?" I asked with concern, as I gazed at them and saw fear in their eyes. I could sense their desperation. Velar shrugged, his expression uncertain. "I'm not sure," he admitted. "Bellamy was about to tell us the plan when you guys showed up."

As we stood around the square, someone suddenly shouted, "What's that?" We all turned to look towards the Emberlynn Forest. A large dark shadow slowly moved its way up the rolling hills, its presence seeming to grow larger and more ominous by the second. My heart started pounding and Velar sensing my unease wrapped his arm around me.

Then, just as suddenly as it appeared, it disappeared into the forest. We all stood still, frozen in fear, unsure of where to hide or what to do next. That's when Bellamy appeared from behind us, his voice calm and reassuring. "I scared it off into the forest," his sudden appearance startled everyone, including me. I let out a shrill scream, my heart racing with fright.

Bellamy apologized for startling some of us, his expression contrite. "I'm sorry, I didn't mean to scare you." Then, he repeated, "I scared it off into the forest. It's not safe to be out in the open right now, until we can figure out what it is and what it wants." His eyes scanned the surrounding area, his gaze lingering on the forest before turning back to us.

The Blackwood's approached and asked to speak with us in private. Bellamy nodded and quickly addressed the crowd, his voice firm and authoritative.

"Everyone go home and lock your doors. Everyone should stay inside unless you hear from me. Stay together if you can, I don't want anyone alone. At least not until we figure this out. And whatever you do- don't answer your doors for anyone." His eyes scanned the crowd, emphasizing the seriousness of the situation.

"We want to leave!" Eudora shouted. I turned to see her and Laven with bags packed. The Rossi family was already heading towards the entrance of the willow tree, eager to escape the ominous atmosphere. They had only paused to listen to Bellamy's message.

Bellamy's face reflected his resignation as he let out a deep sigh. "I won't stand in your way if you're determined to leave," he said, his tone laced with concern. "But let this be a warning to you: guard your secret closely. Never reveal your immortality to anyone. I wish you'd reconsider and stay, but I understand."

His eyes locked onto theirs, his gaze tinged with a desperate plea. "Please, be vigilant. The world is a vastly different place from the one we knew. Mortals are not as accepting as they once were."

My jaw dropped in shock, when I watched Eudora and Laven follow the Rossi family into the tree. I was utterly flabbergasted. Velar noticed my expression and reassured me, "They'll be back." I desperately hoped he was right. Velar's hand rubbed my back to soothe my nerves, his ice cold hand making me shiver.

Bellamy again addressed the crowd, urging everyone to head home and stay together. Ambrette helpfully suggested, "Put salt outside your doors to keep the evil out!" Bellamy nodded in approval, grateful for her assistance. Once the townspeople had dispersed, we returned to Casmira. I was still shaken from the earlier event and hesitated to enter, but Bellamy took my hand and walked me inside.

Eve didn't wait for anyone; as soon as she stepped into Casmira, she bolted for the kitchen and returned with the salt jar. I watched in surprise as she opened the front door and poured a line of salt across the threshold. "Take that!" she exclaimed with a triumphant smirk, but I was too nervous to share her confidence. My anxiety lingered, making it hard for me to feel the same sense of defiance that Eve seemed to embody.

I walked into the conservatory, expecting to see shattered glass and debris from the broken window. But to my surprise, it was already restored. The window was now intact, and the room was filled with the sweet scent of blooming flowers and herbs. I couldn't help but feel a sense of relief and admiration for magic.

Everyone gathered in the living room, where the fire from earlier still crackled and popped. But despite the warmth and light, the atmosphere felt tense and foreboding. It seemed as though Casmira herself was scared, and the usual warmth and comfort of the house was replaced with an unsettling stillness.

As the Blackwood's began to speak with Bellamy, I asked aloud, "Casmira, may I have some tea?" Instead of the usual reply, like the tea appearing on the stove or next to me, a cabinet door flew open, and a box of tea came crashing out, landing on the floor at my feet. It took me a second to process that Casmira, the sentient house, was too scared to perform her usual magic.

Velar let out a loud, belly-shaking laugh, the kind that's infectious and over-the-top. I felt my face heat up with a mix of amusement and embarrassment 'It's okay, maybe later', trying to play it cool while my cheeks betrayed me with a bright blush. I set the tea down and sat next to Bellamy, giving the witches my attention.

Ambrette began, "We did some research on where we believe we picked up this entity." Mesidor added, "We think we landed in the Euphrates River." They paused, expecting us to say something, but our confused faces prompted them to continue.

"The Euphrates River is an ancient river." Mesidor explained further. Ambrette pulled out a giant book from her satchel that she brought with her and plopped it on the table in front of us. In unison we have learned in to read the title.

"In the Book of Enoch, the Euphrates River is portrayed as a symbol of divine judgment, justice, and the struggle between good and evil.

Ambrette continued, "The final judgment, In the Book, the Euphrates is also associated with the final judgment, where the righteous will be separated from the Evil.

"So, what are you saying?" Velar asked with confusion in his eyes. "We believe that the spirit originates from this ancient, imprisoned underworld. Somehow, when we landed there, the entity attached itself to us and then somehow managed to get into Jubilee."

I turned to Bellamy, anticipating a look of confusion or alarm, but instead, he radiated calmness and comprehension. While Eve, Velar and I were struck dumbfounded, struggling to wrap our minds around the revelation. Bellamy seemed utterly unfazed, his demeanor was calm and introspective.

Then Eve finally spoke up, "Are you telling me we landed on a haunted site or something and now we have a ghost?" Ambrette nodded and continued, "According to ancient texts, this was the place where God imprisoned the Watchers."

Mesidor added, "Yes, the Euphrates River is said to be a gateway to the underworld, and the Watchers were believed to be powerful beings who were tasked with watching over humanity but were instead corrupted by their power."

"The watchers?" I asked, trying to keep up.

Mesidor leaned in, his eyes serious. "The Watchers, also known as the fallen angels, were tasked with guiding humanity, but they soon began to teach humans dark magic and forbidden knowledge, among other things."

Ambrette nodded, "They were said to have possessed great knowledge and power, but they used it for evil purposes. God imprisoned them in the underworld, but they cannot die, instead they roam the underworld until judgment day."

Eve's eyes were wide with fascination. "What kind of magic did they teach?"

Mesidor hesitated, as if unsure how much to reveal. "They taught humans how to summon demons, how to control the forces of nature, and how to wield dark energy."

Ambrette's eyes sparkled with intrigue. "You could say that the Watchers were the first witches. They were the ones who initially harnessed the power of the universe and taught humans how to do the same."

Eve interrupted. "So, you're saying that witchcraft originated from the Watchers, like from the Bible?"

Ambrette nodded. "Yes, exactly. The Watchers were the first to tap into the divine energy that surrounds us. They were the first to wield magic."

Bellamy added, "And they were also the first to abuse it. Their actions had consequences."

Mesidor's expression turned somber. "We need to be careful not to repeat the mistakes of the past. We must use our knowledge and power responsibly, just as we already do." His eyes looked to Bellamy's who gave him a nod of agreement.

As I sat back and listened intently, I couldn't help but feel a sense of trepidation. I knew that Ambrette and Mesidor would know the truth, but this was ridiculous to me. My brain could not comprehend what I was hearing. *Fallen angels and an underworld?*

I couldn't contain my confusion and blurted out, "How is this even possible, I mean you are talking about ancient stories, how is this happening?" Everyone's eyes were on me and Bellamy calmly said, "Just look at you baby girl, no one would think you could possibly be here either, yet here you are." His smile widened as he gave me a wink. That surely shut me up.

Ambrette's eyes seemed to bore into my soul as she spoke, her voice filled with a conviction that left no room for doubt. Mesidor's nodding along, his expression serious, only added to the gravity of the moment.

I still couldn't not comprehend what existed just beyond the veil of reality. The Watchers, these powerful beings who had shaped the course of human history, and somehow now they are a part of our world.

But as the truth sank in, I also felt my stomach turning to knots. If the Watchers were real, and they had taught humans dark magic, what does it want from Darlington Circus?

By the end of the Blackwood's' visit, they had agreed to embark on a perilous journey to hunt for the entity in the forest and attempt to commune with it to understand its desires. Bellamy dispatched Velar to gather a few trusted men, including Henry and Briar, to join them on the hunt. The four of them, along with Mesidor, would venture into the heart of the Emberlynn Forest, determined to uncover the truth about the mysterious entity.

That night, the men began preparing for the hunt, as Bellamy called it. They gathered an array of witchcraft items from the witches in Jubilee, including candles, herbs, crystals, pentacles, and surprisingly, a cross and holy water. When the men stepped into the library to do their own research Eve, and I eavesdropped through the door.

We stood quietly with our ears up against the wood and tried to stifle our giggles like little girls.

"But it's a ghost, Bell, a damn shadow for Christ's sake!" Velar exclaimed. "I can't bite into a bloodless being. How the hell am I going to kill a ghost or an angel or whatever it is?"

"Relax, we have Mesidor who's going to communicate with it," Bellamy replied.

"Do you hear yourself right now? Communicate? With a ghost?" Footsteps paced back and forth on the floor.

"Are you scared of a little haunting, Velar?" Bellamy jokes, but Velar wasn't laughing instead his voice raised, 'An angel for crying out loud? I don't even believe in them.'

Bellamy shot back, his tone laced with sarcasm, 'Well, people don't believe you exist either, yet here you are.'

"What do you think you're going to do when you find it?" Velar asked, his tone serious and worried. The room fell silent, and Eve and I held our breath listening for a response. Then, Bellamy said, "I'll use my magic."

Velar's response was immediate and intense. "And kill something that's already dead?"

Eve and I burst out laughing at Velar's response, and just as we did, the door swung open, causing us to stumble and almost fall to the floor.

"Ladies..." Bellamy said, his voice full of amusement since he used his magic to open the door.

We quickly straightened up and walked inside the library, trying to compose ourselves. "So, what's the plan?" I asked, still trying to contain my amusement.

Bellamy smiled mischievously. "Well, first, we need to get near it and Mesidor will communicate with the ghost, spirit, shadow thing and we will figure out what it wants." *Simple enough.*

"What do you want me to do?" I asked, already knowing the answer.

"As for you, I want you to stay here." I rolled my eyes, and Bellamy caught the gesture. He raised an eyebrow, a playful glint in his eye.

"Did you roll your eyes at me, little girl?" he asked, his tone teasing. I smirked, trying to appear nonchalant. "Maybe I did, maybe I didn't."

Bellamy chuckled, his eyes crinkling at the corners. "Oh, I think you definitely did. And I think you know exactly what I'm going to do about it." I raised my eyebrows, intrigued despite myself. "Oh yeah? What's that?"

Bellamy leaned in, his voice taking on a conspiratorial tone. "I'll have to punish you, of course. But don't worry baby girl, I promise it will be a punishment you'll enjoy." I felt a flutter in my chest at his words, and I couldn't help but wonder what he had in mind.

I smiled, and Velar's gaze locked onto me, his emerald eyes burning with an intense scrutiny.

Eve intervened, shifting the conversation back on track. "So, what's the plan if things go south?" She asked, her eyes worried.

Bellamy's grin expanded, his eyes gleaming with arrogance. "We improvise."

CHAPTER
SEVEN

The night before the hunt, Bellamy called me into the playroom, a stern expression on his face. "Time for your punishment, little girl," his voice was firm but gentle.

I felt a flutter in my chest as I entered, the door closing behind me with a soft click. Bellamy was seated in a black leather chair, his eyes fixed on me with a serious gaze.

"Punishment for what?" I asked, trying to sound innocent despite my racing heart. Bellamy sighed, his expression softening slightly. "For rolling your eyes at me, you know I don't tolerate disrespect."

I looked down, feeling a bit ashamed. "I know, I'm sorry." Bellamy stood up, his eyes never leaving mine. "You are forgiven, but you still need a reminder." He walked over to me, his hand reaching out to grasp my arm gently. "Bend over," he commanded.

I felt a blush rise to my cheeks as I bent over, my heart racing with excitement. I felt his magic tickle my body making my panties drop to the floor. Bellamy's hand came down on my bottom with a firm smack, the sound echoing through the room.

I gasped, feeling a sting but also a sense of excitement. Bellamy's hand came down repeatedly, each smack sending a thrill through me. As the punishment ended, Bellamy helped me up, his eyes soft with concern. "Are you okay?"

I nodded, feeling a bit dazed, but also strangely exhilarated. "Yes, Daddy, I'm sorry again for my behavior." Bellamy smiled, "I know you are, baby girl. Now let's get some rest. We have a big day ahead of us tomorrow."

The next morning, everything seemed back to normal in Jubilee. The sky was a bright blue, and the air was crisp and clear. The darkness and cloudiness from the previous day were gone, and a sense of tranquility had settled over the town.

I left my bedroom balcony and headed downstairs, where the men of Jubilee would soon be gathering to embark on the hunt. Casmira was back to her usual self, and the delicious aromas wafting from the kitchen were a testament to her renewed energy. I quickly dressed and scurried downstairs, my stomach growling in anticipation of the hearty breakfast that awaited.

As I entered the kitchen, I was greeted by the warm and inviting atmosphere that Casmira always seemed to create. The table was filled with an array of mouthwatering dishes, and the air was filled with the savory scents of bacon and eggs and freshly baked bread.

The men of Jubilee began to arrive, and I escorted them to the dining room. They left their hunting equipment outside on the porch, then gathered around the table and took their seats in the dining room.

The group had grown far beyond just Velar, Mesidor, Henry, and Briar. I was shocked to see Caleb, Isaac, Hector, and Godfrey had come to hunt, along with several others. United in their determination, they gathered with a sense of purpose.

It was evident that the men of Jubilee would go to great lengths for Bellamy, and it's clear that many of them owe him a debt of gratitude. After the immortality curse, Bellamy went to great lengths to support the immortals, offering sanctuary to vampires and providing a safe haven. Whatever the reason, one thing is certain, the men of Jubilee would willingly lay down their lives for Bellamy, their loyalty and devotion unwavering.

Bellamy stood at the head of the table, his eyes sweeping across the room as he waited for the last of the stragglers to arrive. Once everyone was seated and settled, he began to outline the plan for the day, his voice clear and confident as he detailed the next steps in their quest to hunt down the mysterious entity.

With their strategy session concluded, the group began to eat their fill. Velar and Henry led the other vampires on a quick hunt, probably seeking out a bear to satisfy their primal cravings and quench their thirst for blood.

As the vampires disappeared into the morning mist, the men finished their breakfast, their conversation filled with resolve. They knew that the hunt would be no easy task, but they were ready to face whatever dangers lay ahead.

Bellamy stood when it was time to go. "Alright, men. Let's gear up and get moving. We have a long day ahead of us."

As the men prepared to leave Casmira, I watched with a mix of excitement and concern. I wanted each and every one of them to return safely, so I packed extra food for them to take on their journey. Bellamy whisked me up in his arms and hugged me tightly, his lips meeting mine in a passionate kiss.

"I'll miss you Daddy" His blue eyes peered deep into mine. "I'll miss you more, baby girl," he replied with affection.

I held him close, my arms wrapped around him. I didn't want to let him go, but I knew he had to lead the hunt. "Now remember, you stay here," his voice was firm. "I can't protect you if you don't obey me." With that, he turned and walked out of Casmira, catching up with the other men.

I watched as the men disappeared into the distance, my heart heavy with worry. I knew that the hunt could be dangerous. But I had to trust in Bellamy's leadership and the men's bravery. I took a deep breath and turned back to Casmira, my mind racing with thoughts of what might lie ahead. *Thank God they were immortal.*

I decided to distract myself by reading a book on my fourth story balcony, where I could bask in the warm sunlight and fresh air. It was an absolutely beautiful day, and I couldn't wait to escape into a good book. I grabbed some Lion's Mane tea and conquered the stairs to the balcony, settling into a lush chair with a cozy sigh. As I started to read, the words transported me to another world.

I was so absorbed in my book that before I knew it an hour went by. I stood up and stretched, my eyes turning towards the town square as I peeked through the trees. The town was deserted, not a person in sight, everyone seemed to be obeying Bellamy's orders to stay inside.

I was about to start reading again when a sudden wind gust swept in from the Emberlynn Forest, carrying with it an eerie chill. In the distance, I could see dark clouds gathering over the forest sky, their ominous presence making my heart race.

A knot formed in my stomach as I sensed something was off. The wind began to pick up, rustling the leaves made me begin to panic. Something was bad, and I couldn't shake the feeling that they needed help.

Feeling a sense of trepidation, I wondered what I could do? I'm just a mortal, after all. But I couldn't simply sit back and do nothing. I decided to investigate, just outside the forest. I wouldn't venture in, just a cautious observation to see what was happening.

As I stepped off my front porch, the wind blew, and I suddenly heard Bellamy's voice in my mind, telling me to stay inside. But despite my reservations, my feet kept moving forward, and I found myself walking towards the forest.

My heart raced erratically as I climbed the rolling hills, my pulse throbbing in my throat like a wild animal trying to escape. I felt my breath catch in my chest, and my legs trembled beneath me as I ascended higher and higher, the forest looming before me like an unknown abyss.

Reaching the summit, I turned to face Jubilee, and my eyes swept across the town's tranquil landscape. The usual hum of activity was hushed, the streets eerily still, as if the very town itself was holding its breath.

As I approached the forest's edge, the wind grew stronger, and the trees creaked ominously. I hesitated for a moment, wondering if I should turn back, but my curiosity got the better of me.

I peeked into the forest, my eyes scanning the shadows. At first, I saw nothing out of the ordinary. But then, I noticed a faint rustling in the underbrush. It was subtle, but it seemed to be moving of its own accord. I stood frozen in place watching intently.

Just as fear crept over me, Velar appeared in the clearing. "Velar!" I screamed, startled. "You scared me!"

He looked furious to see me. "Why don't you ever listen?" He stalked over to me, his eyes blazing.

"If you had listened in your past life, you probably wouldn't have been murdered." I was taken aback by his words. *Why was he acting like this?*

"Velar, calm down. I just want to help." He shook his head in disagreement. "I knew you weren't going to stay put like you were told," he said, his voice firm. "You never do Nic." Velar swung a heavy backpack over his shoulder.

"Why aren't you with the others?" I asked, trying to deflect his anger. "I was waiting for you," he stated, crossing his muscular arms over his chest. His demeanor was intimidating, but I stood my ground.

"I just want to help," I repeated. He sighed, his expression unyielding. "You have no idea what's at stake here. You're recklessly putting yourself in danger. There's absolutely nothing you can do, I don't even know what the hell I'm supposed to do."

I felt a surge of frustration. "Well, I'm not leaving." Velar's eyes narrowed and his voice rising, "You have no idea what we are dealing with!"

Our argument was escalating, our voices growing louder and more heated by the second. Abruptly, a sudden noise and movement startled us both, cutting through the tension and silencing our dispute in an instant.

Orlow, the elephant, was running frantically into the forest. "Orlow!" I shouted, but he disappeared into the forest. Without thinking, I took off after him, my heart racing with fear. Velar was right next to me keeping my pace as I chased after my elephant.

As we ran, the forest grew denser, and the shadows deepened. I could feel the weight of the forest's magic bearing down on me, making my skin prickle with unease. But I didn't let fear stop me. I had to find Orlow.

There was a path that wound its way through the edge of the forest, where the homes were, but Orlow didn't follow it. Instead, he ventured into the woods, leaving the path behind and disappearing into the dense underbrush.

We had passed all the homes and were now deep in the dense woods, with no path to guide us. The trees seemed to close in around us, their branches tangling overhead, casting dappled shadows on the ground below. The air was thick with the scent of damp earth and decaying leaves.

"Orlow!" I called out again, my voice muffled by the dense foliage. Velar's grip on my arm tightened. "Shh," he whispered. "Listen." I strained my ears, and soon I heard the sound of rustling leaves and snapping twigs. It had to be Orlow. We followed the sound, our senses on high alert, as we pushed deeper into the woods.

The trees grew taller and the underbrush thicker, making it harder to navigate. I stumbled over roots and fallen branches, but Velar's grip kept me upright. "Orlow, wait!" I cried out, desperately.

But it was no use. The rustling grew fainter, and I feared we were losing him. "Velar, we have to keep going," I urged, my eyes scanning the darkness. "We can't let him get lost." Velar nodded. "Stay close," he whispered. "We don't know what's in these woods."

"What do you mean?" I asked, my voice barely above a whisper. "You're always hunting in these woods, aren't you?"

Velar's expression turned grim. "Never this deep," he admitted. "It's creepy to think what could be in here. All kinds of make-believe creatures."

A shudder went down my spine at his words. The trees seemed to loom over us, their branches like skeletal fingers reaching out to snatch us.

'This isn't right,' Velar whispered. 'It's too quiet. When I hunt, the woods are always noisier, especially at night. I squeezed Velar's hand. Even the forest itself seemed sacred.

"What kind of creatures have you seen in here?" My voice trembled slightly. Velar's eyes scanned the shadows, his hand holding onto mine. "Oh, the tales I could tell you, I've hunted bears and wolves, and I even saw a unicorn once," he said quietly, trying to distract my mind.

I lost all sense of time as we ventured deeper into the woods. Hours blended together, and I couldn't shake the feeling that we'd been wandering for an eternity. The dense canopy above seemed to warp the sun's rays, making it impossible to gauge the passing time.

Before we knew it, we were disoriented and lost. Velar hesitated to admit it, but he too was uncertain of the way back. As the sky darkened and my fatigue grew, I struggled to catch my breath. 'What now?' I asked, my legs refusing to take another step.

Velar surveyed our surroundings, his eyes scouring the woods for a solution. The oppressive silence was unnerving, and fear began to creep in. Even Though it should be daylight the Emberlynn Forest was dark and unsettling. Finally, he declared, 'We'll set up camp.'

Velar swiftly removed his backpack and began setting up a tent with practiced efficiency. I watched in dismay as he finished revealing a compact, one-person tent. *Where's Bellamy's magic when you need it?* I thought to myself. "This is it?" I asked, sounding a bit spoiled.

'Sorry, I wasn't expecting company,' he retorted, his tone tinged with sarcasm. I sighed and nodded, realizing we had no other choice. "Okay, let's get some rest then." I said, trying to sound calm.

It could have been a comedy skit, watching Velar try to squeeze into the tent after me. His struggle to wriggle into the tent was hilarious and had me giggling. I was just relieved to be inside, feeling less vulnerable to be standing out openly in the dark woods.

Just as we were getting settled in the tiny tent, an eerie, high-pitched "OOOOOO-ooooo," sound echoed from outside. I froze, and all the hair on my skin stood on end. Velar's expression turned serious as he gently unzipped the tent, opening it to peer out.

I sat back, holding my legs against my chest, my heart racing with anticipation. The sound sent shivers down my spine, and I couldn't help but wonder what was making it. Velar's eyes scanned the darkness, his gaze intense and focused.

As we waited in silence, the sound grew louder and closer, making my skin crawl. I tried to speak, but my voice caught in my throat. Velar's hand on my arm tightened, his grip reassuring.

Suddenly, the sound stopped, and an unsettling silence fell over the forest. I exhaled slowly, trying to calm my racing heart. Velar's eyes still scanned the darkness, his expression unreadable.

"What was that?" I whispered, my voice barely audible. "I don't know," he whispered back, "but I need you to stay here, I'll be right back."

"What?!" I whispered, my voice rising to a panicked whisper-yell. "No way are you going to leave me here!"

"I have to check it out," he whispered firmly. "You'll be safe here."

I shook my head vigorously, my heart racing with fear. "No, no, no! You can't just leave me here alone! it's dangerous."

Velar's grip on my arm tightened. "I'll be back," he promised. "Just stay quiet and stay here." But I was having none of it. I grabbed his arm, my fingernails digging into his cold skin as I tried pulling him to stay. "Don't leave me, Velar! Please!" I pleaded.

His voice remained firm. "I'll be right back, I promise." And with that, he slipped out of the tent, leaving me alone and trembling with fear.

I sat in silence, my ears straining to pick up any sound in the forest. I couldn't believe Velar had left me alone in this tent. Before long, I heard rustling and rummaging right outside my tent. "Nicole," a voice called out.

I held my breath when I realized it wasn't Velar's voice. It sounded like Bellamy's voice. I listened again, my heart racing with confusion. "Nic?" the voice called out again, sounding more insistent. I was certain now it was Bellamy's voice, but also confused because he never calls me Nic. I hesitated for a moment, then slowly unzipped the tent and peered into the darkness only seeing the night sky.

I tentatively poked my head out of the tent, a dark and malevolent shadow swooped across the entrance, sending me tumbling backward to the far side of the tent. I screamed aloud, my heart racing with terror, and covered my eyes with my trembling hands.

The sudden movement and darkness made me disoriented, and I couldn't see what was happening. But I could feel it. A presence. Lurking. Watching. Waiting.

The rustling and footsteps outside grew louder, more menacing. I heard twigs snapping, leaves crunching, and the sound of heavy breathing. It was getting closer. Closer. CLOSER.

Suddenly, the tent fabric rustled again, and I heard a low voice whispering my name, "Nic..." My blood ran cold.

I heard the tent unzip, and I opened my eyes to see Bellamy's dark outline leaning in. I was so relieved it was him that I quickly wrapped my arms around him, holding tight.

"What are you doing here?" I asked, my voice shaking with fear. "Why are you here?" Bellamy asked, his voice calm and steady. "Let's get you out of here." He took my hand and began to pull me out of the tent.

"But it's still dark, and I'm scared," I protested, my eyes scanning the darkness. "And we're lost."

Bellamy chuckled and pulled me closer to him. "We aren't lost," he whispered. "Come with me." I felt uneasy but I trusted Bellamy. I nodded, and he led me out of the tent, into the darkness.

In the dark forest, I stood frozen, my eyes straining to see beyond the blackness. The forest was terrifying at night, and I wrapped myself around Bellamy's arm, seeking comfort. But he seemed cold and unresponsive, his body stiff and unyielding.

I tried to get him to understand my fear, repeating "I'm scared," in a whisper, but he just kept walking. His grip on my arm was firm and almost painful.

I wondered if he was mad at me or maybe he was scared also. But his silence was unnerving, and I couldn't shake off the feeling that something was off. "What about Velar?" I asked finally, halting my step and looking up at Bellamy's dark silhouette.

"Who?" he asked, his voice a hollow echo of Bellamy's. My body turned to ice as I stared at the familiar figure, my mind filling with terror. My very marrow seemed to quiver with fear as I realized that this was not Bellamy.

CHAPTER

EIGHT

I took off running, just as the figure warped into a shadow and flew after me. His voice echoed through the woods, the words indistinguishable but the mocking tone unmistakable. I didn't dare look back, fearing what I might see. The trees blurred together as I sprinted, my heart pounding in my chest.

Running in the forest at night was treacherous, and I kept stumbling, skinning my knees and bruising my shins. At one point, a searing pain shot through my leg, but I pushed on, driven by pure terror. I ran deeper into the woods, my breath coming in ragged gasps. I didn't scream, fearing that the shadow was closing in.

When I couldn't run any longer, I stopped to catch my breath. I was lost and scared, surrounded by the oppressive darkness of the deep forest. I looked in all directions, but the trees seemed to loom over me, their branches reaching out to snare me.

The forest was eerily silent, as if the very creatures of the night were holding their breath, waiting to see what I would do next. The stillness was unnerving, punctuated only by the sound of my own ragged breathing. I strained my ears, but there was no sign of anyone, no hint of movement or life. I was alone, and the realization sent me falling to the ground.

I grabbed my now aching leg and realized my hands were covered in blood. Tears started forming in my eyes as I panicked. *Am I going to die already?* My mind racing with fear. The blood was spewing out, and I tried wrapping my leg with my ripped shirt, but within minutes, it was soaked through.

I watched in horror as the blood continued to gush, my vision blurring with each passing moment. I felt lightheaded, my body trembling with shock and fear. I knew I had to act fast, but my mind was numb, unable to think clearly. All I could think was, *this can't be happening. I can't die here, alone in the woods.*

I sat there, listening intently, praying for a miracle. But then I remembered, Bellamy could use his magic to create daylight. *Where was he? And why wasn't he doing that already?*

I pondered, my mind racing with questions. *Has something happened to him? Was he even looking for me?* The uncertainty gnawed at me, making my anxiety spike. I strained my ears, hoping to pick up any sound, any hint that Bellamy was near. But the forest remained eerily silent.

Something behind me moved, the sound like a soft rustle. I sat frozen, my heart slamming against my ribcage, too scared to turn around. The darkness seemed to vibrate with an ominous energy, as if something sinister was lurking just out of sight. My skin crawled with goosebumps, my mind racing with worst-case scenarios.

I tried to summon the courage to turn around, but my body was paralyzed with fear. The silence was oppressive. Then, a faint whisper seemed to caress my ear, 'Nic...'

I screamed when I heard Velar behind me. 'Is that you?' he asked, his voice laced with concern. *He must have smelled the blood.*

'Velar! I... I saw the shadow,' I stammered, still trying to process what had happened. 'It pretended to be Bellamy...' I continued, my voice shaking.

Velar came over to me, his eyes widening as he saw me sitting on the ground, my leg bleeding. 'What happened?' he asked, his gaze locked on my leg.

'I cut it running from that ghost shadow thing,' I explained, wincing in pain. Velar's expression turned grim, and he quickly knelt beside me, examining my wound.

"We need to keep moving, we can't stay there." He tore a piece of cloth from his shirt and wrapped my open wound. He lifted me off the ground, and together we walked through the dark forest. I was exhausted and scared, and my leg throbbed with pain.

'I just want to go back to Casmira,' I said, longing for the safety of my home. But Velar didn't respond, he just kept walking, his gaze fixed on some point ahead. I tried to ask him questions, to distract myself from the fear and pain.

'Where did you go after you left the tent?' I asked. 'To look for the others,' he replied, his voice low and gravelly.

'Did you find them?' I asked, a glimmer of hope rising in my chest. But Velar just shook his head, his expression grim. 'No.'

As we walked, I started hearing rustling in the woods and it grew louder, and I whispered hopefully, 'Maybe it's the men?'

But Velar's expression was serious, his eyes gleaming with a warning. 'No, it's the ghost. We need to get away from it.'

I hesitated, unsure, but Velar's urgency was contagious. We quickened our pace, but the rustling kept drawing my attention back to it, the sound of twigs snapping, and leaves crunching isn't the sound the ghost made.

Suddenly, I stopped dead in my tracks. 'Do you hear that?' I whispered. I strained my ears, and then I heard it again, it was voices. It was the men! "Velar, it's them, it's Bellamy!" I went to turn back, but Velar said, 'No, we have to keep moving this way.'

As he turned to urge me forward, a sliver of moonlight illuminated his face, and my heart froze. His fangs, once a distinctive feature, were now nowhere to be seen. A chill coursed through my veins as I stumbled upon a horrifying truth - the person beside me was not Velar.

This was the second time the shadow had tricked me, and instead of fear I was pissed. 'Who are you and what do you want?' The words spilled out of my mouth before I could second-guess myself.

The imposter's gaze narrowed, its eyes gleaming with a malevolent intensity. I stood my ground, my heart pounding in my chest, as I waited for its response.

I watched in horror as Velar's body transformed into the black shadow entity, his form contorting and twisting until he was no longer recognizable. But then, the shadow entity continued to morph and grow, its darkness deepening and solidifying into a towering figure with giant wings.

The being stood taller than any human I had ever seen, its wingspan stretching wide enough to block out the moon. A dark angel stood before me. Its wings were vast and bat-like, with razor-sharp edges. Its body was tall and gaunt, with skin like dark marble that seemed to shift and writhe like living shadows.

The angel's face was a twisted parody of beauty, with high cheekbones, a pointed chin, and eyes that burned with an inner fire. The eyes were the most striking feature, glowing with an otherworldly energy that seemed to pierce through the darkness.

The moment he spoke, the air seemed to thicken, as if the very atmosphere was bending to accommodate his voice. A low, pulsing hum that seemed to emanate from beyond the boundaries of our world.

'I am Shemihazah, leader of the Watchers,' he intoned, his words echoing like a dark, cosmic chant.' One of my angels has defected to your realm, and I will stop at nothing to reclaim him.'

"I stood entranced, my eyes locked on the colossal creature, drinking in every detail. His words of introduction faded into the background as I struggled to comprehend the sheer magnitude of his presence. Surprisingly, I felt no fear.

Instead, I was captivated by him. He was an angel, dark or not, and I couldn't help but be drawn to his majestic being. An angel stood before me, and I was irretrievably drawn to his celestial splendor.

The dark angel's words jolted me out of my trance-like state 'Who is your leader?' he demanded, his voice like thunder in the darkness. 'I'll take you to him,' I stammered.

Instead of moving, I found myself asking, 'So, a watcher like... a fallen angel?' The darkness seemed to pulse around us, and I could sense his intrigue that I knew even that much.

A hint of amusement dancing on his lips. 'So, you have heard of us?' he asked, his tone low and smooth.

I nodded, still trying to process the revelation. 'Yes, I know about the Fallen. The angels who defied God's will and were cast out of Heaven.' I explained remembering Ambrette's words from before. I paused, studying his reaction. His expression was unreadable, but his eyes seemed to flicker with curiosity.

"Whatever stories you've been told, whatever lies you've been fed, they're not the truth. I'm not here to debate or convince you otherwise. I'm here for one of my own, and I require a meeting with your leader. Please show me the way."

I swallowed hard realizing that the fallen angel had no time to waste, and I needed to seek Bellamy. I scanned the darkness, trying to determine which direction to go and which way to find Bellamy. The angel flicked his wings, causing me to startle, but I quickly realized he was just trying to get me moving quicker.

'I don't suppose your leader is one of the humans hunting me, is it?' I swallowed. 'Yes, actually,' I replied, and the angel let out a puff of air, which I assumed was his version of laughter. 'Typical human,' he muttered.

I was still trying to get my bearings when the angel said impatiently, 'Do you want to get out of these woods?'

'Yes!' I gasped, as if that wasn't a foregone conclusion.

Suddenly, the angel transformed into a shadow, and I felt myself being lifted off the ground. I tried to speak, but all the air was sucked out of my lungs. I was unable to breathe, unable to think. Everything went dark.

When I finally came to, I found myself standing outside the forest, back on the rolling hills in Jubilee. I was stunned, scanning my surroundings in disbelief. It took me a moment to realize that the dark angel had magical powers maybe beyond anything Bellamy wielded.

How had he done it? One moment we were in the heart of the forest, the next I was back on the hills in Jubilee, gasping for air. I looked around, trying to get my bearings, but the dark angel was nowhere to be seen. *He vanished into thin air. It didn't take long to notice my leg, no more pain although the dried blood still showed.* My thoughts turned to Orlow, and I couldn't help but wonder if he was safe. I hoped with all my heart that he would find his way back to us.

As I turned to face the opal sea, the dawn's warmth embraced me. The brink of dawn was visible on the horizon, a fiery glow that seemed to herald a new beginning. I decided then to return to Casmira, for I had had my fill of adventure for one night. My mind was racing with the thought of the fallen angel, its presence still echoing within me.

I wondered where the dark angel had vanished to, but my thoughts were soon interrupted by the sight of Bellamy and Eve waiting for me as I arrived back at Casmira. "Where were you?" Bellamy demanded, his voice laced with concern. Eve throwing her arms up in exasperation, "I knew you wouldn't stay put! I came over to your house and you were already gone!"

Before I could even utter a word, the two of them began bombarding me with questions, their voices overlapping in a cacophony of worry and curiosity. Exhausted, I rubbed my tired eyes, the sun's rays peeking through the windows only adding to my fatigue.

When Bellamy yelled, "What do you have to say for yourself?" I gazed at him with weary eyes and managed a meek, "The dark angel would like to speak with you... and I'm going to take a nap."

With that, I turned and trudged up the stairs, my body craving the soft embrace of my bed. The last thing I remembered was collapsing onto the comfortable mattress, my eyelids shutting out the world as I surrendered to a deep sleep.

I woke up to the sound of Velar's raised voice, tinged with a hint of anger. I sat up in bed, straining to hear more clearly. "Let her sleep," Bellamy demanded, his tone firm. "I told her not to leave the tent." Then, I heard some muffled voices, followed by Velar's louder inquiry, "What do you mean a dark angel?"

Realizing that the commotion was about me, I decided to intervene and calm everyone down. I threw off my covers and made my way to the source of the voices, ready to explain the extraordinary encounter I had just experienced.

I followed the voices downstairs into the library. I knocked once on the door interrupting the conversation. "It's time for me to share what I encountered with you," my voice was clear and steady.

"I didn't just wander off... I met the dark angel." The room fell silent, all eyes on me, waiting for me to continue. I took a deep breath and went on to explain the extraordinary events to the three of them.

'The dark angel shifted its form to resemble both of you,' Their eyes locked onto me intently listening. 'It was a trick, but I stood my ground.' I paused, studying their reactions.

Bellamy's face radiated pride, a warm smile spreading across his features. In contrast, Velar's brow furrowed with worry, his eyes clouding over with a mix of concern and uncertainty. Eve's expression mirrored Velar's, her lips pursed, and her eyes narrowed slightly, as if she was bracing herself for what was to come.

'And there's more,' I continued. 'One of the other dark angels is hiding here in Jubilee. Their leader, Shemihazah, is here to take him back, and he wants to speak with you, Bellamy.' I gazed at my husband, expecting him to be worried, but instead, he seemed intrigued.

'Great, I'm ready to get this haunting over with,' Clapping his hands together. 'Where is he?' His enthusiasm was unsettling, and I wondered if he understood the gravity of the situation. "The show must go on." He joked as if reading my mind.

I wasn't exactly sure where Shemihazah was, but I was confident that a dark angel with immense power would be able to hear me call him.

We stepped outside onto the porch, and I remembered his towering height of at least ten feet. I ventured into the grass, gazing towards the enchanted sky, and called out his name. "Shemihazah!" I shouted, my voice echoing through the air.

Eve, Velar, and Bellamy watched me intently from the porch, their eyes fixed on me as I summoned the dark angel. At first nothing happened, and Velar was about to laugh at me. I looked up to the sky and shouted louder, "Shemihazah!"

The sky seemed to tremble in response, and the wind picked up, rustling the leaves with an otherworldly energy. I felt goosebumps on my arms as I waited for a response. And then, a dark silhouette descended from the sky, and in the blink of an eye, Shemihazah stood before us.

His presence was imposing, exuding an aura of mystery and power. The air seemed to be charged with his energy, and I could feel the intensity of his gaze. Eve, Velar, and Bellamy stood transfixed, their eyes locked on the dark angel, as if entranced by his formidable presence.

As the daylight illuminated his face, his features became even more defined and distinct. The ten-foot-tall dark angel tucked his dark wings back and gazed at me with an intensity that made me feel small. His piercing eyes seemed to bore into my soul.

Despite his intimidating presence, I managed to stammer out an introduction, "This is Shemihazah, the leader of the Watchers... and this is Bellamy Darlington, our leader." I smiled at my husband, feeling a sense of pride at having just introduced him to an angel.

Bellamy, unfazed by the dark angel's imposing presence, asked, "Yes, what can we do for you?" His tone was calm and assertive. Shemihazah's gaze shifted to Bellamy, and I sensed a hint of curiosity in his eyes, as if he was sizing up Bellamy.

"When you landed on our entrance to the underworld, one of my Watchers escaped and latched onto your circus. When I went to retrieve him, you had disappeared just as he managed to infiltrate your hidden land." Shemihazah's gaze narrowed slightly, his eyes gleaming with interest. "I must say, your hidden land is quite impressive for a human with little magic."

He paused, his expression unreadable. "My Watcher, Azazel, has been causing trouble in your realm, I presume?" The angel had asked with a subtle dark hint of amusement. "I'll need to find him, and I may require your assistance to do so."

Bellamy nodded agreeably. "Of course, we'll help you. But in return, you must promise that once you find Azazel, you'll leave us in peace. We mean no harm to you or any fallen angel, and we'd like to keep it that way."

Shemihazah's expression turned thoughtful, his dark wings rustling softly in the silence. "I promise that once Azazel is found, I will leave your... circus, and your people, in peace. You have my word as the leader of the Watchers."

He paused, his gaze intensifying. "But know this, if Azazel has indeed infiltrated your hidden land, he may have already corrupted some of your own. You would do well to be cautious, Bellamy. The influence of the Watchers can be... insidious."

My thoughts darted anxiously to Anise, and I couldn't help but wonder if she was safe, wherever she and Miss Poppet were. I pushed aside the unsettling unknowns and focused on the hope that they were both okay, and better off being away from Jubilee.

Bellamy quickly devised a plan, and together Velar and Bellamy worked with Shemihazah. They hatched a strategy to search every home in Jubilee. "We must be thorough and swift," Bellamy emphasized. "No one is to leave the circus until we find Azazel. We can't risk him escaping or causing more harm than he already has."

To ensure everyone's safety, Bellamy set up guards at the entrance out of Jubilee, instructing them to be vigilant. "The angel can easily disguise himself as any one of us, so we must be cautious. If we're not careful, he could slip out unnoticed."

With a sense of urgency, the search party began their systematic sweep of Jubilee, determined to find Azazel and put an end to his mischief. Shemihazah led the charge, his dark wings fluttering ominously as he moved from home to home, his eyes scanning every nook and cranny for any sign of the escaped fallen angel.

CHAPTER
NINE

'I'm done with angel hunting,' I declared, the words feeling like a liberation as I settled into Casmira." Eve opted to stay with me, probably thinking I'd try to sneak off and search for Azazel alone, but I wasn't about to make that mistake twice!

Casmira brewed a soothing tea, and we settled in to savor the warmth. As we sipped our tea, Eve turned to me with a playful smirk. 'I can't help but notice how handsome Shemihazah is,' her eyes sparkling with mischief. 'I mean, for a fallen angel, he's quite the heartthrob!'

I rolled my eyes, 'Eve, he's a fallen angel!' But she just laughed and replied, 'Well, that's true, but he's still utterly captivating, even if he does have a certain...darkness."

I shot Eve a sideways glance, but I couldn't deny the thrill of curiosity that stirred within me. Shemihazah's otherworldly presence was undeniably captivating, and I found myself drawn to his enigmatic aura. The thought of what lay beneath his mysterious exterior made me quiver, and I couldn't help but wonder what deep secrets he harbored.

We dissolved into fits of giggles, our laughter echoing through the air like a pair of carefree schoolgirls sharing secrets. We marveled at the sheer absurdity of it all, the countless wonders that this world held, and the uncanny ability of chaos to seek us out.

'Why does this always happen to us?' I asked, my voice laced with a mix of exasperation and amusement. In that moment, our bond was strengthened by the shared absurdity of our many adventures.

Suddenly, two glasses of rich, vintage wine materialized on the coffee table in front of us, with a giant pepperoni pizza. 'Thank you, Casmira!' Eve exclaimed, her eyes sparkling with delight as she reached for one of the glasses. I smiled, accustomed to Casmira's subtle magic, but still marveled at her thoughtful gesture.

"What's it like when I'm not here?" Eve set her glass down and sighed. "Honestly? It's like the circus loses its magic. I spend all my time searching for you. I mean, I'm talking birth records, newspaper articles."

She paused, taking a sip of her drink.

"And Bellamy? He's a mess. He withdraws into his own world, only coming out for circus and business stuff. It's like he's just going through the motions, waiting for your return. We only have parties when you're here. Bellamy is...different when you're gone. He's not the same. We all feel the sadness, don't get me wrong, but Bellamy is incomplete without you.

Eve's words painted a picture of a man I didn't know existed. I'd always thought of him as a showman, always loud and outgoing, the life of the party. But Eve's description revealed a vulnerable side, one that was hidden from me. It made me sad to think about him that way.

As we sipped our wine and ate pizza we shared stories, the atmosphere was filled with warmth and laughter. We were enjoying each other's company when all of a sudden, the lights in the room began to flicker erratically.

Eve and I exchanged a concerned glance, our merriment momentarily forgotten. I rose from my seat and approached the front bay window, my heart quickening as I gazed outside.

The sky was transforming again, dark clouds boiling over the horizon like a churning sea. The air was electric, and I could feel the storm's approach. 'What's happening?' Eve asked, her voice tinged with a hint of unease, as the lights continued to flash ominously.

'Another storm, it must be Azazel,' I murmured. She nodded in agreement. Without a word, we hastily set our wine glasses aside and made our way upstairs, our footsteps light and urgent.

Reaching the balcony, we pushed open the doors and stepped out into the turbulent air. The wind whipped our hair into a frenzy as we grasped the railing, our eyes scanning the horizon for any sign of the dark angel. The sky was a deep, foreboding gray, and the clouds seemed to twist and writhe like living serpents. Lightning crackled across the sky, casting eerie flashes of illumination on the landscape below. We peered into the distance, our senses on high alert, searching for any glimpse of Azazel's malevolent presence.

As we gazed out into the stormy darkness, a faint dark shadow began to take shape in the distance. The wind howled louder, and the rain lashed down harder, as if trying to obscure our

view. But we stood firm, our eyes fixed on the apparition growing more solid by the second.

Azazel's wingspan was vast, his dark wings beating the air
with a hypnotic rhythm. His eyes glowed like embers from the
underworld, and his gaze seemed to pierce through the veil of
rain and darkness. Eve's hand tightened around mine, her fingers icy with fear. I could feel her trembling, but I stood frozen,
transfixed by the horror unfolding before us.

It didn't take long for us to realize he was heading straight
for us. 'Shit!' Eve gasped, her voice laced with panic. We swiftly
turned tail and sprinted back inside the house, our hearts racing with fear. The wind was deafening, its roar so intense that I
feared the house might be swept away like a leaf.

'Casmira, lock all the doors!' I yelled at the top of my lungs,
knowing it was a desperate measure, but I had to try something,
anything, to keep us safe. I knew it was a futile effort, but I had
to try something.

Eve and I huddled together, our eyes fixed on the windows
as the glass rattled and shook. The wind was a living entity, a
beast that wanted to devour us whole. I could feel its fury, its
evil intent.

Azazel's power was immense, and I knew we were no match
for him. The lights flickered, and I feared the worst. Suddenly,
the front door burst open, and a dark figure loomed in the entrance.

"No!" Eve screamed, her voice hoarse with terror. I pushed
her behind me, my heart racing with fear.

The dark shadow transformed into a dark angel, just like
Shemihazah's had before. But Azazel was different. He was
darker, his presence more menacing. He barely fit inside Casmi-

ra, his massive form straining against the confines of the house knocking everything over in his path.

And then, I felt it. The magic of Casmira, the protective charm that had kept us safe, began to fade. It was as if Azazel's presence was draining the life out of my magical house, leaving us exposed and vulnerable. I felt the ungodly creature's power coursing through the air, making my skin crawl with its dark energy.

'Get out!' Eve shouted, but Azazel just laughed, his voice like thunder. Instead of leaving, he moved swiftly towards us, his dark form looming larger with each step. In one swift motion, he sent Eve flying across the room, her body crashing against the wall with a sickening thud. I knew that if she weren't immortal, she would have been dead on impact. I frantically scanned her body for any sign of movement, but there was none. She lay motionless, her eyes closed as if in death.

Then, Azazel turned his attention to me, his eyes burning wickedly. I backed myself all the way up to the fireplace, my heart racing with fear. I was trapped, with nowhere to go. Fear consumed me, and I fell to the ground, covering my eyes with my hands. I told myself I would return, that I would come back again. But deep down, I was terrified. I prepared myself for the end, waiting for Azazel's final blow.

But just as all hope seemed lost, Bellamy burst through the door, his magic blazing with intensity. The dark angel and Bellamy faced off in a fiery battle, their eyes locked in a fierce stare. The air was thick with tension as they circled each other, their powers crackling at their fingers with energy.

The dark angel sneered at Bellamy, its black wings spread wide. "You are no match for me, mortal," it spat. But Bellamy was undeterred, fueled by determination and anger. He charged forward. The two clashed in a spectacular display of power, their blows shaking the ground.

As they fought, the dark angel unleashed a blast of dark energy, striking Bellamy with a bolt of shadowy force. The attack seemed to have no impact on Bellamy, as if he had absorbed the energy into his body. With a swift motion, he countered the strike, unleashing a powerful force that sent Azazel flying across the room. The dark angel's eyes widened in shock as Bellamy effortlessly deflected the attack and retaliated with a strike of his own, sending Azazel crashing into the wall.

Azazel landed with a thud, but in a flash, he vaporized into a dark mist that swirled around Bellamy like a malevolent vortex. Then, in an instant, he rematerialized on top of Bellamy, pinning him to the ground with an inhuman strength that made Bellamy's struggles seem futile. The air was heavy with the stench of brimstone and decay, and Bellamy felt his very soul being drained away by Azazel's crushing grip.

"You will make a fine servant," it hissed. But Bellamy's response was a fierce cry of defiance. "I will never serve you!" With a surge of newfound power, he broke free from the dark angel's grasp.

As the battle raged on, Bellamy's magic became more pronounced. His eyes glowed with a silver blue, otherworldly luminescence and his movements became faster, more fluid. The dark angel stumbled back, its confidence wavering for the first time.

The fight was ravaging the house, and the walls began to crack and crumble, as if the very foundations of Casmira were being torn asunder. The windows shattered, sending shards of glass flying like deadly projectiles. The roof started to collapse, its beams splintering and crashing down amidst the chaos.

Bellamy's magic wasn't weakening, but his face bore the marks of exhaustion. His eyes seemed sunken and worn, his skin pale and clammy. The lines on his forehead deepened as he gritted his teeth.

I don't know how much more he could take, and the dark angel refused to yield. It unleashed a devastating blast of energy that sent Bellamy crashing through the front wall of Casmira, leaving a gaping hole in the wreckage.

I stood frozen in terror, my heart racing, as Bellamy struggled to rise, his body battered and weakened. The dark angel towered over him, its eyes aglow with malevolent triumph, as if savoring the moment of victory. The house around me was disintegrating, walls crumbling, and debris falling, but the dark angel remained unfazed, its focus solely on Bellamy. 'You are mine now,' it hissed, its voice dripping with malice, the words echoing. The air was heavy with foreboding, and I felt a chill run down my spine as the dark angel's shadow seemed to engulf Bellamy.

As suddenly as Azazel appeared, he vanished into thin air, leaving behind a swirling cloud of dust and debris. And in his place, Shemihazah materialized. Velar and the others rushed to Bellamy's side, their faces etched with concern and worry as they helped him sit up and assessed his injuries.

Meanwhile, I hurried to Eve's aid, carefully turning her over and cradling her head in my lap. Her eyes fluttered open, unfocused and dazed, as she struggled to catch her breath. I gently helped her sit up, and she gazed around in confusion, her eyes scanning the destruction and chaos as if trying to piece together the fragments of her shattered world. The air was thick with the acrid smell of smoke and dust, and the sound of groaning wood and crumbling stone filled the air. A haunting scene of devastation surrounded us.

"What happened?" Eve stammered. I took stock of our surroundings, the house reduced to rubble. Walls cracked, furniture splintered, and debris scattered everywhere. Velar rushed in and helped Eve to her feet.

Shemihazah approached Bellamy just as I was getting to him. "We arrived just in time," His voice was gravelly. "Azazel was about to deliver the final blow." Bellamy nodded, his eyes scanning the destruction. As we looked back at the house, I knew our troubles were far from over. I knew Bellamy was running on empty after his fierce battle, and I could see the exhaustion etched on his face.

But even in his worn state, he was still concerned about me, his eyes scanning me with a gentle intensity. "Are you okay?" His voice is low and soothing. I nodded, still trying to process the chaos that had unfolded. Shemihazah stepped forward, his voice ringing out across the clearing. "It seems Azazel vanished into the forest again, I'm going to track him, can't let him escape." Velar agreed to join the hunt.

Bellamy nodded, his eyes clouded with fatigue, but his spirit unbroken. As Shemihazah and Velar disappeared into the darkness, Bellamy turned to me, his eyes softening. "We'll get through this," his voice a gentle promise.

I knew Bellamy was too weak to rebuild Casmira with his magic, so Eve offered us to stay with her in her townhome for the evening. I trailed behind Bellamy as we made our way through the town square, while also lending a supporting arm to Eve, who was still recuperating from her injuries. The two of them were still regaining their strength after the ordeal.

I had just gotten comfortable when Bellamy came over to me and whispered, "Baby girl, I am going to help the others." I instantly sat up, my heart racing, and pleaded, "No, please don't go!" I couldn't believe he was already trying to get involved again after his battle.

I begged him not to go, but he insisted, "Shhh, it's okay. The Blackwood's put a protective spell over the house, and we have guards all around. If they see anything, they'll siren me, and I'll be back so fast." Bellamy nodded at me reassuringly, as if soothing a child to sleep.

As the door closed behind him, my eyes met Eve's, and she simply shrugged her shoulders. "You should get some sleep," she insisted, her voice gentle but firm. My eyes felt heavy, and I couldn't resist the exhaustion any longer. I closed my eyes and let sleep take over, surrendering to the weariness that had been building up.

The knocking on the door was like a death knell, shattering the silence and sending my heart racing. I screamed aloud, my voice hoarse with fear. "Eve!" My eyes wide with terror.

Eve rushed downstairs, her face pale and her eyes haunted. We stared at the front door, our bodies frozen in fear. The knocking grew louder, more insistent. Bellamy was still gone, and I knew we were alone and vulnerable. "Maybe it's them," I whispered, my voice trembling. Eve shook her head, but her eyes betrayed her fear. We waited, our breathing the only sound, as the knocking grew more frantic. Then, a voice called out from the other side of the door, "Mrs. Darlington, are you in there?"

I recognized the voice, but couldn't place it "It's Prudence," Eve said, her voice barely above a whisper. I instantly suspected that Azazel was behind it, pulling another one of his mischievous stunts. I grabbed Eve's arm, my nails digging into her skin.

"Don't answer it," I hissed. "It's not her." Eve's eyes went wide, and she nodded. We waited, our hearts pounding, as the knocking grew louder, more insistent. Whatever was on the other side of the door was not going away.

"Prudence?" Eve asked, her voice cautious. The knocking stopped, and we were met with silence. "Yes, Eve, is Nicole with you?" Prudence replied from the other side of the door.

"When was the first time we met?" Eve asked, her tone probing. She hesitated for a moment before responding, "What do you mean?"

Eve explained, "Tell me, so I know it's really you." Prudence quickly replied, "I met you when you auditioned to be an acrobat for the circus, right after Nicole joined."

Eve, whose eyes were wide with contemplation, her brow furrowed in concentration as her mind sprinted through thoughts.

From the other side of the door she pleaded, 'Evangeline Milton, please let me in!" Eve's expression changed, and she nodded, seemingly satisfied with Prudence using her full name. She quickly opened the door.

Prudence stood in the doorway, her long blonde hair disheveled, and her face etched with distress. It wasn't fear that radiated from her, but a deep sadness. Her brown eyes looked as if she had been crying for hours.

Eve immediately sensed her distress and ushered her inside with a gentle touch. "What's wrong? Are you okay?" Prudence slowly made her way to the kitchen table, her movements heavy with emotion.

I was taken aback by her anguish, and my instincts kicked in, prompting me to call out, "Casmira, make some tea!" But my command was met with Eve's warm chuckles, which brought me back to reality.

"Oh, um, Eve, make some tea," I corrected myself, feeling a bit awkward. Eve stopped laughing and immediately started preparing the tea, her movements efficient and soothing. I walked over to Prudence, my concern growing, and asked, "Why were you looking for me?"

Prudence looked up, her red-rimmed eyes locking onto mine, and said, "I have a confession." Her voice trembled, and her words hung in the air. I sat next to her, my eyes locked on hers, and said, "You can tell me anything." But her gaze darted to Eve, as if seeking permission.

"Is Bellamy here?" she asked, her voice laced with a hint of desperation. "No, it's just us," I replied, my tone firm. "Well, can you be the one to tell him?" Eve joined us, her expression skeptical. "Tell him what?" she asked, her patience wearing thin.

Prudence's eyes fluttered closed, and she took a deep breath before speaking. "Well... I have something to confess. Azazel is here because of me." She paused and looked downward. "I thought I had fallen deeply in love with him, but it was all a ruse. Now, he won't leave me alone." Her voice was laced with embarrassment and a hint of desperation.

"Don't worry, Bellamy will make him leave," I said, trying to reassure her. But Prudence's expression turned distant, and she hesitated before speaking. "It may not be that easy." Her voice was laced with uncertainty, and she seemed nervous, as if she was hiding something.

Eve noticed it too and pressed for more information, "What is it, dear?" My eyes traced the gentle curve of Prudence's hand as it protectively cupped her belly, a telling gesture that spoke volumes. And then, my gaze rose to meet hers, and I was met with a flood of tears. The realization hit me like a wave, crashing over me with a mix of shock and compassion.

"Oh, fuck."

CHAPTER

TEN

"Prudence, when and how did this happen?" I asked gently. She took a deep breath before explaining, her words tumbling out in a rush.

"He deceived me, Prudence said, her voice trembling with anguish. He didn't resemble a dark angel at all - just a man. And I, foolishly, believed him. I must have been drugged because everything's a haze, but the memory of us having sex haunts me. And... and he sneaked into Jubilee." Her voice cracked as she revealed the shocking truth, her eyes welling up with tears. I offered what little reassurance I could, "Don't worry. They'll find him soon, and it will all be over."

I gazed out the window at the star-studded night sky, the darkness seeming to press in around us. "Why not just enchant the sky to stay daylight?" I asked aloud.

"He is in the darkness," Prudence's enigmatic reply left me pondering the secrets she might be hinting at. Her words terrified me.

"In the meantime, we'll stay together in this house, protected by guards and a powerful spell."

But my reassurance was short-lived, as Prudence's next words made my heart sink. "What guards?" She asked, her voice laced with concern. Fear crept in and I wondered what had happened to the guards who were supposed to be protecting us. Had they been compromised or overpowered?

"Don't panic, don't panic," Eve muttered aloud, pacing back and forth across the room. "We just need to stay calm." I finally had to grab her arm to stop her frantic pacing. "We're still protected by the witches' magic," I insisted.

"The angels themselves have magic!" She spat back. "Ladies," Prudence interrupted, her voice low and urgent. She whispered, "It's Azazel." Just then, a loud thud echoed from above, as if someone had landed on the roof. "Oh God," I breathed, my heart racing with fear.

Prudence's eyes darted towards the ceiling, her face pale. "He's here," she mouthed, her voice barely audible. Suddenly, the air seemed to vibrate with an otherworldly energy. The lights flickered, and the shadows on the walls appeared to twist and writhe like living things.

Azazel's voice boomed from above, "Prudence, my love, I've come for you!" The sound of his voice made me freeze. Footsteps echoed from the roof, growing louder with each passing moment. It was as if Azazel was descending into our midst, his presence suffusing the air with an electric sense of anticipation.

"We have to get out of here, now!" Prudence urged, grabbing our hands and pulling us towards the door. But it was too late. Azazel shattered through the ceiling, his wings unfurled and his eyes blazing with an inner fire. He was a vision of terrifying beauty, and I felt my heart quail in fear.

"Prudence, my beloved," Azazel declared, his voice dripping with passion. "We are going to be together forever." Prudence stood frozen, her eyes locked on Azazel's face.

As Azazel's words hung in the air, Prudence's gaze seemed to glaze over, her eyes fixed on some point beyond his shoulder. I felt a chill run down my spine as I realized she was entranced, her mind ensnared by Azazel's otherworldly charm.

"Prudence, No!" I shouted, trying to break the spell. "Don't listen to him!" But she didn't respond, her body swaying towards Azazel as if drawn by an unseen force. I grabbed her arm, trying to pull her back, but she shook me off, her eyes still fixed on Azazel's face.

"Az," she whispered, her voice barely audible.

Azazel's wicked smile grew wider, his eyes blazing with triumph. "Yes, my love," His voice dripped with seduction. "We will be together forever."

With a wave of his hand, the room seemed to dissolve around us, the walls melting away like wax in a furnace. I stumbled backwards, my mind reeling as the world around me disintegrated.

I found myself standing in a vast, empty plain, surrounded by towering mountains that stretched up to the sky. "Welcome to our new home," he said, his voice dripping with malice. "For eternity."

The scene around me was like nothing I had ever witnessed before. It was utterly terrifying, and I couldn't help but wonder if I was in the depths of hell or the underworld. The eerie landscape seemed to stretch on forever, and I felt tiny and vulnerable in its midst.

"Prudence!" I called out, my voice shaking with fear. But she didn't respond. Her eyes were fixed on Azazel, entranced by his presence. She was about to take his hand when suddenly, the world around us shattered like fragile glass. The scene exploded in a kaleidoscope of colors and sounds, and I felt myself being pulled back into reality.

When my vision cleared, I found myself back in the town house. As the dust settled, I gazed around at the townhouse in total ruin, realizing that Shemihazah had once again scared Azazel off leaving nothing but destruction in his wake. The memory of that terrifying scene lingered, etched in my mind haunting me.

I was shaking uncontrollably when Bellamy reached me. "It's okay, baby girl, you're safe," holding me close to him. I looked around and saw Eve with Prudence, who was also trembling.

Shemihazah explained, "Azazel is mimicking your world and trying to create his own. We must stop him, or I fear he will disappear forever."

As I tried to process what was happening, Bellamy's warmth and comfort enveloped me, slowly easing my trembling. I gazed at Prudence, concerned about her well-being after being entranced by Azazel. Eve's supportive presence beside her was reassuring.

"We have to act fast," Shemihazah urged, his eyes scanning the area as if searching for any sign of Azazel's next move. "We can't let him continue to manipulate your world."

Bellamy nodded in agreement, his expression resolute. "Let's gather our strength and come up with a plan. We can't take him down alone."

Eve spoke up, her voice firm. "I'm with you. We can't let Azazel win." Prudence, still looking shaken, nodded silently, her eyes fixed on Shemihazah.

Velar burst through the door, his expression urgent. "Bell, we need to evacuate Jubilee immediately. We can't afford to wait any longer."

I expected Bellamy to refuse, but to my surprise, he nodded in agreement. "I want you to go too," looking at me. "But why can't you come with us?" I asked, hesitant to leave Bellamy behind. "I need to stay and help fight the evil," Bellamy replied, his jaw set in determination. "I'm staying with you, then," I said.

Bellamy enveloped me in an extra-long hug, and I knew he was saying goodbye. Before releasing me, he placed a tender, lingering kiss on my forehead. Then, turned to Eve and instructed, "Take her and get them all to safety."

It seemed Bellamy had already made up his mind, and I knew arguing with him would be futile. Eve gently took my arm, and I reluctantly followed her, knowing Bellamy would face the dark angel once again.

As we emerged from the town house, the sun was rising over Jubilee, casting a golden glow over the chaotic scene. Many people were already hurrying towards the willow tree, eager to evacuate the town. I trailed behind Eve, my feet heavy with reluctance. I couldn't believe I was leaving, and the thought of possibly never seeing it again left me feeling utterly dreadful.

Tears pricked at the corners of my eyes as I gazed around at the familiar sights, now tinged with a sense of loss. This was my home, my sanctuary. How could I leave it behind?

Sadness took over, and I felt my legs give out from under me. Planted on the ground I gazed at my enchanted world that was now haunted by the dark angel. Velar was helping the others escape, his movements swift and urgent. I watched in slow motion as people scurried about, their faces etched with fear.

Towards the shadowy expanse of the Emberlynn Forest, a storm was gathering momentum. Dark clouds boiled with huge bolts of lightning, their leading-edge slashing towards Jubilee like a malevolent scythe. The tempest's fury would soon unleash its full wrath upon Jubilee once again.

This can't be happening, I thought, my mind reeling in disbelief. Jubilee, the place I loved, was being torn apart by darkness. And I was leaving Bellamy behind, my love.

My heart felt heavy, weighed down by the uncertainty of it all. Would I ever see *Bellamy again? Would Jubilee ever be the same? Would I reincarnate?* The questions swirled in my mind like a maelstrom, threatening to consume me.

Eve pulled me to my feet, and I followed in a daze, everything felt like it was in slow motion. I am trailing behind the crowd up the spiral stairs to the circus. Everything seemed to blur together, and I stumbled. Eve's grip on my hand was the only thing that kept me moving forward.

Everyone quickly followed the same path to the front gate. I was disoriented and had no idea where we were in the world.

The troupe poured out of the circus like a river, and I was swept along with them, unable to resist the tide of bodies. We spilled out onto the city sidewalk with brightly lit streetlights, and I blinked, my eyes adjusting slowly to the darkness. The sudden transition from morning to night was a disorienting and overwhelming experience.

As the crowd dispersed, I found myself standing on a familiar city street in New York City. I gazed up at the street sign, my eyes widening in surprise and when I saw the green and white sign displaying seventy sixth street. I was close to home.

Eve walked up behind me and said, "Bellamy thought it would be best if you stayed with your mom until it was safe for you again." I nodded numbly, still trying to process everything that had happened.

But then I turned to Eve and asked, "Do you want to stay with me?" I already knew her answer, but I had to ask. Eve's expression was sympathetic, but firm. "You know I need to stay," her voice was gentle but resolute.

"I'm walking you home," Velar said, walking up from behind Eve and me. He stepped closer to me on the street corner. I hesitated, unsure if I wanted to leave, but Velar's kind eyes and reassuring smile put me at ease. "No arguments, Nic," he added, his tone playful but firm, as he gestured for me to start walking.

I began to walk slowly in the direction of my mother's apartment. "Can you stay with me?" I already knew the answer.

'Someone has to save Bells ass,' he said with a shake of his head, his tone a mix of amusement and resignation. I nodded slowly, understanding. They had to go back to Jubilee, to help Bellamy and the others. And I had to stay here, in the safety of my own world. But it was hard to let go. I felt helpless.

Eve's expression softened, "Don't worry, we'll be back for you." Velar nodded in agreement, adding, "We always do."

Before I could respond, they both wrapped me in a warm embrace. I hesitated for a moment, then reciprocated, holding them tightly. The hug was a mix of comfort, reassurance, and sadness. We all knew that our paths were parting ways, at least for now.

As we pulled back, I saw a determined look on their faces. They had a mission to complete. I watched as Eve turned and walked away, disappearing into the crowd.

Velar took my hand and walked me home, and I was happy to be seeing my mother. But my heart was heavy with sorrow, leaving behind Jubilee and Bellamy. We didn't talk much on the way, but I had to ask Velar,

"How are you going to defeat a dark angel?" Velar's expression turned somber, and he shook his head, "Hell if I know," he admitted. "But we'll find a way. Bellamy always figures some way." A slight chuckle escaped Velar's lips, his eyes gazing into the distance as if reminiscing about past memories of their time together.

Defeating a fallen angel seemed like an impossible task. I felt a lump form in my throat as I thought about Bellamy, Eve, and the others who were staying in Jubilee, fighting against the forces of pure darkness. *If people only knew.*

As we reached the front door, I bid Velar farewell, but my mother's excited scream cut our goodbye short. "Nicole!" she exclaimed, sweeping me into a warm embrace. "You're back!" she said, her eyes shining with joy. "Yes, for a little while," I replied, hoping that was true.

I introduced Velar to my mother as the circus's strongman and I could almost see him struggling to keep his fangs hidden. When I noticed my mother carrying her purse I asked, "Where are you going?"

"To church, there's a late service on Saturdays, why don't you both come?" I knew Velar would decline. Velar declined with a gentle smile, his mouth closed tightly as he shook his head.

My mother, oblivious to the subtle exchange, beamed with enthusiasm. "Well, Nicole, are you coming with me? We can go for dinner after, I'm so excited you're here!" Her eyes sparkling with excitement.

My mind began to wander. In this lifetime I grew up Roman Catholic, and it has been a significant part of my life's journey so far. I found myself thinking about church. Which, of course, led me to thoughts of God. And that's when it hit me - a sudden spark of realization.

Hearing my mother talk about church, a sudden spark ignited within me, and I was transported back to my childhood.

Memories of church services, sacraments, and sacred rituals flooded my mind. The scent of incense, the sound of hymns, and the feel of worn pews all came rushing back.

And then, like a flash of lightning, I remembered God - the constant presence in my life, the source of comfort and guidance. The spark of memory had lit a fire, and I felt the warmth of nostalgia wash over me.

"Nicole?" My mother said, snapping me out of my daydream. "No Mom, I'm so sorry, but I forgot something! But I'll be back!" I exclaimed, grabbing Velar's arm and sprinting back towards the circus.

CHAPTER

ELEVEN

'No way, you're not going back in there!' Velar yelled to me outside the circus gate. At this point, a crowd was starting to gather around the perimeter of the circus. Although they couldn't get inside, it was attracting a lot of unwanted attention.

'I know how to defeat the Dark Angel!' I shouted to Velar over the din of the city, my voice carrying a sense of determination and urgency.

Velar urging me to stay, clearly not taking me seriously. But when he saw the determined look on my face, he asked calmly, 'How?' I didn't have time to explain, so I blurted out, 'I need the Blackwood's' help!'

Just as we were about to reenter the circus, Orlow burst through the gate and ran out into the city traffic, causing chaos and accidents in his wake. "For Pete's sake!" Someone shouted from the sidewalk, as I called out, 'Orlow!'

The poor elephant was terrified, and his panic led to a trail of destruction, with him backing into cars and knocking over various objects. "Get Lost!" An angry taxi driver startled the elephant more causing him to back up and destroy cars in his path.

I calmly approached him, and when he saw me, he relaxed slightly, allowing me to reach him. Velar kept the gathering crowd at bay as I carefully guided him away from the mayhem. Once Orlow felt secure, he hoisted me onto his back, and Velar quickly ushered us back to the circus, amidst shouts and yells from the bystanders. 'We needed to jump right away,' Velar said, his voice laced with urgency, but it was too late, we'd already drawn too much attention.

Once inside the circus, Velar swiftly secured the gates and led us to the majestic willow tree, its branches swaying gently in the sunlight. Orlow's trumpet blast was a clear indication that he had no intention of returning to Jubilee, so Velar carefully bound him in the backyard of the circus, ensuring his safety. Then, together, we descended the spiral stairs hidden within the willow's trunk.

Jubilee was shrouded in gloom and turmoil. We huddled inside the tree trunk, seeking refuge from the torrential rain that had suddenly turned to hailstones the size of golf balls. The wind howled and buffeted us, making it impossible to see more than a few feet in front of us. The gray sky cracked and boomed with thunder, and lightning bolts illuminated the chaos, casting eerie flashes of light on the tumultuous scene. The storm raged on, its fury unrelenting.

As the hail subsided and turned to rain, we seized the opportunity to make a dash for the Emberlynn Forest. 'Did the Blackwood's stay?' I quickly asked Velar, my voice laced with urgency. Most people had fled, but if I knew the witches like I think I did, they would have stayed.

'I think so!' Velar yelled above the storm, his voice barely audible over the thunder's roar. Just then, a lightning bolt streaked across the sky, its electrifying crack making us both jump.

Without hesitation, Velar swept me up in his arms and unleashed his vampire speed, hurtling us through the torrential rain towards the witch's cottage. We reached the doorstep in a blur, the storm's fury still raging around us.

Velar burst through the door with urgency. Within seconds Mesidor stood before us.

Mesidor hastily closed the door behind us. 'Be very quiet,' he instructed, his voice barely above a whisper. That's when I noticed that all the lights in the cottage were off, plunging us into darkness.

Ambrette and Clove entered the room shortly after, their faces illuminated only by the faint glow of a candle. Velar quickly filled Clove in on Orlow's whereabouts, but I interrupted before he could finish. 'But that's not why we're here,' I said with urgency.

The Blackwood's gazed at me intently, their eyes burning with curiosity. Even Velar leaned in, his interest piqued. 'I know you can communicate with the dead and the spiritual world,' I began, my voice steady. 'So, is it possible to communicate with an angel?'

Velar raised an eyebrow. 'Another angel?' he asked. 'Not just any angel,' I clarified in a whisper, 'but The Archangel, Michael.' Ambrette's eyes lit up, and she nodded enthusiastically, glancing at her husband. Mesidor's expression turned thoughtful, and he asked, 'Why him?'

I took a deep breath, recalling childhood memories. 'I remember going to church with my mom, and according to the Book of Revelation, Archangel Michael defeated Lucifer and the fallen angels. He's already done it before,' I said, my conviction growing."

Ambrette's eyes sparkled with determination. "I believe we can. We've worked with the spiritual realm before, and I'm quite confident we can make contact with him."

She turned and looked at Mesidor, giving him a playful slap on his chest, "Why didn't we think of that?" She whispered. Shrugging his shoulders he gave his wife a playful smile.

Clove joined the conversation, his curiosity piqued. "Mom, how can we—" he began to ask, but before he could finish, I interrupted him with a gentle "Shhh." Clove's eyes widened, and he nodded, his voice barely above a whisper. "How?"

Ambrette smiled, her expression thoughtful. "We'll need to prepare a sacred space, cleanse our energies, and focus our intentions. Then, we can use a combination of meditation, prayer, and invocation to reach out to the Archangel Michael."

Mesidor nodded in agreement. "And I'll mix a special blend of herbs to enhance our connection."

Velar's eyes narrowed slightly. "I'll keep watch, make sure we're not interrupted." I took a deep breath, feeling a sense of excitement and trepidation. "Let's do it. Let's call upon Archangel Michael."

The Blackwood's began preparing the space, their movements fluid and practiced. I watched, fascinated, as they worked together seamlessly. Ambrette lit candles, Clove burned incense, and Mesidor sprinkled herbs around the room. Velar stood guard, his eyes scanning the shadows.

As they finished, Ambrette beckoned me to sit with them in a circle. "Join hands, everyone. Let's connect our energies and call upon Michael." We sat, hands clasped and closed our eyes. Ambrette began to pray.

"Saint Michael the Archangel, defend us in battle.
Be our protection against the wickedness and snares of the
devil.
May God rebuke him, we humbly pray;
and do thou, O Prince of the Heavenly Host,
by the power of God, cast into hell Satan.
and all the evil spirits who prowl throughout the world
seeking the ruin of souls.
Amen."

As I clasped hands with the witch family, their warmth and energy enveloped me, and I felt the weight of their genuine devotion. Their whispers of ancient incantations and tender prayers stirred the air, and I couldn't help but ponder the cruel irony of a world that often-shunned witches, yet desperately needed their brand of kindness and compassion.

The Blackwood's embodied the very essence of unconditional love, standing by us through trials and tribulations, their support a beacon of hope in the darkest corners of Darlington Circus.

And in that moment, I realized that the labels we assign to one another - witch, believer, or mortal or immortal - are mere illusions, fading into insignificance before the radiance of our shared humanity. For in the eyes of the divine, we are all equal, our hearts beating as one, our souls yearning for connection and understanding.

Ambrette prayed,

"Saint Michael the Archangel, defend us in battle.
Be our protection against the wickedness and snares of the
devil.
May God rebuke him, we humbly pray;
and do thou, O Prince of the Heavenly Host,
by the power of God, cast into hell Satan.
and all the evil spirits who prowl throughout the world
seeking the ruin of souls.
Amen."

The Blackwood's continued to pray, their voices unwavering despite the wind's fierce howling against their cottage. Velar and I joined in, our voices trembling at first, but growing stronger as we repeated the words alongside them.

I prayed with every fiber of my being, every inch of my body calling out to Saint Michael to come save us. My bones vibrated with the urgency of my plea, my heart racing with fear and hope.

The wind howled and the cottage creaked, threatening to lift off its foundations. But whenever the storm intensified, the witches' voices grew louder, their prayer more fervent. I tried to match their intensity, chanting the prayer alongside them, my voice rising with each repetition.

Just when it seemed like the cottage was about to take flight, the door burst open and Bellamy and Eve rushed in, their hair and clothes disheveled by the wind. Ambrette's grip on my hand tightened, and I continued to chant, my voice merging with the others.

Bellamy and Eve joined in, their voices blending with ours, and slowly, they reached out and took our hands, forming a circle of unity. Together, we prayed to Archangel Michael, our voices a beacon of hope amidst the Pandemonium.

Then, a familiar voice boomed from outside, making our blood run cold. 'I wouldn't do that if I were you,' Shemihazah growled, his tone dripping with malice. 'Stop now, or I'll have no choice but to destroy you.'

Ambrette's chanting faltered, but the others continued, undeterred. 'He's trying to stop us from summoning Michael,' Ambrette whispered urgently, 'but it's our only chance.' With renewed determination, Ambrette joined the chant once more. Louder.

Bellamy was a man of his word, and he rarely went back on his promises. Ambrette knew this about him and quickly reminded him, 'Remember whose side you're on, Bellamy.' Her words were laced with a hint of urgency, as if to snap him out of his momentary hesitation. Ambrette's gaze locked onto Bellamy's, her eyes burning with an unspoken message: 'Don't let Shemihazah get to you. We need you.'

He nodded resolutely, knowing what he had to do. He began to pray to Michael, his voice steady and strong. But just as he started, Shemihazah unleashed his dark powers, and the cottage around us began to crumble.

Just as Bellamy began to pray, Shemihazah unleashed his dark power, and a devastating blast struck the cottage. The impact was catastrophic, tearing the structure apart and sending us all flying. Our hands were ripped apart, breaking the circle and silencing our prayers. I felt myself hurled through the air, my senses reeling from the force of the explosion.

As I struggled to regain my footing, I saw the others scattered around me, our eyes wide with shock and fear. The cottage, once a symbol of hope and refuge, now lay in ruins from Shemihazah's merciless wrath.

We scrambled back to each other, Bellamy positioning himself protectively in front of me. We huddled together, united in our determination. Ambrette grasped our hands, and with a fierce urgency, began praying to Michael once more. We all followed her lead, our voices merging in a desperate plea for protection.

Just as we prayed, a dark cloud hurtled towards us, and I recognized the ominous form of Azazel. Shemihazah didn't hesitate to launch another attack, but this time, Bellamy raised his arm to the sky, and a brilliant lightning bolt exploded in front of us, deflecting the dark magic. The two forces collided in a spectacular display of light and sound, sending shockwaves through the air.

We clung to each other, our hands intertwined as we prayed, but an unseen force sought to tear us apart. We held fast, our grip on each other tightening as the pressure grew.

Azazel materialized before us, his dark form coalescing into a twisted, nightmarish visage. With a flick of his wrist, he unleashed a dark energy that wrenched us from each other's grasp, sending us tumbling to the ground. We landed hard, our bodies sprawled in different directions, our connection broken.

Pain ravaged my body, making every attempt to rise excruciating. I laid there helpless, as Bellamy stood tall, his eyes blazing with determination. He wielded his magic with precision, striking the fallen angels with a fierce intensity, despite the agony etched on his face.

I prayed to Michael, my heart racing with fear, as I watched Bellamy absorb every brutal blow the angels delivered to him. His body trembled, his steps faltered, and I thought, 'This is it. He's going to actually die.' The thought had me screaming out for him in agony.

I tried to rise again, but the pain was too intense, forcing me back down. 'Bellamy!' I cried out in despair, my voice trembling as I lay helpless. I frantically scanned the area, my heart sinking as I took in the devastation. Eve and Velar lay motionless on the ground, while Mesidor, Clove, and Ambrette were buried under the rubble, their bodies still and lifeless.

My gaze returned to Bellamy, and I watched in horror as he stumbled under a final, brutal blow from the dark angels. He crumpled to the ground, and I screamed his name, 'BELLA-MY!'

Flipping onto my stomach, I crawled towards him, but the dark angels closed in, their sinister forms looming over him. I couldn't bear to look, fearing what they would do to him next. I buried my face in the ground, overcome with fear and grief, as the dark angels stalked towards him, their ominous shadows looming larger with each step.

Just as all hope seemed lost, a radiant light illuminated the dark angels, forcing them to recoil in discomfort. The air seemed to vibrate with an otherworldly power as Michael, the archangel, descended upon the scene. His presence was like a whirlwind, dispersing the shadows and filling the air with an electric sense of purpose.

The dark angels snarled and bared their teeth, but Michael stood tall, his eyes blazing with a fierce inner light. He raised a hand, and a shaft of pure energy shot forth. Striking the dark angels and sending them stumbling back. The ground shook beneath his feet as he strode towards Bellamy, his gaze burning with a fierce determination. I felt a surge of hope and strength flow through me, and I knew that Michael had come to turn the tide of this desperate battle.

With a gentle touch, Michael reached out and grasped Bellamy's hand, pulling him to his feet. Bellamy's eyes fluttered open, and he gazed up at Michael with a mix of awe and gratitude. Michael's face was stern, but his eyes shone with a warm light as he spoke in a voice that was both commanding and comforting.

'Rise, Bellamy. We must stand strong against the forces of darkness.' As he spoke, Michael's back shimmered with a soft, ethereal light, and his magnificent wings unfolded from his shoulders. Feathers of purest white and gold rustled softly as he stretched them wide, casting a protective shadow over us. Bellamy nodded, his strength seeming to have returned with Michael's words.

Together, they turned to face the dark angels, who were now advancing with renewed ferocity. Michael raised his hand once more, and a brilliant light enveloped us, protecting us from the dark angels' attacks. I felt a surge of energy and hope flow through me, and I knew that we were not alone in this fight.

As the dark angels closed in, Michael's wings beat powerful and slow, creating a whirlwind that sent them stumbling back. The air was filled with the sweet scent of vanilla and the sound of soft chanting, and I felt a sense of peace wash over me. Bellamy stood tall, his eyes shining with a newfound strength, and together they approached the dark angels.

Michael's sword flashed in the dim light, striking true and sending the dark angel fleeing in disarray. And then, in the midst of the chaos, I saw Azazel, the fallen angel, his eyes blazing with hatred and his wings dark as coal. He sneered at Michael, and I knew that this was the moment of truth.

The battle raged on, Michael's sword clashing with Azazel's dark magic. Bellamy wielded all his magic once again, but Azazel's power was formidable. Just when it seemed like they were losing, Michael grasped Bellamy's arm and yelled, 'Now!'

With a swift motion, Michael shackled the dark angels in chains of pure light. 'You will not escape this time,' Michael declared, his eyes blazing with authority.

And then, with a swift gesture, Bellamy reached up to the sky. Jubilee vibrated beneath us, jumping us out of NYC. A second later I knew exactly where we had landed.

I watched, Velar, Eve, Ambrette, Clove, and Mesidor struggled to their feet, their faces etched in pain, but thankfully, all still alive. Bellamy followed close behind Michael, who was leading the way, tearing a seam through the air with his sword. I was amazed by the sight, but quickly followed as they escorted the fallen angels back to their rightful place.

The eerie glow of the Euphrates River, the entrance to the underworld stretching out before us. The water was a sickly shade of green, like a festering wound, and it seemed to writhe and twist like a living thing.

The air was thick with the stench of decay and corruption, and I could feel a malevolent presence lurking just beneath the surface and I didn't need to be told, we had arrived in the realm of the damned. Shemihazah and Azazel struggled against their chains, but Michael's power was unwavering.

As Michael raised his sword to condemn them to hell, Azazel's voice echoed through the air, 'You'll be interested to know, Saint Michael, that one of the humans is carrying a Nephilim child.' Shemihazah and Azazel's wicked laughter and mockery made my skin crawl, but Michael's expression remained unfaltering.

With a swift motion, he wielded his sword to part the water in the river, then parted a crack in the earth, he banished them to the underworld, sealing the ground and water above them. Back to the underworld for them, to await judgment day.

CHAPTER
TWELVE

As Bellamy conversed with Saint Michael, The Archangel, I turned to see Velar and Eve approaching us. But Michael's stern tone commanded my attention. 'You're not destined for immortality or magical powers,' his eyes narrowed on Bellamy. 'However, I don't sense any malicious intent from you. So, I'll overlook it… for the time being.'

Then, as suddenly as he appeared, Michael bid us farewell. We thanked him profusely as he vanished into a brilliant white light, his departure as majestic as his arrival. The light enveloped him, and in an instant, he was gone, leaving us to ponder the mysteries of the world.

As we gazed around, the circus lay in ruins. Destroyed and crumbling. Bellamy exclaimed, "Let's jump out of here now!" I knew he wanted to escape far away, never to return to this side of the world ever again.

We hastily made our way through the devastation, back to the weeping willow tree, the sole structure still standing amidst the wreckage. Down in Jubilee, a palpable sadness hung in the air.

Many people had vacated the area, while others slowly emerged from their homes, shell-shocked, to survey the destruction. Devastating barely scratched the surface of what Jubilee had become after the fallen angels' annihilation.

Bellamy took my hand, and together we gazed around at the devastation. I knew that the quickest way to restore everything would be through Bellamy's magic, but I had no idea how long it would take him to rebuild everything. My heart felt heavy as I watched people gathering their belongings from their homes, which looked like they had been ravaged by a tornado. The scene was heartbreaking, and I couldn't help but wonder how long it would take for our community to recover.

With a sweeping gesture, Bellamy raised his arms to the sky, and in a flash, we were transported to a new location. The familiar vibrating sensation washed over me, and I felt the thrill of Bellamy's magic coursing through the air.

"Wow, I feel... I feel myself again," Bellamy said, his eyes shining with wonder. He strode confidently towards the town square, his footsteps filled with purpose. With a deft flick of his wrist, a brilliant flash of white light burst from his fingers, illuminating the devastated area.

"Thank you, Saint Michael," Bellamy called out as he used his magic. The light danced across the ruins, and the air hummed with energy as the town square began to rebuild itself, stone by stone, before our very eyes.

With a burst of energy, Bellamy sprinted towards the town homes, his magic at the ready. With a swift gesture, he wielded his power once more, and astonishingly, the town homes began to rebuild themselves. The walls rose from the rubble, the roofs took shape, and the windows sparkled into existence, all in a matter of moments. The air was filled with the sound of hammering and sawing, but it was Bellamy's magic that was doing the work, restoring the homes to their former charm.

Eve, Velar, and I watched in utter amazement as Bellamy zigzagged across the town, his magic bursting forth in a dazzling display. With each swift gesture, he blasted his power at anything that needed repair, and in an instant, the damaged structures transformed before our eyes. Buildings, homes, and even the smallest details were recreated with precision and speed, as if Bellamy's magic was unraveling time itself.

When the town was fully restored, Bellamy returned to us, beaming with pride. "Time to go home, baby girl," his smile radiated. We all sprinted together towards the destroyed Casmira, its walls blasted out, and my belongings scattered across the yard. But Bellamy was ready to work his magic once more.

With a confident stride, he approached my beloved house and raised both hands, unleashing a brilliant white light that enveloped the structure. Piece by piece, the house began to reassemble itself, walls reforming, windows reshaping, and doors rematerializing, all in a matter of moments.

After dedicating a significant amount of time to restoring Casmira to its earlier majesty, I assumed Bellamy would be drained of energy. However, to my surprise, he flashed a vibrant smile and exclaimed to Velar, "I need to fix the Emberlynn Forest!"

Velar nodded and without hesitation, the two men took off towards the hills, leaving me to stay behind with Eve at Casmira. I nodded in understanding, knowing that Bellamy's determination to repair the damage was unwavering.

Eve and I strolled up the steps to Casmira, and as we reached the entrance, the door swung open, welcoming me back home. "Welcome back, Casmira!" I exclaimed, my voice filled with excitement as we walked inside. Instantly the sound of pots and pans clanging from the kitchen, and I knew instinctively that Casmira was preparing something delicious to eat.

As we entered the cozy main room, a warm and inviting fire roared to life, casting a golden glow across the space. Eve and I settled into our favorite spots on the oversized suede leather couch, feeling the softness immersed us.

Just as we were settling in, two glasses of wine materialized on the coffee table before our eyes. I reached for a glass, gratefully, and called out, "Thank you, Casmira! I'll never take you for granted!" Eve nodded in agreement, smiling. We both savored our first sips, feeling the warmth and relaxation spread through us.

We had finished our first glass when Velar and Bellamy returned, their faces beaming with smiles. Bellamy walked over to me, his eyes shining with love and adoration. Without a word, he gently cupped my face in his hands and leaned in, planting a passionate kiss on my lips. As our lips touched, I felt a surge of happiness and relief wash over me.

When he finally pulled back, my eyes slowly opened to see him smiling at me, his eyes sparkling with joy. "Everything is fixed, baby girl," his voice full of emotion. Overcome with happiness, I threw my arms around him, hugging him tightly. Velar, meanwhile, took a seat next to Eve, and Bellamy and I joined them, our faces still aglow with triumph and exhaustion.

"I can't believe what we just went through," Velar exclaimed, still trying to process the enormity of their experience. Bellamy smiled knowingly. "Well now, I think it's time for you to start believing," his voice filled with conviction. Velar nodded slowly, a look of wonder still etched on his face, as if he was only just beginning to grasp the true nature of their reality.

As we sat around talking about fallen angels and Saint Michael, our minds began to wander to the others who had left. "I think it's time we bring everyone back home," I said to Bellamy, and he agreed with a nod.

"Can we make a quick stop in NYC first?" A hint of longing in my voice. Bellamy's eyes softened, and he smiled knowingly. "Yes, my dear," he replied, his voice gentle.

As the circus settled back into the vibrant city of NYC, Eve, along with a few others, set out to gather our family members who had evacuated. I was eager to reunite with my mom for a couple of days and spend some time with her.

We went to our favorite diner, and roller skated. We strolled through familiar streets and shopped, laughing, and reminiscing. I told her about some of the incredible experiences I'd had and the unbreakable bonds I'd formed with Bellamy and the others. My mom listened with tears in her eyes, her heart overflowing with pride and joy.

When it was time to leave, I hugged my mom tightly and said goodbye once again, but I knew I'd be back to visit soon. I was excited to get back to the routine of the circus, to the thrill of the performances.

Bellamy was waiting for me across the street from my apartment, and my heart skipped a beat as I saw him. "Daddy!" I exclaimed aloud, my excitement drawing curious glances from passersby. But I didn't care, I was too thrilled to see him. I ran across the street, throwing my arms around him in a tight embrace.

Bellamy and I strolled hand in hand into the closed circus. Bellamy was about to close the gate when a familiar voice called out, 'Bellamy!' He turned, his eyes scanning the crowd, and a hint of surprise crossed his face.

With a warm smile, he opened the gate wider, and in walked Prudence, her radiant presence commanding attention. But it was her noticeable baby bump that caught my eye.

Prudence hesitated inside the gate, her eyes seeking Bellamy's reassurance. He offered a warm, encouraging smile and said, 'Don't worry, we're here for you.' His words seemed to melt away her uncertainty, and a gentle smile spread across her face. With a newfound sense of confidence, she nodded, and we all strolled together towards Jubilee.

CHAPTER
THIRTEEN

The vibration faded as we strolled into the town square, replaced by a soothing tranquility that enveloped us, bringing a welcome sense of relief. I didn't care where our next destination was; I was just thrilled to be done with the fallen angels.

Upon our return, the town square was abuzz with everyone gathering, eager to welcome us back. I beamed with excitement as I spotted the Rossi family among the returnees. Bellamy and I walked hand in hand, greeting each familiar face with warmth.

'Welcome back!' I exclaimed to Giuseppe and the entire Rossi family, my voice filled with joy. The atmosphere was electric, with everyone marveling at Jubilee's remarkable restoration. The very essence of the town had been revitalized, and magic danced through the air.

Henry joined Bellamy and Velar, and together we stood amidst the cheerful crowd, chatting with friends and welcoming everyone back to Jubilee. Hugs and laughter filled the air. It was a truly heartwarming reunion, with everyone thrilled to be back in the safety of our beloved town.

Many of the immortals' conversations were laced with disgust and disappointment as they discussed the outside world. Their words were tinged with a sense of relief and gratitude for being back in Jubilee, away from the chaos that lay beyond our borders.

As Henry recounted his tale of Azazel, his words trailed off, and his gaze locked onto something in the distance. We followed his gaze and were met with a sight that took our breath away. Eve emerged from behind the weeping willow tree, followed by Anise and Miss Poppet. Henry's eyes widened, and his mouth hung agape, until Velar's playful taunt broke the spell. 'Go get her, you fool!' Velar exclaimed, and Henry took off in a sprint, racing towards Anise.

We watched, entranced, as he swept her into his arms, twirling her around and planting a tender kiss on her lips. The scene was pure love, like something right out of an Audrey Hepburn movie. The crowd in the square erupted into cheers.

I felt a tear roll down my cheek, much to Velar's delight. 'You're such a sap Nic!' he teased, as Bellamy wrapped me in a warm embrace. Together, we watched as Henry and Anise strolled towards us, hand in hand, their happiness shining brighter than the sun.

I wrapped Miss Poppet in a tight hug, expressing my gratitude for her unwavering care and protection of Anise. Her eyes scanned the surroundings, and I reassured her, 'It's okay, the dark angels are gone.' Her tense expression eased, replaced by a gentle smile. 'I better get baking then!' Her eyes twinkled with excitement.

Then, Bellamy's voice boomed through invisible magic speakers, his words electrifying the air: 'Tomorrow, the circus opens!' The crowd exploded into cheers, and I found myself jumping up and down with uncontainable excitement. I was ready, but as I looked around at everyone's beaming faces, I realized we all were.

As everyone dispersed, Bellamy offered his arm to escort me home. I was reluctant to end my conversation with Eve, but he gently took my hand and said, 'It's time to go home,' his politeness tinged with a hint of playfulness. I smiled as he subtly pulled me away from Eve, and we strolled together in comfortable silence. Nearing Casmira, I knew what my husband's intentions were, and my heart skipped a beat in excitement.

As Bellamy opened the door to the playroom, I felt a rush of anticipation. I was nervous but aroused. As he undressed me, his voice filled with emotion.

"Being with you is not enough, I need to own you." Not a question but a statement, which made me weak in the knees.

He moved closer, his sea blue eyes locked on mine, and I sensed his desire. Taking my arm, he led me to a black leather table with restraints. With gentle care, he helped me onto it and started to buckle my ankles and wrists. I started trembling as I waited patiently. Bellamy saw me and placed his hand on my neck. His touch soothed my nerves with his magic. "Oh, baby girl, it's been too long," he moaned. Standing in front of me he slowly lowered his pants exposing his true masculine radiance.

Without needing words, I knew what he wanted. I opened my mouth, inviting him in. Our connection deepened, and I felt his passion. My mouth watered as I took him deeper and deeper until he was making me gag. Bellamy roared like a hungry beast.

As he tenderly pulled away, he traced his fingers down my spine, sending shivers down my back, leaving me craving his hands. His hands explored my body, teasing and tantalizing me. I begged for more, and he obliged.

Our bodies merged, and I arched my back, feeling his presence. "Oh, Daddy," I moaned, lost in the moment. Bellamy's gentle thrusts intensified, and I felt his excitement build. As we reached the peak, Bellamy's body trembled, and his magic swirled around us. A soft, baby blue glow enveloped us, leaving me tingling and satisfied.

With a flick of his finger he released me from my restraints, then he scooped me up and carried me down the hall to our bedroom.

Before I knew it Bellamy was snoring softly, and I lay in bed savoring the cozy feeling. Just when I was going to reach for a book to read, a tray of late-night snacks appeared in front of me.

I quickly sat up and started to indulge in a delicious elephant ear. The dough was so perfectly balanced with cinnamon and sugar that I knew it had to be one of Miss Poppet's famous treats from her bake shop. Just as I finished my snack, a glass of milk appeared, and I drank it down, savoring it's refreshing coldness.

When I was tired and my eyes began to close, I snuggled close to Bellamy, who was unaware of my touch as he was deep asleep. I heard an abrupt noise downstairs. I lay still, about to wake Bellamy, but then I heard laughter. The voices sounded familiar, and I quickly jumped out of bed and tiptoed down the three flights of stairs.

As I approached, I could hear Eve and Velar's voices growing louder. When I reached the landing, I asked, "What are you guys doing?" Velar flashed a mischievous smirk as he caught my eye, and Eve exclaimed, "We didn't get to celebrate your return, so we are sneaking you out to have some fun! Velar said, "We miss having fun with you, and now that we aren't being haunted by angels, I think we all deserve a night out."

I stared at Eve with a beaming smile, unsure of what to do. "Get dressed!" she snapped, and I finally nodded and tiptoed back upstairs trying not to wake my snoring husband. I slipped into the closet and changed into a little black dress. I added a headband to complete the look.

I really missed hanging out with my friends! While we always have a great time with Bellamy, it's a different dynamic when it's just the three of us - Velar, Eve, and myself. When Bellamy's around, it feels like we need to be on our best behavior, but when he's not, we can relax, be ourselves a bit more, and we always have a blast together!

I was so excited to get to the town square, I wondered who else would be awake and out at this hour, especially since we were opening the circus tomorrow. I crept past Bellamy, stilettos clutched in my hand and tiptoed towards the bedroom door.

Just as I was about to slip out the door, I heard Bellamy's gentle voice call out, "Have fun." I paused, turned back towards the darkness, and made my way to his bedside. Leaning down, I gave him a soft kiss goodbye, feeling the warmth of his smile beneath my lips. I knew he truly meant it. He wanted me to let loose and enjoy my time with friends. With that loving sendoff, I slipped out the door and down the stairs.

When I got downstairs, I expected to see Velar and Eve waiting for me, but they were nowhere to be found. I listened carefully, but the house was silent. I slipped on my heels and stepped outside into the crisp night air, and that's when I saw them. Sitting on the porch swing, waiting patiently for me. "Are you ready?" Velar asked, and I nodded eagerly. Eve chimed in with an excited "Let's go!"

We followed the porch steps down and through the iron gate as it opened up for us. We strolled along the pine straw path through the dense forest, the moon casting silver shadows on the ground. As we emerged from the woods, I headed towards the town square, but Eve and Velar suddenly stopped in their tracks. I turned around, curious, and asked "What's going on?" Velar stepped closer, a mischievous glint in their eye, and said "We're going out." My mind raced - surely, they didn't mean to leave Jubilee.

Eve started walking towards me. I shook my head vehemently, realizing they wanted to venture out into the real world, beyond the safety of Jubilee. I knew Bellamy would never approve.

"No way," I said firmly, trying to sound convincing. But Eve was persistent, her eyes sparkling with excitement. "Come on, Nic, have some fun for once!" she urged. I hesitated, feeling a knot form in my stomach.

"Guys, you know Bellamy wouldn't want me leaving," I protested. But Velar was quick to reassure me. "We'll be back before he's even awake," he promised. "We're just going to sightsee, get a feel for where we are. We're opening up the circus tomorrow, after all." Eve said as she pulled me towards the willow tree.

Velar's voice dripped with sarcasm as he said, 'I won't tell Daddy.' The way he emphasized 'Daddy' made it clear he was mocking my relationship with Bellamy. I felt a surge of annoyance, but Eve's excited chirping distracted me. 'Come on, Nic, it'll be fun, I promise!' she said, tugging on my arm.

Velar's smirk grew wider showing both his sharp fangs as he added, 'Yeah, Nic, live a little. Bell won't even notice we're gone.' Despite my reservations, their enthusiasm eventually wore me down, and I reluctantly agreed to join them on their adventure. Who am I kidding, I love an adventure!

Eve grasped my hand, and we darted towards the weeping willow tree, its branches swaying ominously in the cool night breeze. We climbed the stairs, our footsteps echoing on the deserted circus cobblestones. As we slipped out the circus gate, I couldn't help but think I should have changed into something more practical. But I pushed that thought aside, focusing on the thrill of the night.

I gazed out at the unfamiliar surroundings. A street sign read: Melrose Avenue. It must have been around nine pm, the streetlamps casting long shadows across the sidewalk. Neon signs of the coffee shops and record stores flickered like fireflies.

While the darkened windows of the head shops and psychedelic poster stores, adorned with Day-Glo colors and Peter Max-inspired artwork. A group in mod dresses and bell-bottom jeans, appeared like ghosts drifting through the misty veil of the LA night. Sounds of Jimi Hendrix and The Doors drifting from the nearby clubs.

Just then, a sleek, cherry-red 1962 Ferrari swooshed by, its engine purring like a contented beast, followed by a gleaming, midnight-blue 1963 Corvette Sting Ray, its exhaust notes echoing off the buildings as it disappeared into the night, leaving behind a trail of excitement.

"Where are we?" I asked. Velar's smile grew wide, "LA, baby!" His deep voice sounding mischievous. The twinkling city lights made me miss New York City, but only briefly. I was too excited to explore this city for the evening. Velar smiled as he nodded his head for us to follow him, and Eve and I trailed behind, my mind racing with possibilities. *What did he have planned for us?*

Velar turned onto N. La Brea Avenue, the city lights of the street casting a colorful glow on our little trio. He led us on a short wild goose chase, finally coming to a stop at a small hot dog stand. 'You guys wait here,' he said with a sly grin, disappearing into the queue. Eve and I exchanged a curious glance, our anticipation building.

Before long, Velar returned, triumphantly holding three steaming hot dogs smothered in chili and toppings. 'Behold!' he announced, 'These are the legendary Pink's Hot Dogs!' He handed one to each of us, and the aroma of sizzling meat and spices filled the air, making our mouths water in unison.

"Delicious!" I exclaimed, savoring the first bite of my Pink's Hot Dog. The flavors danced on my tongue, a perfect blend of salty, sweet, and spicy. I turned to Velar, curious about his choice of destination.

"Why did you bring us here if you can't eat food anymore?" I asked, nodding towards his own hot dog, which remained untouched. Velar shrugged, a hint of nostalgia in his eyes.

"This place is iconic," he said, his voice filled with reverence. "It's been here since the thirties, and also because I knew Betty and Paul, the original owners. They were friends of mine." He smiled wistfully, lost in thought about a different time.

I gazed at my dear friend, Velar, the strong man of the circus. His emerald eyes sparkled with a youthful vigor, betraying no hint of his true age. Despite his rugged physique and chiseled features, he appeared to be in his fifties.

A testament to the immortal curse that had frozen his aging process. But I knew the truth. He was turned into a vampire in fifteen-fifty. Velar was actually a staggering four hundred and fifteen years old! I marveled at the disconnect between his appearance and his long existence. He didn't look or act a day over fifty, yet his eyes held the wisdom and secrets of centuries.

I struggled to wrap my head around the fact that Bellamy was actually older than Velar, despite appearing to be about half his age. While Velar looked middle aged, Bellamy seemed decades younger, not looking a day over thirty.

"Can't go home empty-handed," Velar said with a chuckle, wrapping his untouched hot dog in a bag. I nodded in agreement, thinking about Bellamy's likely reaction if he knew we were sneaking out to grab hot dogs. "Good idea," I said, imagining the look on his face if we showed up at the circus with Pink's Hot Dogs in hand.

After leaving Pink's, Velar hailed a cab, and as we waited, a checkered taxi pulled up. Just as we opened the door, a woman with bright hair was exiting the cab. Velar held the door for her, and I was astonished to see none other than Julie Andrews! "Julie Andrews?" I squealed, startling her.

Eve and Velar seemed perplexed, but I was too starstruck to notice. "I'm such a big fan!" I stammered. "I just watched The Sound of Music with my mom, and you were lovely in it!"

The beautiful actress smiled sweetly and replied, "Thank you so much for your support, dear." I was left speechless, my mouth agape in wonder. Velar, trying to conceal his fangs, nodded politely and said, "Okay, time to go."

Eve helped me into the cab, still looking confused. Once the door closed, I asked, "Don't you know who that was?" Apparently not, but the cab driver replied nonchalantly, "Yeah, she sure loves this place."

This was the grooviest night of my life. My excitement grew as we sped through the streets. I had no idea where we were headed, but I was thrilled to be along for the ride. As we drove, the Hollywood sign came into view, perched in the hills like a legendary beacon. I rolled down the window, eager to soak up the atmosphere, and breathed in the night air. It smelled of smog, but I didn't care, I was too busy grinning from ear to ear.

The cab finally stopped outside a darkened house, its occupants presumably asleep. As we got out of the taxi I asked, "Whose house is this?" Velar scanned around before saying, "Wait here," his eyes glinting with mystery. *Again?!* I thought, my patience piqued.

So, Eve and I waited on the sidewalk, the two of us gazing up at the nice house. Moments passed, and then I heard strange noises coming from the garage. Suddenly, Velar pushed open the massive garage door, and with a flourish, he drove out a brand-new sleek Ford Mustang.

My eyes widened as I gazed at the sports car. Velar was grinning, clearly pleased with himself, despite his massive frame struggling to fit into the small car. Fortunately, the black Mustang was a convertible, providing ample space and eliminating any concerns about feeling claustrophobic.

Without a word, Eve and I slipped into the tight back seat, and Velar hit the gas. Before I knew it, we were flying down the street, the wind whipping through our hair. I glanced at the speedometer and gasped when I saw that we were well over a hundred miles per hour!

I didn't care where we were headed, and I had no clue what our destination was, but I didn't let that bother me. As we cruised through downtown LA, I was too busy enjoying the scenery to worry about the details. The vibrant city lights, the bustling streets, and the iconic landmarks all blended together in a thrilling blur.

Before I knew it, we were pulling into The Paramount Drive-in movie theater. I hadn't been to one since I was a little girl, when my mom drove us all the way to New Jersey from NYC.

"You can't have a proper night out without catching a film!" Velar yelled from the driver's seat, his excitement infectious. We pulled in and parked among the other cars, and soon everyone was checking out Velar's sleek new ride. We pulled up to a massive white screen and parked, ready to enjoy the show under the stars.

We arrived too late to catch the first movie, so I asked, "What's playing next?" Eve checked the poster by the snack bar and announced, "Looks like it's a horror night! Far Out! The Birds just ended, and then Psycho is playing next!" Velar turned around to face us, his eyes gleaming with excitement. "Sounds like my kind of movie!" he said.

Psycho was all the craze right now and had a lot of controversy and for that reason alone I was excited to see it. I was curious to see what all the fuss was about, especially since I'd always been a fan of Janet Leighs' movies.

Just as the movie was starting, a group of guys strolled over to admire Velar's car. Velar stepped out of the car and removed his leather jacket, which reeked of pine and leather. The guys approached us, wearing white shirts with rolled-up sleeves, and smoking cigarettes.

"Hey, doll face!" One Of the guys said, smiling at Eve. She smiled and thanked the young man, but I knew Eve well enough to recognize that he was no match for her. Still, she seemed to enjoy the attention.

"I'm craving a malt, want to come with me?" He asked Eve. *A malt?* Eve turned to Velar for understanding. "A Milkshake," Velar clarified. Eve nodded and she happily went off with the handsome stranger.

As they headed toward the snack bar, Velar warned, "Be careful."

The young man with Eve yelled back, "Don't worry, she's in good hands."

Velar quickly retorted, "I meant you." Eve laughed it off, pulling the guy away, assuring him, "He's only kidding."

As the snipes began, the guys who were chatting with Velar returned to their cars. Velar hopped back inside and said, "Move up front." I slid into the passenger seat, glancing around for Eve, but Velar reassured me, "She'll be back. Let her enjoy herself tonight."

He adjusted the radio to the drive-in movie station, and the sound of the previews filled the car. I nodded understandingly, knowing that Eve's immortality gave her a unique perspective on life. We would have been the same age if I hadn't died. Instead, Eve had been stuck in her twenties since the curse in seventeen-ninety. Velar turned up the volume, and we settled in to watch the movie.

As the opening credits finished rolling across the drive-in movie screen, I turned to Velar and whispered, "I have a feeling Eve won't be back for a while." Velar nodded in agreement, "She can have a little fun for tonight." his eyes fixed on the film.

Just then, a chilly gust of wind swept through the drive-in, sending shivers down my arms. Velar noticed my discomfort and quickly draped his leather jacket around me. I snuggled into the warmth of the jacket.

He wrapped his arm around me, but his body did not put off any heat, he was cold to the touch. Despite the chill, the jacket provided a cozy shield from the wind. We both refocused on the movie, engrossed in the eerie atmosphere of Hitchcock's thriller.

We were both entranced by the movie, our eyes fixed on the massive screen as Marion Crane's fate unfolded. Suddenly, the shocking shower scene played out. Marion was stabbed by Norman Bates' mother! I let out a loud scream and instinctively flew into Velar's shoulder, seeking comfort.

Velar burst out laughing at my frightened reaction, his shoulders shaking with amusement. "I can't believe you're so scared!" he teased, his eyes sparkling with delight. "How can you face off against evil dark angels, but scared of a little movie?"

I playfully hit him on the arm, still trying to process the intense scene we had just witnessed. As the movie played on, Velar's comments about the plot grew less frequent, his attention shifting from the screen to me. His gaze lingered on my face. He smiled.

"Are you enjoying being back with us?" he asked, his voice low and gentle. I nodded, slightly confused by the question, but my heart skipped a beat at the sincerity in his tone.

"Of course," I replied, "You're my family." Velar's grin softened. "Well, I'm glad you're back," his voice filled with emotion. "We wouldn't have defeated the dark angels if it wasn't for you." I smiled, feeling a warmth spread through my chest.

"I'm happy to help," I said. Velar's eyes locked onto mine, his emerald gaze piercing through me like a ray of sunlight. I tried to look away, but I was captivated by the intensity of his stare, my heart racing with a mix of excitement and nervousness. It was as if he was seeing right through to my soul, and I couldn't help but feel drawn to him, like a magnet to steel.

Velar's gaze held mine, "You're always saving us, saving me." I was entranced, unable to look away as he leaned in, his fangs slowly emerging from behind his lips. The air was electric with tension, and I felt my heart racing. Suddenly, my popcorn fell to the floor, breaking the spell.

I sat up confused and disoriented, as Eve and her new friend returned, jumping into the back seat. Velar quickly moved to help me gather the popcorn, his muscular arm brushing against my legs as he worked. "I'm sorry," I stammered, feeling flustered and unsure.

Eve noticed the awkward exchange and asked, "What's going on?" Velar and I exchanged a glance, and in perfect sync, we replied, "Nothing." The rest of the movie passed in silence, the tension between us palpable, like a living thing. I could feel Velar's eyes on me, burning with an inner fire.

As we pulled out of the drive-in, Eve suggested heading to downtown, despite the late hour. I was thrilled to explore the city. Velar reluctantly agreed, though he mentioned it would be best to head home sooner rather than later. Eve's enthusiasm was infectious, and we set off towards downtown LA.

Velar pulled over, and Eve and I got out to explore the closed shops. I wandered along the storefronts, gazing into the dark windows, when I spotted a beautiful blue dress hanging in one of them. I stood there, mesmerized by the way the dress seemed to shimmer in the dim light.

Eve wandered off, and Velar appeared behind me, his voice low and husky as he said, "That dress was made for you." I smiled, still staring at the dress, unsure how to respond after our last exchange.

"It's pretty," I said, trying to sound casual. But my heart was racing as Velar's reflection appeared in the window, his image dwarfing mine. I couldn't help but want him to touch me. He moved closer, as if reading my mind, his body pressing against my back. I stood still, unsure what to do, my heart pounding in my chest.

I started searching for Eve, but Velar turned me to face him, his hands on my arms, and I felt a jolt of electricity run through my body. "I want to kiss you, Nic," he whispered, deep with desire.

I tried to resist, but my body betrayed me, leaning in towards him. "Velar, I can't... I'm with Bell, he would..." But my protests were lost in the fervor of Velar's kiss, his lips claiming mine with a passion that left me breathless. My entire being ignited, and I felt myself getting lost in the depths of his desire.

His kiss was like a wildfire, consuming me whole being, and I couldn't help but surrender to the flames. When he finally pulled away, I was left gasping for air, my heart pounding in my chest. Eve's return snapped me back to reality, but the embers of Velar's kiss still smoldered within me, refusing to be extinguished.

Eve, still bubbling with excitement, exclaimed, "I found a cocktail lounge!" She spun around and darted towards it, leaving Velar and me to follow in her wake. I eagerly trailed behind her, my heart still racing from the intense moment we'd just shared.

The lounge was packed with people seeking late-night revelry. I quickly abandoned Velar and made a beeline for the bar, where Eve was already perched on a stool.

As she began to order, I jumped in. "Two shots of vodka, please!" The bartender raised an eyebrow but hastily poured two shots, which I downed in quick succession. Eve watched in surprise, her eyes sparkling with amusement. "Another!" I shouted, and the bartender nodded, pouring me another shot. The vodka burned down my throat, but I welcomed the distraction from the tumultuous emotions swirling inside me.

I downed the cocktail and was about to order another when Eve stopped me. 'What's gotten into you?' she asked. The jukebox was loud, and I knew Velar could hear me wherever he was with his vampire heightened senses.

I gave Eve a look that hinted something was off. She nodded knowingly, just as Velar sauntered over to the bar, looking sharp in his leather jacket. Eve cupped her hand around her mouth and yelled to him, 'We need to powder our noses!' He nodded and took a seat at the bar. Eve grabbed my hand, and we squeezed through the crowd to the powder room.

As soon as we stepped inside, Eve asked, "What happened?" I blurted out, "Velar kissed me!"

Eve's jaw dropped, and she exclaimed, "Oh my god, I knew it!" She threw her arms up in the air and started pacing. "What do you mean?" I was surprised.

"I knew he was into you the moment we found you again!" She shook her head in an amusing way. "Ya know, it was his idea to get you out of town tonight."

I blushed, feeling a flutter in my chest. "But Eve, I'm married to Bellamy. This is a disaster! And I... I don't like him like that!"

Eve's expression turned serious. "Well just tell him that." A smile spread across her lips, "You know you can't stop a vampire from claiming what he wants!" I gave her a nudge with my elbow.

"Velar is one of my oldest friends and that's not the point. The point is, I'm married, and I can't just go around kissing other men!"

Eve nodded understandingly. I sighed, feeling torn. Eve hugged me tightly. "We'll figure it out together, okay? Now let's go back out there and face the music. Or should I say, face Velar?" I didn't laugh at her joke.

As we returned, Velar had vanished from the bar. We searched the interior, but he was not there. Soon the crowd rapidly began to exit the lounge. A confrontation was brewing, and the crowd was on the verge of eruption. We pushed through the sea of bodies, our senses on high alert, as Velar's voice rose above the din.

Velar was tangled in a fierce argument with someone I couldn't see because of the large crowd growing. Eve pushed our way to the front of the crowd and my eyes landed on a sight that made me sober up instantly. Bellamy.

CHAPTER
FOURTEEN

I swiftly intervened, wedging myself between the two men, my hands firmly planted on their chests. "Stop it!" My voice echoing through the night air. Bellamy's face was inflamed with rage, his blue eyes blazing with a fierce intensity as he lashed out at Velar.

"What the fuck were you thinking! Do you think her life's a joke?"

I knew Bellamy's wrath wouldn't easily subside, so I quickly fabricated a reason to deflect his anger. "It was my idea," Trying to sound convincing.

He wasn't buying it, but I continued, "I've always wanted to see downtown LA." The lie tasted bitter on my lips, but I hoped it would suffice.

Bellamy's gaze narrowed, knowing I lied, but he seemed to be trying to figure out why I was standing up for Velar more than anything. His expression softened slightly, his voice still catching his breath whispered in my ear, "You will be punished for this."

With that, he turned to Eve and Velar, "You've had your fun, it's time to go." He pivoted and walked away, his long strides forcing us to hurry behind to keep up. The tension was palpable, the air thick with unspoken threats and unresolved conflicts. Bellamy only paused to let Velar take the lead, guiding us to the parked sports car.

Velar and Eve occupied the front seats, while Bellamy and I settled in the back. I felt like I was being scolded by a parent, with no one daring to utter a word. We crossed Melrose Avenue and returned to where the circus was set up. Velar pulled the car up to the main gate. The three of us exited the car and watched as Velar sped away.

The sports car's engine sound faded into the distance, growing fainter and fainter, leaving me again wondering whose vehicle it was. Once we walked into the circus, Eve quickly slipped away to Jubilee, probably eager to avoid Bellamy's lecture.

We started to walk home but the silence was too much for me to bear. Finally, I grasped his hand, trying to get him to talk to me. He slowed down feeling my hand in his. "I just worry about you," he said softly with concern.

I felt a pang of guilt, thinking about Velar's kiss. *Had I kissed him back?* I couldn't remember, and I didn't want to admit it to Bellamy. I couldn't bear the betrayal that would dawn on his face if he knew.

So, I pushed the thought away, telling myself it was just a momentary lapse. Velar was probably just caught up in the moment, or maybe he was thirsty for my blood. I'm sure he wouldn't want to mention it again, and neither would I.

As I crossed the threshold into Casmira, Bellamy instructed "You know where I want you to be." I did. I knew exactly what he meant. The playroom on the third floor, where I would assume the familiar position of submission, kneeling on the floor waiting for Sir. The towering grandfather clock, its face gleaming in the dim light, stood like a sentinel, its ticking told me that we had returned during the witching hour.

I waited for Bellamy to head towards the kitchen before I made my way up to the third floor. Taking my time up the flights of stairs admiring the pictures that adorned the walls. In the dim and sultry playroom, I stripped out of my little black dress down to my lingerie.

Then carefully I knelt on the ground, assuming the pose that Bellamy had taught me many lifetimes ago. As I waited, I couldn't help but wonder if the prolonged position itself was the punishment. *Was this my punishment? Leaving me here to wait naked and uncomfortable.* My muscles aching and my mind fogging with anticipation.

The thought made me whimper aloud. I had been in this position before, but never for so long. I was starting to lose my focus. My body trembled with the effort of maintaining the pose. Just when I thought I couldn't hold it any longer, the door opened. I quickly readjusted myself into my sub pose. As the door shut behind him, I lowered my head in submission.

I was ready to submit to Bellamy's desires. As his shoes came into view, I felt myself become instantly wet and aroused. He tilted my face to look up at him, I saw a glint in his eye that made me wonder if I was in for more than I had bargained for.

As I pondered the situation, my anxiety spiraled out of control. Velar's kiss still lingered on my lips. Maybe the punishment was exactly what I needed. A stark reminder that I am Bellamy's.

I hoped that the sudden jolt of discipline would free me from the persistent thoughts of Velar. Bellamy took my arm, making me rise before him. He led me to the bed, his eyes burning with an unspoken intensity.

'Bend over,' he commanded. As I yielded, the leather belt bit into my skin, its sting a sharp shock that coursed through my veins. I arched my back in pain. Each successive strike was a crescendo of intensity, a symphony of pleasure and pain that left me breathless.

The belt sliced through the air, its leather tongue licking my skin with a sharp crackle. Tears filled my eyes. I screamed in pain as the belt struck my flesh, my body trembling with each impact. I could feel my skin growing tender and swollen.

I instinctively moved my hands to protect myself, but he ordered me to move them. I hesitated, fearful of the consequences. 'Move them, or I'll punish you harder,' he warned. I quickly complied, bracing myself for the next strike. The final blow sent me crumbling to the floor, my body aching and my spirit shaken.

Bellamy gently lifted me onto the bed, his touch gentle. I avoided eye contact, tears streaming down my face. He laid beside me, caressing and soothing my tender skin from his belt. He held me close until the pain subsided. 'Baby girl,' he whispered softly as he kissed my head.

When I finally met his gaze, his blue eyes shone with compassion. His hand wandered, tracing a path down my thigh, as he explored every curve. A tingling sensation radiated through my body, and I knew he was using his magic to soothe me and to turn me on. It was working. Our lips met in a passionate kiss, and I felt myself responding, lost in the moment. "Daddy," I moaned.

Bellamy mounted me, his passion grew kissing me deeper. Our eyes locked and I saw the desire of a beast that wanted to ravage me. As he slid himself inside me, I knew my punishment wasn't over just yet. His intensity grew and he became fierce and ravage, his movements strong and unrelenting.

I felt overwhelmed, and when I couldn't take it anymore, he shifted our position, his thrusts becoming more insistent. I cried out, pleading for him to stop, but he continued, his passion consuming us both.

He was a ferocious beast, untamed and unbridled, with a primal energy that couldn't be contained. And I didn't want to tame him - I wanted to unleash the wildness, to surrender to the raw magical power that pulsed through his veins. I craved the passion, the unrelenting intensity, and the unapologetic ferocity that made him a force of nature.

As Bellamy's passion reached its peak a primal sound escaped his lips. Exhausted, we laid together, entwined in each other's arms. Moments later, his gentle touch and soft kisses reassured me that the intense moment had passed. He tenderly cared for the welts on my skin and reiterated his love for me. The beast within him had retreated once again, leaving me blissfully sore.

Bellamy roused me from slumber before the sun's ascent, his considerate nature evident in the tonic he'd left on my bedside table. A thoughtful remedy for the previous night's indulgences. Bellamy was already dressed in his Showman attire, opting for a jet-black tailcoat. He exuded an air of dashing sophistication.

Today the circus was reopening, and despite yesterday's turmoil, I was eager to begin my official return. 'No flying for you today,' Bellamy said with a knowing smile. I understood his reasoning. He hadn't yet witnessed my skills yet in this life, and I required practice before taking to the aerials. Nonetheless, I was thrilled to be back in the circus even if I was just practicing.

I skipped the tonic and asked for coffee instead, and to my delight, the tonic transformed into a steaming cup of black coffee. Just how I liked it. "Thank you, Casmira." I slowly got out of bed and wandered towards my closet, but my laziness got the better of me.

I turned to Bellamy, who was about to exit our bedroom, and pouted in a playful tone, 'Daddy, can you help me find something to wear?' Bellamy's smile turned wicked as he replied, 'My pleasure.'

He stood before me, gazing up and down my body like I was on display. With a flick of his wrist, I was suddenly adorned in a stunning black and white wavy dress that matched the circus tent pattern. 'Now everyone will know you are Mrs. Darlington,' I smiled as I looked at my reflection in the oversized mirror.

As I admired my dress, Bellamy was enamored, 'You are stunning, baby girl.' He slowly stepped behind me and gathered my hair into his hands. Pulling tightly my head tilted back, my neck exposed, as his lips brushed against my skin.

The sudden rush of pleasure made my heart race. Magic was tingling my scalp as he styled my hair into an elegant updo. A few loose strands framed my face, and he tucked a stray lock behind my ear. 'Utter perfection,' He offered his arm, and I took it, feeling like his queen as we walked out of the bedroom.

I knew we had to get to the circus to open, but my growling stomach had other plans. I made a quick detour to the kitchen and snatched a warm hand pie that I found resting on the countertop. I savored the first bite as the flaky crust and sweet filling melted in my mouth. Just as I was about to take another bite, Bellamy called out from the front door, 'Time to go!' I grabbed another pie and took off running to catch up with him, the warm pastry clutched in my hand like a sweet treasure.

We strolled along the wooded path, joining the throng of performers and crew heading towards the majestic willow tree, our gateway to the circus. Velar and Eve caught up with us just as we reached the tree, and together we ascended the winding stairs.

Eve and I found ourselves walking in tandem, and she whispered with a sly grin, "Did you get in trouble?" I rolled my eyes playfully, and she chuckled, glancing ahead at Bellamy and Velar.

Once we reached the top, we stepped out into the circus. "Nicole's not performing today, just practicing," Bellamy announced, his eyes locking onto Velar to make his point heard.

"So, keep a close eye on her and make sure she doesn't hurt herself. That shouldn't be too difficult a task for you to handle, should it?" Bellamy's tone was firm, as if daring Velar to defy him.

Velar's expression turned stoic, his jaw clenched, and he nodded curtly. "I'll take care of her." I swallowed at his response.

Before I could contribute anything, he turned and planted a quick kiss on my lips. I caught Velar's gaze as Bellamy pulled his lips away from mine. His expression was unfazed. 'It's show-time!' Bellamy exclaimed, his eyes sparkling with excitement.

He sure loved what he did, and his passion was infectious, making everyone around him love it too. I watched in awe as he disappeared towards the front gate, ready to open it and welcome the eager crowd.

Soon the circus was abuzz with excitement. The crowd poured in, and the performances started. Velar took me to the backyard of the circus for a private aerial practice session. The backyard was for circus staff only. Climbing the ladder to get into position I saw Velar on the other side waiting for me to start. I took my first leap into the air. I reached for the trapeze flying towards me, but I missed completely and fell into the net, a curse word escaped my lips.

By the time I crawled out of the net and landed on the ground Velar's playful teasing met me, 'Nice jump.' I was about to climb the ladder again when I felt his hand on my arm. Stopping me.

A sly grin appeared on his face, 'Did you get punished last night?' The way he said 'punished' implied he thought the idea was absurd.

I shot him a look, knowing he was the one who'd put me in this state. 'Nothing I can't handle,' I retorted, trying to brush it off. But Velar persisted, his grin mischievous, 'I hope he went easy on you.' I searched his eyes, wondering if he was serious, and found a spark of sincerity.

This flirtatious side of Velar was new to me, and I struggled to respond. 'You should have been the one punished,' I finally said, trying to sound stern. Velar chuckled, 'I was. That's why I'm not performing today.' I raised an eyebrow, intrigued by his admission.

Again, I took the trapeze in my hand and leaped just as another was coming towards me. I grasped for the trapeze, my fingers slipped, and I tumbled into the safety net below.

Again. And again. Velar's frustration grew with each failed attempt, his words laced with a hint of exasperation. "Damn girl, something on your mind?" he asked, his eyes narrowing as if he knew my mind.

And he was right. My thoughts were a thousand miles away, replaying the kiss we shared like a broken record. I couldn't shake the feeling that our lips were still touching, the spark between us still crackling. *Why did he kiss me?*

After I fell again, Velar helped me out of the net, his hand brushing against my arm. "Let's take a break," he suggested, his voice low and smooth.

He handed me water, his eyes probing mine for a question or a reaction or something I couldn't detect. I didn't know exactly. I just stared back at him, my mind a jumbled mess of emotions.

He stepped closer, invading my personal space, but I didn't back away. Instead, I gazed up at him, the memory of our kiss burning bright in my mind.

Was he testing me? Did he have feelings for me? I'd only ever seen him as a friend before, but now I wasn't so sure. He stared at me, almost forcing me to speak. I tried to shake off the thought, but he kept looking at me.

'I think I'm done for the day.' I turned to walk away, but he grabbed my arm. 'Nic, I want to show you something tonight,' He stepped closer. 'Not now, but tonight.' I looked at him, even more confused.

I started to shake my head no, but before I could reject his request, he added, 'It won't take long, and Bellamy has a meeting tonight.' My stomach was screaming no, but I couldn't think of a simple reason to reject him.

I walked away and stepped into a tent where Eve and Anise were performing. I watched in awe as they delivered a breathtaking performance on the aerial silks. They soared through the air, their bodies bending and twisting in impossible ways, like ethereal creatures dancing on the wind.

Their silken fabrics shimmered and flowed like water as they wrapped themselves in intricate poses, their strength and grace mesmerizing the crowd. I gasped as they executed a series of daring drops, plummeting towards the earth before catching themselves at the last second, their movements utterly unbelievable. The crowd erupted into applause as they landed a final, show-stopping pose, their faces radiant with joy and triumph.

When Eve finished her performance, she came over to me. "Amazing performance!" She gave me a playful bow. 'Hey, how are you feeling after last night?'

I hesitated, looking around to make sure no one was listening. 'I'm fine,' I whispered, 'Velar wants to see me tonight while you and Bellamy are at a meeting.'

Her mouth opened in surprise, but then she gave me a blank stare. 'Just see what he wants,' she said nonchalantly, like it was no big deal. I was taken aback by her casual response.

'Eve, this is crazy! I shouldn't meet him, right?' But she just shrugged and said, 'Just hear him out. See what he wants. It's just Velar after all."

I felt a nagging sense of unease, like something was off. Was Eve aware of something she wasn't letting on? Before she left for her next performance, I stopped her and asked point-blank, 'What are you not telling me?'

Eve's face betrayed her, and I knew she was hiding something. But she just smiled sweetly and said, 'Have fun tonight!' Her evasion only fueled my curiosity.

I watched as she walked away, her secrets trailing behind her like a mysterious cloak. I couldn't shake the feeling that she knew more than she was letting on.

As I made my way back to Jubilee, I passed Velar, who was in conversation with Henry. As I walked by, I could feel Velar's eyes on me, and I turned to catch his gaze following me. I felt a flutter in my stomach, and my heart skipped a beat as I wondered what he wanted to show me. *Maybe another stolen kiss?*

The thought sent a thrill through me, but I quickly pushed aside the excitement, feeling guilty for indulging in such thoughts. I turned once more to see if he was still watching me. And he was. Like I was his prey.

CHAPTER
FIFTEEN

I'd been waiting for the knock at the door all afternoon, my anticipation growing with each passing hour. Now, with night having fallen and Bellamy still tied up in a meeting at the circus, I was ready. Eve's whispered words echoed in my mind, 'Have fun tonight,' as I opened the door to reveal Velar's chiseled physique in a tight t-shirt that made my heart race. His perfect features seemed to gleam in the dim light, making my knees weak. 'Aren't you going to invite me in?' he asked, his mischievous grin flashing like a challenge.

I stepped aside, and he entered. It was then I noticed he was carrying a gift bag. As we approached the main room, a fire crackled to life, creating a cozy atmosphere. Soft music began to play. *Was Casimira setting the mood?*

We sat down, and two glasses appeared, one with wine and the other with a deep red liquid that seemed to move of its own accord - blood. I cringed, and Velar noticed, his eyes sparkling with amusement.

As I took a sip of wine, Velar handed me the gift bag. 'I think you'll like it,' his emerald eyes intensely. Moving my hand through the tissue paper I pulled out a blue dress. My mouth dropped when I realized it was the same one I had admired in the downtown LA store window. 'Oh my god, this is the dress!' I exclaimed.

I held the dress up against my body imagining it on my body. Velar's expression was pleased as he told me. 'I told you, it was made for you,' his voice was low and smooth.

'Thank you,' I said, swallowing hard. "But why?" I paused looking at him for a reason. 'Like I said, "It was made for you," his tone was serious, his eyes gleaming with an intensity that made my heart race. I felt a blush rise to my cheeks.

As Velar closed the distance between us, his expression transformed, his emerald eyes burning with an intense gaze that left me breathless. I felt paralyzed, my heart racing with anticipation, as he reached out and placed his hand on my thigh.

The touch sent shivers coursing through my body, and before I could stop myself, I blurted out the question that had been haunting me, 'Why did you kiss me last night?' Velar's response was a simple, yet powerful statement, 'You kissed me back.'

The truth hit me like a wave, and I knew I couldn't deny it. I had kissed him back, and the memory of it still lingered on my lips. His other hand wrapped around me, pulling me in with a gentle yet unyielding force, and I knew he was going to kiss me again. This time, I was ready. This time I wanted it.

He leaned in, his face inches from mine, and I mirrored his movement, my heart racing with anticipation. But just as our lips were about to touch, he tucked the same strand of hair behind my ear that Bellamy had that morning. The same gesture, once tender, now felt like a betrayal. I instantly pulled away, 'I'm sorry,' I stammered, my voice barely above a whisper.

Velar's reaction was swift and intense. He grasped my face with urgency, his hands cradling my cheeks as he claimed my lips with a fierce passion. The kiss was a whirlwind of sensation, leaving me breathless and wanting more. It was as if he had been waiting for an eternity to kiss me.

The depth of his emotion was overwhelming. I felt my heart soar, my resistance melting away under the tender yet ardent pressure of his lips. I could feel his fangs. Time stood still as our mouths moved in perfect sync, the world around us fading into oblivion. I was lost in the infinity of his kiss, unable to pull away even if I wanted to.

As he slowly pulled away, I remained frozen, my lips still tingling from the intense kiss. 'Now you can say I kissed you again,' His eyes knew. I stared at him in shock, my mind reeling with the implications. *What have I done?*

Guilt washed over me like a wave, and I felt my face flush with heat. *Why was he doing this to me?* He obviously knew I kissed him back with equal passion, if not more. I felt ashamed. It was as if he could read my thoughts, understand my turmoil. Maybe he could. His gaze seemed to hold a deep understanding, as if he knew the secrets I hadn't even admitted to myself.

"I've been waiting forever to kiss you." I looked at him, trying to comprehend his words, but they seemed to come from a place I couldn't understand. "I'm with Bellamy," I stated flatly, as if he didn't already know. But Velar's response sent my mind reeling. "How many lifetimes are you going to be with the same man, Nic?"

I felt like I'd been punched in the gut. No one had ever questioned my relationship with Bellamy like that before. Bellamy was my husband, my partner for countless lifetimes. We were the Darlington's of thee Darlington Circus.

The idea of being with anyone else was unfathomable. I stood up, shaking my head in disbelief. "I'm with Bellamy," I repeated, trying to sound convincing. But Velar stood next to me, his towering presence making me feel small. He looked down at me with a fierce gaze. "I want my turn," his voice dripped with desire. "I've waited longer than you know."

Just as Velar leaned in to kiss me again, a sudden knock at the door interrupted us, mere inches from our lips touching. I leapt up with a surge of relief. I thought I heard a low growl emanate from Velar's throat, a primal sound that made me quiver. But I welcomed the unexpected interruption, using it as an escape from the intense moment.

I swung open the door to find Miss Poppet standing on the threshold, her eyes gleaming in the moonlight. I turned to Velar, who was now gazing into the fire. Probably adjusting himself for company. "Come in," gesturing to Miss Poppet, who stepped aside to reveal Prudence behind her.

My eyes widened as I took in Prudence's swollen belly, her pregnancy seemingly advanced. "We need your help," Miss Poppet said, her voice low and urgent. I nodded, my mind racing, and called out towards the main room, "Velar, we have a situation!"

He entered the room, I caught him muttering under his breath, "Always something." But his nonchalant demeanor quickly shifted when he laid eyes on Prudence's protruding belly. His eyes widened in surprise, and he exclaimed, "ugh, I...I'll get Bell!" With vampire speed, he darted out of the front door, leaving me to attend to our unexpected guests.

I ushered Miss Poppet and Prudence into the main room, trying to compose myself despite the sudden commotion. "Please, have a seat. Can I offer you some tea?" I asked, trying to maintain a semblance of hospitality amidst the chaos.

Prudence's swollen belly seemed to herald an ominous presence, the baby she carried was half dark angel, an entity whose nature we couldn't quite comprehend. The rapid progression of her pregnancy was unsettling, to say the least. She had only just conceived, yet her belly seemed full term, straining against her frail body.

Her once-radiant complexion now appeared pale and wan, her eyes sunken and dark, like two voids that seemed to suck the light out of the room. Her fragile frame looked woefully unprepared to withstand the rigors of childbirth, and I couldn't shake the feeling that she might not survive the ordeal.

Miss Poppet tenderly attended to Prudence, asking if she wanted more water, but Prudence's response was barely audible, her voice a faint whisper. My heart went out to her, seeing her in such a frail and vulnerable state. As she started to shiver, I quickly wrapped a soft heavy blanket around her shoulders, trying to comfort her.

As the warmth from the blanket and the fire enveloped Prudence, her eyes seemed to glaze over, and her body relaxed slightly. Miss Poppet continued to tend to her, speaking softly and offering words of comfort just like a mother. I watched, feeling a sense of helplessness wash over me.

Velar returned with Bellamy, who immediately went to Prudence's side. "What's happening?" Bellamy asked, his voice laced with concern. "Her pregnancy looks like it was accelerating," I replied.

Bellamy's eyes narrowed, his gaze scrutinizing Prudence's frail form with a mix of concern and determination. He leaned in close to Velar, whispering something in his ear, and Velar quickly nodded before hurrying out of Casmira with a sense of urgency. Bellamy turned back to Prudence, his expression softening as he offered a reassuring smile. "We will handle this, and you will be okay," he said, his voice gentle and comforting.

Prudence looked up at him, her eyes filled with a deep sadness, and asked, "Will the baby be, okay?" Her voice trembled, and I could sense the fear and uncertainty beneath her words. I felt a surge of impatience, thinking, *who cares about the dark angel's baby?* But before I could express my thoughts, Bellamy intervened, his expression empathetic. "We will do whatever we can," he promised, his voice filled with conviction. "You have my word."

Minutes later, Mesidor and Ambrette Blackwood arrived, accompanied by Velar. Bellamy swiftly ushered them into the library, their faces stern and serious, hinting at the gravity of their discussion. I was about to follow when Eve burst through the door, her entrance like a whirlwind.

"What's going on?" she demanded, her voice sharp and urgent. But before I could respond, her gaze landed on Prudence, and her expression transformed from irritation to shock. "Oh my…" she trailed off, her eyes wide with concern.

Ambrette's eyes locked onto Prudence as she returned from the library. "May I?" Her hand hovering over her swollen belly. Prudence nodded, and Ambrette's hand made contact, her eyes flashing with a knowing glance at Bellamy.

"She will give birth to a Nephilim," Ambrette declared. Prudence's tears burst forth like a dam breaking, and Miss Poppet's comforting embrace couldn't stem the anguish.

I turned to Bellamy, my mind racing with questions, but his expression was grim. "Sit," he commanded, his voice firm but laced with a hint of desperation. We obeyed, our eyes fixed on Mesidor as he opened The Book of Enoch, its yellowed pages crackling with an otherworldly energy.

"Because you are pregnant by a Watcher, the spawn will be a Nephilim, a giant," Mesidor intoned, his voice heavy with foreboding. "You won't survive childbirth. We must act swiftly, for the baby wants to come out."

I turned to Bellamy, my eyes asking, "What are we going to do?" But he didn't answer, instead pacing back and forth like a caged lion. Velar stood beside me, and I tried to push aside the disturbing thoughts of what had just transpired. "We have to get it out of her," Velar blurted with urgency.

Ambrette's expression turned grave. "We need to be careful. If it senses we intend to kill it, it may retaliate against Prudence." The room fell silent, the weight of her words sinking in.

Velar's face darkened, his voice rising. "What do you mean? It's a baby, for fuck's sake!" Bellamy snapped at Velar. "Show some compassion!"

Velar's expression remained resolute. "Compassion? We're dealing with dark angels, Bell. We can't afford to waste time."

Eve intervened, her voice calm and soothing. "Calm down, everyone. We need to think this through." Prudence's voice trembled, cracking with each word as she spoke through tears. "I should have stopped him... I should have tried to fight him..." Her body shook with sobs, and Miss Poppet quickly wrapped her in a comforting embrace.

"This isn't your fault, Prudence!" Miss Poppet exclaimed, her voice firm and reassuring. "This could have happened to any of us. Don't blame yourself!"

We all felt Prudence's fear and were scared ourselves. I noticed Bellamy's eyes landing on the dress and gift bag. I hastily pushed it back into the gift bag, shoving it under the table. I couldn't think about that right now; our priority was saving Prudence.

CHAPTER
SIXTEEN

Ambrette proposed the idea of performing a ritual to protect Prudence and safely deliver the baby. After weighing their options, they decided this was the safest approach. Although we weren't certain if it would succeed, Bellamy and Ambrette reassured Prudence that she would survive due to the immortality curse.

"We'll get through this, Prudence," Bellamy said, his voice calm and resolute. "You're immortal, and you'll come out of this unscathed."

Ambrette nodded in agreement. "The ritual will protect you and the baby. We'll ensure your safety." Prudence looked uncertain but seemed to draw strength from their words.

Millie, a seasoned midwife witch from the Emberlynn Forest, joined us, bringing a warm and reassuring presence. With gentle hands, she examined Prudence's belly, her eyes closed as if tuning into the baby's energy.

After a moment, Millie smiled, her face aglow with wonder. "This little one is strong." Prudence looked at her with concern. "Will I be able to deliver safely?" she asked, her voice laced with worry.

Millie's expression turned comforting. "With our combined magic and my expertise, we'll ensure a safe delivery," she said, her hands still cradling Prudence's belly. "But we must prepare for any unexpected challenges.

Bellamy sprang into action, swiftly gathering materials and instructions from Millie and Ambrette. I could hardly believe what was unfolding before my eyes. We hastily decided to transport Prudence to the town square, where our makeshift "hospital" was located. While it wasn't a real hospital, it was stocked with basic supplies and equipment. Bellamy, however, needed to supplement these with his magic, conjuring additional necessities to ensure the ritual's success.

As we carefully made our way through the streets, Ambrette briefed Bellamy on the specifics of the ritual. "We'll need a circle of protection, Bellamy. And a binding spell to restrain the Nephilim's influence."

"Understood," Bellamy replied, his eyes flashing with determination.

Millie walked slowly with Prudence asking questions like a real doctor. When we arrived at the square, Bellamy swiftly set to work, his hands weaving intricate patterns in the air as he invoked his magic.

I knew my role was largely supportive, but I was determined to be there for my friends in any way I could. I watched with rapt attention as Bellamy's hands danced through the air, his magic swirling around him. Mesidor worked in tandem, carefully crafting a salt circle that seemed to shimmer with a protective energy.

Ambrette's voice cut through the tension, her words crisp and clear. "It's time." Bellamy nodded to me, Velar, and Eve, and we stepped outside. Our only view was through the small window that peered into the surgical room.

As we waited, I couldn't help but wonder what would unfold. Would the ritual successfully shield Prudence and her unborn child from the darkness that threatened to consume them?

As we waited, the air inside the circle began to shift and swirl, like a vortex pulling everything towards its center. The energy building inside was evident.

Suddenly, a burst of light exploded from the circle, sending us all stumbling backward. I caught myself against the wall, my heart racing with surprise. When I looked through the window, I saw Ambrette and Bellamy exchanging a tense glance.

"What's happening?" I yelled, my voice barely above a whisper. "The ritual is pushing back against the Nephilim's influence," Millie replied, her eyes fixed intently on the circle. "But we need to be careful. This could get out of hand quickly."

Bellamy nodded in agreement. "We need to contain this energy before it's too late."

And with that, they stepped forward, their hands raised to guide the swirling power. As they worked to contain the energy, the air around us began to charge with an electric tension. I could feel the hairs on my arms standing on end, and my skin tingle with anticipation.

Suddenly, a loud crash echoed through the room, making us all jump. We turned to see that the circle had exploded, sending salt and candles flying everywhere. "What happened?" I exclaimed, my heart racing with surprise.

"It's too strong," Ambrette yelled, her face grim. "We need more energy." Bellamy nodded in agreement. "We need more power to bind the Nephilim's energy." Hearing her words I pushed open the door and the three of us stepped inside.

Ambrette and Bellamy guided us into the circle. They instructed us to hold hands and focus our energy on the spell. As we did, I could feel a surge of power building within me.

"Channel your energy into the circle," Ambrette directed. "Visualize a bright light enveloping Prudence and protecting her from harm." We concentrated, and a warm, golden light began to emanate from our joined hands. The light grew stronger, filling the circle and the space around us.

We stood in a circle, holding hands and focusing our energy on the spell. Prudence was at the center, her belly swollen with the Nephilim baby she was carrying. Our goal was to protect her and the baby from any harm.

As we channeled our energy, a warm, golden light surrounded Prudence and the baby. The air seemed to vibrate with magic, and I could feel the power of the spell building.

Ambrette's voice rose above the din, her words clear and authoritative. "By the power of the elements, protect Prudence! May the Nephilim's own power be turned to protection!"

The golden light grew stronger, enveloping Prudence and the baby in a warm, protective embrace. I could feel the magic coursing through me, a sense of wonder and awe at the power of our combined energy.

As the spell reached its climax, Prudence's belly began to glow with a soft, pulsing light. The Nephilim baby was responding to the magic, its own power stirring within.

"We've done it," Bellamy breathed, his eyes shining with relief. "The baby is protected." But as we turned to leave the circle, I noticed something strange. Prudence's belly was still glowing, the pulsing light growing stronger by the second.

"What's happening?" I asked confused "I don't know," Ambrette replied, her eyes fixed on Prudence's belly. "But I think the baby is trying to communicate with us." Millie reached out a hand to touch Prudence's belly.

"I feel a strange sense of connection to the Nephilim baby." As soon as she made contact, she started to convulse back and forth. I gasped in horror, as I watched the horrifying scene. Her hand never left Prudence's belly.

She stumbled back, overwhelmed by what just happened. "I saw it, I...I saw the baby, it was a giant monster, rampaging through Jubilee, leaving destruction in its wake. Buildings crumbled, trees were uprooted, and the skies grew dark with smoke and ash." Millie plunged herself into a chair that was close to her, and I instantly went to her aid.

"I felt the baby's rage and frustration, its desire to break free from the constraints of its mother's womb. I felt its hunger for destruction, its need to unleash its power upon the world." Her eyes filled with tears as she continued, "Whatever it is, is not meant for our world."

Prudence grasped my arm, her eyes wide with concern. "Please help it, it's just a baby," her voice trembling.

I struggled to find words, still reeling from Millie's visions. "It's going to destroy everything." Millie's face was grim. "We need to act fast," Ambrette interjected. "We can't let that happen." Prudence's face was set in determination. "I want the baby to be safe," she said, her voice firm. "I won't let it be harmed."

As they prepared for the delivery, I couldn't shake off the feeling of dread. I knew what was coming. We waited once again outside the room as Ambrette and Millie prepared for the delivery.

Prudence's screams were like razors, slashing through the air as she writhed in torment, her body convulsing in agony. The pain was a living entity, a malevolent force that ravaged her womb, threatening to consume her very soul. Every contraction was a fresh hell, a scorching blaze that incinerated her insides, leaving her a quivering, sweat-soaked mess. If mortality's cold hand had claimed her, it would have been a mercy, a sweet release from the unrelenting anguish that tore her asunder.

After a moment of eerie silence, a tiny cry pierced the air, heralding the arrival of a new life. We three stepped forward, our hearts racing with anticipation, to behold the giant creature that had emerged. I pushed open the door just as Millie had wrapped the giant baby in a cloth.

Just as Millie was about to hand it to Prudence, Bellamy stepped forward, his eyes cold and hard. "I'll take it," his voice firm. His eyes on Millie ordering her. Prudence pleaded, "No Bellamy, please. It's my baby, it's only a baby" She sobbed begging for her newborn.

I attempted to intervene, but Bellamy swiftly carried the gigantic baby out of the room. I chased after him, "Bellamy, no," I screamed out in desperation, but Velar restrained me, preventing me from following.

Miss Poppet was tending to Prudence, while Millie and Ambrette cleaned her up. Prudence's sobs were heart-wrenching, and I could feel her anguish deeply. As her sobbing reached its peak, I broke free from Velar's grasp and chased after Bellamy, determined to stop him from harming the baby.

CHAPTER
SEVENTEEN

As I ran after Bellamy, I felt the familiar vibration that signaled him jumping us to a new location. I spotted him exiting through the willow tree and called out, "Bellamy!" But he didn't stop. I chased after him, finally catching up at the circus gate just before he was about to exit. "Stop!" I pleaded, breathless.

Bellamy turned around, his expression firm. "Go back to Jubilee, now, and stay there." My eyes widened in astonishment as I gazed at the massive baby in his embrace. It started to cry.

Its appearance was unlike anything I'd ever seen. It possessed a peculiar quality that I couldn't quite describe. Bellamy swayed back and forth trying to soothe it.

"Prudence..." I began, trying to protest. Bellamy cut me off sharply. "This is not a baby for her." I felt the blood racing to my face.

"What are you going to do with... it?" I asked, trying to find the words. "I'm taking it to the undying council." His tone left no room for argument. "I'll be back. Stay here. I am not asking Nicole." And with that, he walked away, leaving me standing there, feeling frustrated and helpless.

Velar emerged behind me. I turned to see him gazing at me with a thoughtful expression. "How's Prudence?" I asked, already knowing the answer.

Velar stepped forward, "He had to do what he did, you know that right?" He said sincerely with justification. I bristled, feeling a surge of defensiveness. "Why are you sticking up for him? Weren't you just trying to seduce me a couple of hours ago?"

His expression was almost patronizing. "If I wanted you, I would have you." I rolled my eyes not believing his words.

Velar's gaze was unfamiliar, his eyes seeming to regard me with a newfound condescension. For a moment, he looked at me as if I were a child, his expression almost patronizing. "Little girl, this has nothing to do with us," his tone dismissive.

Before I could react further, he appeared in front of me, his vampire speed startling. His piercing emerald eyes locked onto mine, burning with intensity. "Someday, I'll be the one to punish you," he whispered, his voice low and husky, "but I doubt you'll be able to handle it."

I crossed my arms, my protest instinctive. "What makes you think I'd even want you to be the one to punish me?" I shot back, my voice laced with defiance.

Velar's gaze narrowed. His voice low and seductive, "you have no idea what I'm capable of. I can see the fire in your soul, the spark that sets my own heart ablaze. You'd beg for my mercy, and I'd delight in denying it."

He leaned in closer, his breath caressing my skin, sending shivers down my spine. "But don't worry, I'll savor the moment… for now." With a sly smile, he turned and walked back to the tree, leaving me breathless and bewildered.

Back at the hospital, I found Prudence in a state of utter distress. Her emotional pain was visible, and I could only imagine the depth of her suffering. I offered my support, but Miss Poppet gently advised that rest was what she needed most.

Ambrette administered an elixir, which seemed to calm her mind and ease her tears. My heart went out to her, yet I couldn't help but wonder why she would want a dark angel's baby. But I checked myself, recognizing that I couldn't truly understand her perspective. It's a pain that's uniquely hers, one that I can only attempt to empathize with.

As we departed, Eve assured me, 'We'll return to check on Prudence tomorrow morning.' Eve and I strolled back to Casmira in contemplative silence, struggling to grasp the events that had unfolded. 'She'll need our support now more than ever,' Eve's concern for Prudence is evident. I nodded in agreement, understanding her situation.

As we approached Casmira, Velar approached us, but I subtly indicated to Eve that I didn't want to engage with him. She intuitively understood and intercepted Velar, allowing me to continue into the house without interruption. It was clear she had dissuaded him from following me inside.

Eve and I spent some time together, snacking and unwinding, but as the evening wore on, I began to feel the weight of exhaustion. The events of the day had taken their toll, and I was ready to call it a night.

As I trudged up the stairs, I felt the familiar vibration that signaled Bellamy's return. I knew he had jumped us to a new location, but I didn't wait to find out where. I wasn't ready to face him, so I decided to take a shower, hoping the warm water would wash away my fatigue and concerns.

Despite my reluctance to see my husband, he joined me in the shower, his presence unsettling. *My mind raced with questions, what had he done with the baby? Had he harmed it? I* couldn't shake off the gruesome thoughts.

Avoiding his gaze, I tried to hide my fears, but he lifted my chin, forcing me to meet his eyes. 'What did you do with it?' Unsure if I wanted the truth.

'I took care of it,' he replied coldly. 'Baby girl please, stop looking at me like I'm a monster.' But I couldn't help it; I saw the man I loved, the one who had ripped a newborn baby— dark or not—away from its grieving mother. I was lost, unsure how to process my emotions or look at him anymore.

Bellamy's sudden embrace overwhelmed me. My mind reeled from the kiss with Velar, and the guilt of betrayal threatened to consume me. Tears streamed down my face as Bellamy held me close, his warmth and affection a stark contrast to the turmoil within.

I couldn't bring myself to reveal my secrets. He held me tightly, his touch a gentle comfort that only heightened my sense of guilt. As my tears subsided, I desperately tried to convince myself that Velar was just a friend, that the kiss meant nothing. But the weight of my deception lingered.

By the next morning, I couldn't bear the thought of being intimate to Bellamy. I slipped out of bed before he could wrap me in his arms, a routine I'd grown accustomed to. I quietly got dressed and tiptoed down the stairs, desperate not to wake him. When Eve arrived, I felt a wave of relief wash over me. She had come to accompany me to check on Prudence, and I was grateful for her timely presence.

As we stepped outside Casmira, I turned to Eve and said, 'I need to talk to you in private.' She nodded knowingly, likely already aware of what was weighing on my mind. Together, we strolled towards the Emberlynn Forest, the trees' gentle rustle beneath our feet a soothing accompaniment to our footsteps. When we'd walked far enough to escape prying ears, I finally opened up to my best friend. 'Velar kissed me,' I confessed.

'Again?' Her brow arched in surprise. I nodded, a sheepish grin spreading across my face. 'I think I kissed him back,' I admitted, my cheeks flushing with embarrassment.

'Girl, don't be too hard on yourself," her tone was gentle but firm. 'Honestly, if you knew how long Velar has been waiting...' Her voice trailed off, as if she was guarding a secret. 'What are you not telling me?' I stopped walking, and I turned to face her, my breath catching in my throat from walking up the steep hills.

'It's not my secret to tell,' she said, 'but I don't think you should worry about it too much. You tend to get wrapped up in your thoughts, and I know you're still mortal...I think that has a lot to do with it.' Her words were cryptic, but I let her continue.

'Do with what?' I asked, my confusion evident. 'Well, you see, I don't think like I used to anymore,' she explained. 'After you live so long, you look at relationships differently, and all kinds of things differently.'

I didn't fully understand what she was saying, but I let her talk. Before I knew it, we'd walked to the cemetery. Jubilee's highest hill was home to my very own cemetery. I studied the five beautiful headstones that stood in a perfect row.

What a peculiar feeling it be looking at your own graves. I stopped at the most recent one. The last one read 'May 5th,

1949.' It seemed so long ago. I tried to remember who I was then.

I turned to Eve, and she was standing behind me, her gaze also fixed on the row of graves. 'I bet it's weird to see your own tombstones,' I nodded yes. It was surreal, to say the least.

I turned to face her again, searching for guidance. 'What do I do about Velar?' I asked. 'And do I tell Bellamy?' Eve's smile was gentle yet hinting at a deep wisdom.

'You're like a child, seeking answers to questions you're not even sure you understand,' her eyes crinkled at the corners. I felt a flush rise to my cheeks, knowing she was right. After all, she has lived for over one hundred and eighty years now, while I was still grappling with the complexities of immortality.

'Let go and flow, that's my advice,' Eve said, her voice like a gentle brook. 'You worry too much, look at the life you live.' She gestured to the world below us, vibrant and full of wonder. 'And if you're worried about Bellamy, tell him,' She added, as if it were that simple.

I shook my head vehemently, my mind racing with the impossibility of it. 'I can't,' I said, trying to convey the depth of my concern. 'I can't let Bellamy down, I can't do that to him." He's everything to me, I'm his, I belong to him. "He owns me, Eve." I emphasized my words, hoping Eve would understand the weight of it. But maybe she didn't, maybe she couldn't grasp the complexity of my situation.

I knew I wasn't getting through to Eve, so I suggested we check on Prudence. At the hospital, we found Bellamy engaged in a heated conversation with Prudence. I thought they were resolving their issues, but then Prudence dropped a bombshell: she was leaving the circus and Jubilee.

'You can't go!' I exclaimed, my heart racing with concern. Bellamy noticed my arrival and asked, 'Where have you been? I thought you'd be here already.'

Eve intervened, 'I needed her help with something at my place.' Bellamy nodded understandingly and suggested, 'Let's give her some time, she's been through a lot and shouldn't be making decisions right now.' With that, he left. Millie and Ambrette were trying to reason with Prudence, but they seemed just as distraught as I was.

Prudence refused to look at me, her anger and sadness clear. But beneath those emotions, I sensed a deeper loss, a feeling of being utterly lost. I tried to persuade her to stay, even suggesting a vacation to help her clear her head, but she rejected the idea. She wanted nothing to do with the circus, Jubilee, or me.

A WEEK LATER, EVE AND I WAITED OUTSIDE PRUDENCE'S home. We received the news late last night that Prudence would be leaving us. Bellamy emerged from her steps, his expression stern and unreadable.

As he approached me, he announced, 'She's made her decision.' Without another word, he left us standing there. I didn't know where he was headed, but I knew Prudence had chosen to leave.

I wondered where she would go and what would become of her. Miss Poppet opened the door and helped Prudence outside, treating her with the tender care of a daughter. Velar followed behind, carrying her bags and suitcase.

'Prudence,' I called out as she tried to brush past me without a glance. She was taking her anger towards Bellamy out on me. 'Please,' I begged, finally getting her to pause. But her gaze was icy, and she snapped, 'You let him take my baby.'

I wanted to explain that I don't control Bellamy, that he's his own man who does as he pleases, regardless of my wishes. But all I could do was watch as she walked away, my head bowed in sorrow. Velar followed, his eyes avoiding mine. I felt a deep sadness wash over me once again.

The weeping willow tree stood tall, its branches swaying gently in the breeze, as everyone gathered around to bid Prudence farewell. A small group volunteered to accompany her to her desired destination, help her settle in, and then return to the circus.

As we said our goodbyes, Prudence instructed Velar on where she wanted to go, her voice inaudible from where I was standing. She avoided eye contact with Bellamy and me, her silence speaking volumes.

Velar relayed the information to Bellamy, who nodded and instantly lifted his hands to the sky, feeling the vibration of the jump made it feel more real, she was actually leaving us.

As she left the tree Bellamy walked over to me and gave me an empathetic smile. "She will be back, they always do."

CHAPTER
EIGHTEEN

It's been a month since Prudence left, and everything has returned to normal at the circus. So far anyway. I'm performing again. I think about Prudence and hope she's finding happiness living her immortal life to the fullest.

I've just finished my second act for the day when Velar approached me. Since our heated exchange, things have cooled down between us, and we've managed to maintain a friendly relationship.

I've made sure to keep things platonic, avoiding solo hangouts, and it seems he's respected my boundaries. He hasn't made any further attempts to pursue me romantically, and I'm relieved we can continue working together amicably.

I was in the backyard practicing. I'd been struggling with a particular performance. The first flip is a forward somersault. My arms and legs tucked in tight as I spin through the air.

The second flip is a twisting motion, my body rotating horizontally as I reach the apex of their trajectory. And the third flip is a show-stopping double layout, with my body stretched out in a straight line as I spin twice over, with my arms and legs extended in a graceful arc.

As the day progressed, I continued to scrutinize my performance, determined to improve. Anise was assisting me, but she had to prepare for her own show. 'Keep up the great work, girl!' she encouraged, her voice carrying up from below.

With renewed focus, I directed all my energy towards the ropes and made a bold jump. However, just as I was about to grasp the rope, I spotted Velar walking into the backyard, and my concentration was broken. I missed the rope entirely and tumbled into the safety net.

Velar's hearty laughter echoed through the air as I awkwardly plunged into the net. He kindly held it steady for me to crawl out of, and then effortlessly lifted me into his arms, gently placing my feet back onto solid ground. Despite my embarrassment, I couldn't help but laugh along with him, my frustration momentarily forgotten in the face of his charming smile and chivalrous gesture.

Velar handed me some water, and I realized how sweaty I was, while he seemed utterly unfazed. I caught myself watching him disassemble the trapeze equipment and acrobatic gear, his strength and ease mesmerizing. He moved everything effortlessly, his muscles rippling beneath his skin. When his eyes met mine, I quickly looked away, feeling uncomfortable and flustered. My heart raced, and I tried to shake off the sensation, focusing on my act instead.

As I handed the water back to Velar, our fingers touched briefly, and I felt a jolt of electricity run through my body. I quickly pulled my hand back, trying to brush off the sensation. "Thanks," I said, trying to sound casual.

Velar nodded and smiled, his fangs peeking out. "No problem. Let's try again, shall we?" He gestured to the equipment, and I nodded, taking a deep breath.

We spent the next hour practicing, Velar offering words of encouragement and advice. I was determined to master the triple flip, and with Velar's help, I finally started to get the hang of it.

As the sun began to set, we called it a day, and I thanked Velar for his help. "Anytime," he said, smiling. "You're a natural." I blushed, feeling a sense of pride and accomplishment. As we packed up the equipment, I couldn't help but steal glances at Velar, his strength and skill leaving me in awe.

I felt a strong urge to talk to him more, but before I could say anything, someone interrupted with a cheerful, "Hey Velar, have fun in Alaska!" I was taken aback, having completely forgotten about his trip. Velar's annual visit to the vampire festival in Alaska had slipped my mind.

He noticed my surprise and explained, "I was going to tell you, but we got caught up in rehearsals and I..." His voice trailed off, and I finished for him, "It's okay, I totally forgot. When do you leave?"

Velar replied, "Tonight, after the circus closes." I nodded, unsure how I felt or what to say. I settled for a simple, "Have fun," trying to sound genuine. Velar smiled, but his eyes seemed to cloud over for a moment. "Yeah, I'll try to," he said softly. "I'll bring you back some souvenirs." He paused, then added with a hint of playfulness, "Maybe even some vampire fangs." I laughed, trying to lighten the mood. "Sure, that would be great."

We stood there awkwardly for a moment before he glanced at his watch and said, "I should get going. I have to pack and get ready for my trip." I nodded, feeling a pang of disappointment.

"Yeah, okay. Have a safe trip." he smiled and nodded, then turned and walked away. I watched him go, feeling a little lost and unsure of what to do with myself.

As the circus began to close up, I was pinged with the faint tang of goodbye. Velar was leaving for a month, and the thought of not seeing him every day felt like a physical ache.

Bellamy, resplendent in his ringmaster suit, approached me with worry in his eyes, his voice low and soothing. "Still rehearsing, my dear?" I shook my head, unable to speak. "I thought you would be back in Jubilee by now." I didn't respond.

My thoughts were racing, and Bellamy stopped me before I could climb the ladder again. "Baby girl…" he said, pausing for me to explain, but I just felt sad. Then he asked, "Do you want to come with me to say goodbye to Velar?" I looked at him, his sea blue eyes appeared to know more than his words let on. "Sure."

We strolled towards the gate, the setting sun casting a warm, golden light over the scene. "Won't you be jumping him somewhere?" I asked, wondering how Velar would make it to Barrow. Bellamy smiled and shook his head. "Velar will fly overnight to Alaska. He'll be safe, my love."

As we approached, Velar was already bidding farewell to others. His emerald eyes gleaming in the fading light. When he saw me, he paused, his gaze locking onto mine with an intensity that made my heart race. I felt a flutter in my chest, my feet rooted to the spot, as the crowd parted to create a pathway between us.

The scent of leather and pine wafting towards me like a siren's call. Bellamy stepped in front of me, his bro hug interrupting the moment, and said, "Have a great time at Vamp Fest!" with a grin that seemed to hold a secret.

Velar's eyes never left mine, his gaze burning with an inner fire that made my skin prickle with awareness. Finally, Bellamy stepped aside, and I moved forward to embrace Velar.

His massive arms wrapped around me like a vice, his scent enveloping me, and I felt my body light up with a warmth even though his body was cold to the touch. As he pulled away, whispering in my ear, "Don't miss me too much."

As Velar vanished into the night, Bellamy's grasp on my hand tightened, and he swept me through the crowd with a sense of urgency. People reached out to him, but he brushed them off. His eyes were fixed straight ahead. I stumbled alongside him, my heart racing with curiosity. To others he must have looked like he was on a mission, and perhaps he was.

What was going on? Where were we headed? The answers remained elusive until we returned to Jubilee, and Bellamy's stern expression made my stomach twist with anxiety. "What's wrong?" I demanded, but he just pulled me up the stairs of Casmira, his silence more unsettling than any words.

Finally, we reached the front door. He released my hand, his eyes burning with an intensity that made my stomach knot. "Baby girl," he growled, his accent sending shivers down my spine, "I need you to go to the playroom. I'll be up shortly."

I didn't bother to get into my usual position. Instead, I settled into the plush couch, I couldn't help but feel a sense of unease. The warm, golden light that filled the space seemed to mock me, making me feel like I was trapped in a gilded cage. I had been waiting for what felt like an eternity for Bellamy to arrive, my mind racing with worst-case scenarios.

Suddenly, the door creaked open, and he strode in, his presence commanding attention. But it was what he held in his hand that made my heart skip a beat. A black wooden paddle. My eyes fixed on it, my mind racing with questions. *What was it for? Was I in trouble?*

Bellamy's eyes locked onto mine, his gaze burning with an intensity that made my skin prickle. "We need to talk." He sat down beside me, his arm around me, but his hand holding the paddle rested on my knee.

As he spoke, his hand tightened around the paddle, his knuckles white with tension. He pulled me closer into him with his other hand around my back. I felt a surge of fear mixed with anticipation, my heart racing with every word. 'It seems I must teach you a lesson,' his voice low. 'I'm going to punish you.'

I'm confused about why Bellamy thought I needed punishment. Could he read my thoughts about Velar? I'm not even sure what I'm even feeling myself. I'm unsure if I should be guilty or if it's just a misunderstanding. I wish I could clear the air and understand Bellamy's perspective.

"Why do you need to punish me? What did I do?" I asked, confusion etched on my face. Bellamy's smile was enigmatic as he turned to face me. "Baby girl, you didn't do anything wrong. Sometimes, I just need to remind you who you belong to."

My mind raced with all the scenarios I'd shared with Velar, and I wondered if Bellamy could sense my hidden feelings. I looked down, avoiding his gaze. *This was because the way Velar was looking at me or maybe it was because of the way I was looking at him.*

Bellamy gently lifted my chin, his eyes locked on mine. " I own you," he said, his voice firm but smooth. "But do you?" I nodded, my heart racing. "Yes," I whispered. "Yes, what?" he prompted.

"Yes, Daddy," He nodded again, this time more emphatically. "Good girl," his expression softened. "Now, bend over."

I SAT AROUND THE DINNER TABLE WITH EVE AND BELLAMY, exhausted but relieved to finally have a break from the circus's grueling schedule. Eve and I chatted about our latest aerial stunts, while Bellamy tried to focus on his food, still looking a bit bothered by a recent headline from this week.

Just as we were all relaxing, I accidentally knocked over my glass of water, spilling it all over the table and Eve's lap. We all burst out laughing at the sudden chaos. In the midst of the commotion, I turned to Bellamy and said, "Velar, can you—"

Bellamy raised an eyebrow, correcting me, "Bellamy, actually."

My face turned bright red as I realized my mistake. "Oh, Daddy, I'm sorry," laughing it off.

Eve giggled and patted my hand. "It's okay, we know you're tired!" But Bellamy couldn't let it slide.

"Actually, baby girl, that's a punishable offense," he said with a sly grin. My eyes widened as he quickly rose, taking my hand, leading me away from the table.

"Time for a little trip to the playroom." Eve's laughter followed us out of the room, and I couldn't help but feel a bit aroused...

CHAPTER

NINETEEN

Today was the day Velar would finally return from Alaska, and I couldn't believe how quickly the time had flown by. It felt like just yesterday I was bidding him farewell, and now, a month had already passed.

I had been performing non-stop all month long, pouring my heart and soul into every show, and Velar hadn't crossed my mind once. I was starting to get used to him being away, adapting to the new rhythm of my life without him.

But it seemed like Eve had other plans. All day, she kept reminding me about Velar's return, asking me if I was excited, if I had missed him, if I was nervous. And with each passing conversation, my mind started to wander back to him. I couldn't help but wonder what he'd be like after a month away, if he'd changed, if he'd missed me too. I wondered how our friendship would resume.

As the hours ticked by, my anticipation grew. I found myself rehearsing our reunion in my head, imagining what I'd say, how I'd act, what I'd wear. It was like my brain was trying to prepare me for a performance, but this time, it was a performance of emotions, of vulnerability. *Was it more?*

And now, as the night draws near, I can feel my heart racing with excitement and nerves. I'm not sure what the night will bring, but I know one thing for sure - Velar's return is going to change everything.

After my last show ended, I headed back to Jubilee early, eager to prepare myself. I stopped by the Big Top to let Bellamy know about my plans, and I couldn't help but watch in amazement as he performed. Everything about Bellamy was pure perfection - his wisdom, his grace, his words, his undeniable sex appeal. I was getting turned on just thinking about him.

As the face of the circus, he had a way of captivating the audience, and I was no exception. Most people were obsessed with him, he was a legend after all. I felt blessed to call him mine.

As I watched him perform, I couldn't help but feel a pang of guilt about my feelings for Velar. It was a strange sensation, like my heart was torn between two different emotions. I pushed the thought aside as Bellamy ran over to me as soon as his act ended.

"Daddy, I'm heading home," looking up at Bellamy with a smile. He gazed back at me curiously but smiled. "Okay, love," he replied, his voice warm and gentle. He leaned in to kiss my forehead, his lips soft and comforting. As I turned to leave, he gave my ass a playful pat, sending a flutter through my chest.

I made my way through the crowd, which was gathering around Bellamy, eager to meet him and get his autograph. I knew he'd be busy for a while, so I slipped away, thinking to myself that he wouldn't miss me too much.

As I settled into my cozy chair on the fourth story balcony of Casmira, the soothing warmth of peppermint tea in my hands, I gazed out at the bustling scene below. The performers and crew were returning from the circus, their faces aglow with the thrill of the day.

I watched as Miss Poppet returned and made her way to her bakery, chatting with people along the way. I felt a sense of contentment wash over me as I watched them, my heart still basking in the joy of my own performance.

After losing myself in the pages of my beloved book, I decided it was time to prepare for Velar's return. A flutter of excitement stirred within me as I thought about seeing him again. I wanted to look my absolute best, to shine like the stars on a clear night sky.

With careful hands, I styled my hair and applied my makeup, savoring the quiet moment to myself. No need for Bellamy's magical assistance tonight. I wanted to present myself to Velar as authentically me. As I slipped into my closet, my eyes landed on the breathtaking blue dress Velar had gifted me after our night in downtown LA. It was the first time I'd worn it, and it fit me like a glove, as if tailored specifically for this moment.

I felt a thrill of anticipation as I admired myself in the mirror, the dress shimmering in the soft light like a celestial whisper. I couldn't wait to see Velar's reaction when he saw me in it. With a final touch to my hair, I was ready.

Bellamy's sudden presence behind me made me jump, and I hadn't realized he was also admiring me through the mirror. Our eyes met in the reflection, and I swiftly turned to face him, restraining my surprised demeanor. 'I don't think I've ever seen you wear that before,' his gaze roamed over my outfit with interest.

I felt a blush rise to my cheeks, 'It's new.' He raised his eyebrows, 'Oh?' His expression is playful and teasing. 'Eve got it for me,' I lied, trying to sound nonchalant despite the flutter in my chest.

His hard heavy arms encircled me from behind. He turned me to face the oversized mirror, our eyes locking in a sultry gaze. 'Absolutely gorgeous,' his hot breath danced across my skin. 'You will always be mine.'

The possessiveness in his voice sent a thrill through me, and I couldn't help but wonder if it was a threat or a promise. Either way, I was his, and I knew it. I turned to kiss him, and he devoured me, his magic surging with excitement. I tried to step back, but Bellamy pulled me closer, his hand slipping down to my ass, sending sparks flying.

He let me go, leaving me panting, and I knew it was just a tease of what was to come later. With a sly smile, Bellamy adjusted himself, 'Shall we go get our friend now?' I nodded, still reeling from the intensity of the moment.

Velar's arrival was imminent, and Eve and I waited with bated breath by the weeping willow tree on the Jubilee side. Bellamy had jumped us to wherever Velar was, and he would escort him back to us. As we waited, Eve complimented my dress, knowing full well I wore it to impress Velar.

We giggled like schoolgirls, and for a moment, I let go of my worries about my feelings. So, what if I was married and had a crush on Velar, Bellamy's best friend? We were all friends for many lifetimes, and this unconventional life we led wasn't traditional, but maybe I was starting to finally accept that.

Our laughter and whispers ceased abruptly as we heard the footsteps coming down the stairs, signaling Velar's arrival. The air seemed to vibrate with anticipation as we waited for him to appear.

It had only been a month, but the anticipation of seeing him again felt like an eternity. It's strange, I didn't even think about him that much when he was away for a month, but now it feels like he's constantly on my mind, it's like my brain is making up for lost time.

I couldn't wait for him to lay eyes on me in the stunning dress he had gifted me. I knew he would be thrilled. The memory of his thoughtful gesture made my heart skip a beat, and I felt like a schoolgirl on prom night. Eve's compliments on my dress only added to my excitement. The footsteps grew louder, my nerves dissipated, replaced by an electrifying sense of excitement.

Bellamy emerged first, making his way to me. Velar followed, his eyes burning with an intensity that made my heart race. I stepped forward to greet him, but my words were swallowed by shock when I saw a petite blonde walking beside him, her hand clasped in his.

My mind reeled as I struggled to process the scene before me. Velar froze, his gaze locking onto mine with a fierce passion, his eyes scorching me from head to toe. Obviously seeing the dress on me.

The air was electric with tension as Eve intervened, her voice slicing through the silence like a knife. "Welcome home, Velar. And who is this?" she asked, her tone dripping with curiosity.

Velar and I continued to stare at each other, the silence between us crackling with unspoken questions. Finally, I found my voice and extended my hand to the young woman, my heart pounding in my chest.

"I'm Nicole," I said, trying to sound calm despite the turmoil inside me. The young blonde stuck out her hand and I took it. Ice cold. She smiled, "I'm Marcella," as her smile grew, I noticed her fangs. Vampire.

'Velar met Marcella at Vamp Fest, she's a newly turned vampire and was looking for a safe place to live. Velar kindly told her all about Jubilee. I think we can help her out, can't we ladies.' Bellamy said to us, noticing our shocked silence. Eve and I nodded but remained speechless.

I couldn't believe what I was hearing. All this time, I thought Velar was interested in me, but now he was with this... this...vampire instead. Marcella. I couldn't even look at her. I felt betrayed, hurt, and angry all at once.

What was going on? Why was Velar doing this? I didn't know what to do or say, but I knew I didn't want to be there. I needed to get out of there, fast.

With a sweeping gesture, Bellamy raised his arms to the sky, prolonging sunset throughout Jubilee. He immediately started to give Marcella a tour of our magical town which felt like a twisted knife in my heart. Eve's gentle back rub was the only thing that kept me from unraveling. Velar's hasty release of Marcella's hand when he saw me only added fuel to the fire raging inside me. I couldn't bear the thought of him with her.

I couldn't help but compare her to myself, wondering if it was her vampiric nature that drew Velar to her, or perhaps it was the fact that she wasn't married to his best friend. She was petite and adorable, and her presence made my stomach twist with a mix of emotions, a pang of jealousy and a dash of insecurity.

I made a hasty excuse and bolted, my feet pounding the ground in a desperate bid for escape. Eve distracted Bellamy and Marcella while I quickly walked off.

Velar's voice called out to me, 'Nic, I... I didn't know...' but I refused to listen. I ran up the stairs to Casmira, slamming the door behind me like a declaration of war. Casmira felt my anger. *Didn't know what?*

About forty minutes later Eve burst into Casmira holding two wine bottles. 'Time to drown our sorrows...or at least, your sorrows,' she declared. 'They are now showing Marcella the Emberlynn Forest.' She pronounced it 'Mar-CELL-La', drawing out the syllables in a mocking, high-pitched tone, making me laugh. I couldn't help it, but partly because I was two sips away from sobbing uncontrollably. Again.

We spent the next hour drinking, laughing, and making poor life choices...like singing 'I Will Survive' at the top of our lungs. By the end of the night, I didn't care about Velar, Marcella, or even my own name. It was glorious.

I must have blacked out because I don't remember Bellamy coming home, but he must have been the one to clean me up and put me to bed. I woke up to a horrible headache. On the nightstand, there was a drink, which I desperately needed since my head was throbbing and my stomach was churning. I downed the concoction, which tasted like orange juice, and within seconds, I felt better.

'Thank you,' I called out to Casmira, but to my surprise, Bellamy replied, 'You're welcome.' He was sitting in the chaise lounge across from the bed, and I hadn't noticed him there before. I assumed he had just gone to open the circus early this morning.

As I sat up and grabbed my head, not because of the pain but because of my racing thoughts, Bellamy walked over to me. His eyes seemed to know exactly what I was thinking. Thoughts about Velar and Marcella, my feelings, and Bellamy himself. 'Baby girl,' he said softly, his scent carrying the salty sea air from his recent swim in the Opal Sea. 'How are you doing?' he asked.

I knew Bellamy was aware of the situation with Velar and why I was distressed. Feeling embarrassed, I hesitated, but he gently encouraged me to open up. 'Talk to me baby,' sitting beside me. I sat up, apologizing profusely, but Bellamy's nod indicated he wanted more.

'I understand you were upset seeing Velar with someone else,' he began, 'but I didn't realize your feelings ran so deep. You've been hiding your emotions from me, and that is unacceptable.' His expression showed a mix of concern and disappointment, making me feel even more ashamed.

'So, tell me. How long have you been in love with Velar?' I gasped, my eyes widening in surprise. 'I am not...' 'I'm not blind, baby girl,' he said with a gentle smile. 'I've seen the way you look at him. But I had no idea it was this serious.'

I hastily added, 'I don't love him, Bellamy. I don't know what I feel, and it doesn't matter anyway. He has a girlfriend, I'm married, so it's not like anything can happen between us.' I hoped my words sounded convincing, but Bellamy's knowing gaze made me wonder if he saw right through me.

Bellamy's expression softened, and he chuckled, "Oh, you're so adorable when you're trying to navigate immortal relationships." He pulled me into a warm embrace, "It's okay, little one. You'll always belong to me, no matter what."

I felt a mix of comfort and confusion. As an immortal, Bellamy didn't view relationships like mortals did. To him, time was endless, and connections were fluid. But for me, reincarnation made things complicated. Each life was a new start, and memories of past lives were hazy at best. I struggled to grasp the concept of eternal belonging.

Bellamy sensed my unease and pulled back, his eyes sparkling with amusement. "Don't worry, I love you. And besides, you're mine, always." His voice tightened when he said always. Deep down, I knew I still had much to learn about immortal love and loyalty.

1974

"The distinction between past, present, and future is only a stubbornly persistent illusion."

—Albert Einstein

CHAPTER
TWENTY

As the clock struck midnight, I shouted 'Happy New Year!' Bellamy's lips crashed into mine, the passion in his kiss leaving me breathless. The room erupted in cheers and applause, but I only had eyes for him. I knew he was eager for our guests to depart, so he could have me all to himself. I watched as magically the champagne filled the crystal flutes that were sitting on the dining room table.

I gazed around at the familiar faces of my dear friends, feeling grateful for their presence. Henry was beaming as he held Anise close, while Eve twirled across the dance floor with Eudora. Bellamy and Velar were bickering about what performance acts drew the most crowds.

Although Miss Poppet had stopped by earlier, she had already bid us farewell for the evening. Clove, meanwhile, was deep in conversation with Marcella. It filled my heart with joy to see everyone I'm closest to in one place, surrounded by love and laughter.

Bellamy cleared his throat, preparing to give one of his beloved speeches. 'Happy New Year, my dear friends!' his eyes sparkling with enthusiasm. 'I hope this year is our best one yet!' I felt a flutter in my chest as I gazed at my immortal friends, their faces aglow.

For a moment, I worried about my own mortality. Another year older while they remain the same, I pushed the thought aside, not wanting to tarnish the magic of the night. Marcella handed me a flute filled with champagne, and I noticed hers contained a thick red substance that seemed to glow in the dim light.

She walked off and I watched as she gave another blood-filled glass to Velar, who toasted with her. I looked away before he kissed her, not out of jealousy but because I didn't want to intrude on their intimate moment.

It had been years since I last harbored any romantic feelings for Velar. Right before he met Marcella, I was in a state of confusion, wondering if he might be developing feelings for me. But I was wrong. The moment he brought Marcella to meet our close-knit group, I realized my mistake. I saw the way he looked at her, and it was clear that his heart belonged to her.

At first, I was a bit disheartened, but I soon came to terms with the fact that Velar and I were meant to be just friends. Marcella, despite being the new person in our circle, quickly won me over with her kindness and warmth. Although she lives alone in a cozy cottage built by Bellamy, she and Velar are incredibly close.

Marcella approached me, her hands full with her and Velar's empty blood-stained glasses. 'Where should I put these?' she asked, her voice raised above the music. I nodded for her to follow me, and we made our way to the kitchen, the pulsating beat of the music growing fainter as we escaped the crowd.

As we stood at the sink, I turned to her with a mischievous grin and slurred my words, asking, 'What's your New Year's revolution... I mean, res-o-lution?' Marcella's eyes widened in surprise, and she looked taken aback, like she'd never been asked that before.

She shrugged her shoulders, and finally said, 'I want to suck people's blood without killing them.' I couldn't contain my expression, and my eyes widened in surprise, but I quickly covered with, 'Good one!' and a playful laugh.

Then, she asked me the same question, likely feeling obligated to reciprocate. I thought for a moment before responding, 'I'm going to start aerial ropes again.' Marcella nodded enthusiastically and said, 'Yeah, Eve mentioned you were going to do that.'

It hit me then, I'd only been the Circus' Ring mistress for the past few years, content to be Bellamy's second. I remembered that I'd changed roles once Marcella joined our community. It was Bellamy's idea, but I knew I did it to create distance between Velar and myself, to redefine my role and get rid of any feelings that I thought I had for that handsome vampire.

What surprised me most was how quickly Marcella, and I became friends. It wasn't immediate, and I'd be lying if I said it was easy. But over time, we grew closer, and now our friendship feels completely natural. She's even starring in a thrilling stunt performance in the circus, which has been an exciting new chapter for her.

Her story was heartbreaking, forced to become a vampire at a young age, witnessing her entire family's brutal murder. The trauma and pain in her eyes were palpable as she first shared her tale with me. She had only come to Vamp fest seeking solace, hoping to find others like her and escape the dangerous life she'd been living.

Everyone who heard her story, including me, was deeply moved. We couldn't help but feel a sense of sorrow and empathy for what she had endured. I was so grateful that we had saved her from that struggling existence, and I knew Velar would have done the same for any vampire in need.

He was that kind of selfless person. His compassion and kindness knew no bounds, and I admired him all the more for it. He may appear rugged and tough on the outside, but on the inside, I believe he's a gentle soul.

I still remember the early days when she first joined our ranks as a new vampire. She struggled to come to terms with her newfound immortality, and the thought of feeding on blood was utterly repugnant to her. But now, as I watch her raise the blood-filled goblet to her lips and drink without even a hint of hesitation, I'm struck by how far she's come. She's long past the struggles that once defined her and has embraced her new existence.

It's remarkable to see how she's adapted to this immortal life, and how seamlessly she's integrated into our little community here in Jubilee. She's no longer the tentative, uncertain newcomer she once was - now, she's a confident, self-assured immortal, living life on her own terms.

Velar and I have also rediscovered the joy of our unbreakable friendship, just like in the good old days. The fact that we've emerged even stronger and more united than ever is a testament to the unshakeable foundation of our friendship. We've always been able to laugh together, support each other through thick and thin, and celebrate each other's triumphs.

I'm so grateful that we could navigate this new reality without any issues, and that our connection has only deepened as a result. It's a beautiful reminder that true friendship can withstand even the most significant changes, and that with love, trust, and mutual support, we can overcome anything that comes our way.

I won't sugarcoat it, it wasn't easy for me to warm up to Marcella at first. In fact, I used to avoid her altogether, even hiding in my house to escape her presence. But Velar kept bringing us together, almost forcing me to interact with her.

I have to admit, I initially put on a facade of friendliness just to appease Bellamy, who threatened to kick her out of Jubilee and the circus if I didn't get along with her! But, as time passed, something remarkable happened. I genuinely started to enjoy her company. Fast forward years later, and here we are.

"I was looking for you!" Eve clinked her champagne glass against mine with a joyful clink. I couldn't help but laugh at my drunken friend as she stumbled her way around the room, doling out New Year's hugs to anyone within arm's reach. Her bright smile and infectious laughter had everyone in stitches, but as she made her way back over to me, her legs suddenly gave out from under her, and she began to fall.

In a flash, Velar sprang into action, swiftly catching Eve before she hit the ground. "Alright, lady, time to get you home," he said with a chuckle, scooping her up into his arms. He gave me a warm smile, and I smiled back nodding in agreement. Marcella followed close behind them, her eyes shining with amusement, as they made their way towards the front door of Casmira.

As the last of the partygoers departed, the room grew quiet, and soon it was just Bellamy and me left standing amidst the glittering decorations and scattered party favors. The sudden silence was a stark contrast to the lively atmosphere that had filled the room just moments before. I turned to Bellamy, and we shared a knowing look.

Bellamy and I have been engaging in a thrilling game of cat and mouse, and it's undoubtedly added a spark to our sex life. Without warning, I darted out of Casmira, sprinting towards the back of the house wildly. The cold, wet grass beneath my bare feet was invigorating, and I didn't care that I was barefoot. I heard the front door close, and my heart began racing with anticipation.

I listened intently for Bellamy's footsteps, holding my breath and remaining silent. When I heard him heading in the opposite direction, I tiptoed back to the front of the house, thinking I could outsmart him. But just as I thought I had the upper hand, I heard a noise behind me. I sprinted ahead, looking over my shoulder, until I ran straight into Bellamy's arms. I screamed with delight as he caught me, his wicked smile revealing that he had outmaneuvered me once again.

"I got you!" he exclaimed, throwing me over his shoulder and carrying me back into the house. I couldn't help but laugh at the thrill of the chase and the excitement of being caught. Our game of cat and mouse had become a tantalizing ritual, ending with me being caught.

Once inside, Bellamy sets me on my feet, but not before giving my ass a playful slap. I glance around and notice that Casmira is spotless, with no signs of the party that had just taken place. I loved that my house magically cleans itself. Bellamy takes my hand. I follow him up the four flights of stairs, my heart racing with anticipation.

Instead of stopping at the playroom door, Bellamy continues on to our bedroom. Just as he opens the door, the bathtub water starts to run, filling the room with the soothing sound of flowing water. I raise an eyebrow, intrigued by the surprise. Bellamy gives me a sly smile, and I know that he has something special planned. He leads me into the adjoining bathroom, and I see that the room is lit with candles, casting a warm and intimate glow. The bathtub is filling with bubbles, and I can't help but feel a sense of excitement and relaxation wash over me.

Bellamy gently undressed me, his fingers tracing my skin as he guided me towards the half-filled tub. I sink into the perfect hot temperature, feeling my muscles relax and my senses come alive. Then, Bellamy removes his clothes, revealing his already-aroused state. His eyes lock onto mine, burning with desire like a wild animal.

I slide into the water in front of him, and he sits behind me, pulling me onto his wet, hard body. I feel his erection against me, and he rubs my breasts and kisses my neck as the bubbles fill the tub around us. 'Happy New Year, baby girl,' he whispers, his voice full of desire. I turn to repeat the word to him, but stop when his hands slowly make their way down to my pussy.

As I lean back, Bellamy's embrace envelops me, his lips tracing tender kisses on my neck. His gentle bite sends shivers down my spine, and I can't help but whine with pleasure. The warmth of the tub and the champagne's effervescence still coursing through my veins, I surrender to the sensation.

Bellamy twists me around, and I straddle him, the water sloshing over the tub's edge as we move in unison. His hands explore my body, and I melt into his touch, our lips meeting in a passionate kiss. The world around us fades away, leaving only the two of us, lost in the intimacy of the moment.

As we move together, Bellamy's hands guide me, positioning me to fit perfectly onto him. I moan softly as I slide down, our bodies becoming one. The warmth of the water, the softness of his skin, and the gentle pressure of his embrace all blend together, creating a sensation that's both exhilarating and serene.

Our lips meet again, and our kisses deepen, the passion and desire between us growing with each passing moment. I feel myself getting lost in his eyes, drowning in the depths of his love, and I know that I'm exactly where I'm meant to be.

As Bellamy's passion intensifies, his magic swirls around us, his grip on me tightens, and his thrusts become more fervent. The water in the tub churns and foams, splashing over the edge onto the enchanted ground, where it disappears in a mist of glittering droplets. Our bodies move in perfect harmony, our pleasure building in tandem.

Just as I reach my peak and moan in ecstasy, Bellamy lets out a primal roar, his voice echoing through the mystical realm. His release is explosive, and I feel his warmth spread through me.

I step out of the bathtub, my legs a bit wobbly from the champagne and the intense pleasure we shared. My body is sore, but it's a good kind of sore, a reminder of the passion we've just shared. I smile to myself, feeling a sense of satisfaction and happiness.

As I turn to leave, Bellamy's voice stops me. "Are you running away again?" he asks, a playful glint in his eye. "Why? Do you want to chase me again?" I turn back to him, a sly grin spreading across my face. "Always." He grins back and I answer him. "The only thing I'm running to is our bed."

CHAPTER
TWENTY-ONE

Winter in Jubilee was always a brief affair, lasting no more than a month. I'm convinced that Bellamy conjures up the snowflakes just for me. Every day for a month, the skies are painted with a gentle hue of white, transforming the hills of the Emberlynn Forest into a snow-covered playground.

The entire town gathers there, and for a while, everyone becomes a kid again - including me! Eve and I sneakily spiked the punch, the secret ingredient everyone's been eagerly anticipating. Meanwhile, Mesidor works to build a roaring bonfire, it's almost the size of the one at my Samsara Ritual. These were truly enchanted days, filled with laughter, snowball fights, and my very favorite, sledding.

I couldn't help but laugh watching Bellamy, all bundled up, flying with his magical staff towards Eve and I, carrying the sled I had asked him to find in our attic. He wasn't about to trudge through the snow.

'Baby girl, put on a heavy jacket, you're going to get sick,' his eyes twinkled with concern. Eve and I were already laughing, our cheeks frozen and bright red from the cold. We were having the time of our lives, and Bellamy's arrival only added to the fun.

Just then, Velar and Marcella flew down the hill, their sled flipping over right next to us. Eve had to jump out of the way to avoid a crash. Velar, seemingly unfazed, boldly questioned, 'Bell, you came to have some fun for once?' Bellamy shook his head no, "This is not my kind of fun." Then turned back to me handing me the sled.

With a flick of his wrist, a snow suit jacket appeared in his hands, and before I could protest, he quickly wrapped it around me and zipped me up in it. His hands on my cheeks instantly warmed them. The toasty magic lingered after he pulled his hands away.

"Get her home at a reasonable hour, would you?" Bellamy said to Velar, as if he was my personal babysitter. I opened my mouth to protest, but Velar quickly replied, "Yes, sir!" before sprinting up the hill with Marcella by his side. Their speed was incredible, like lightning flashing through the snow.

Bellamy turned to me, his eyes sparkling with magic, and kissed me on the lips. I felt a tingling sensation, as if his lips had left a trail of sparks on my mouth. As he slowly floated away, Eve and I grabbed the sled and followed after Velar and Marcella, trudging up the snow-covered hill with laughter and excitement.

The snow crunched beneath our feet, and the cold air invigorated our senses. We reached the top of the hill, and Velar and Marcella were already there, waiting for us with huge grins on their faces. They were patiently waiting for us to join.

We plopped down on the sled, with me in the front and Eve in the back. I took a moment to gaze out at the breathtaking scenery below. The snow-covered town square, the majestic willow tree in the distance, and the rolling hills stretching out as far as the eye could see. It was a winter wonderland, and I felt like I was on top of the world.

As I took in the view, it started snowing again, and I gasped in delight. I knew Bellamy had made it snow just for me, and the magic of it all filled my heart with joy. But before I could gaze around any longer, Eve gave us a push, and we were flying down the gigantic hill!

As the icy gusts tore across my face, I let out a joyful scream, the kind that bursts forth from the pure exhilaration of being fully alive in the present moment. My screams of delight mingling with the howling gale.

As we sped down the hill, the snowflakes danced around us, and the world became a blur of white and green. When we reached the bottom of the hill, our sled spun around in circles until it finally came to a stop. Eve and I laughed so hard that our sides ached. Velar and Marcella helped us up off the ground.

"Why don't we call it a night?" Velar suggested, and I knew it was because of Bellamy. But I wasn't ready to end the fun yet. "No, not yet," I pout. Velar spat out 'Save that for Bell' and I crossed my arms, my eyes narrowing in defiance. There was no use, they seemed to have already made up their minds. "We'll be back here tomorrow," Marcella said, and Eve nodded in agreement.

Marcella took off towards the forest. "I'll see you later," she said to Velar. As the three of us walked towards the town, we laughed and chatted, taking in the beautiful snow-covered scenery. But as the temperature started to drop, I began to feel the cold seeping in.

It was as if Bellamy was gently nudging me towards home. When we reached the town square, Eve said her goodbyes and took off running towards her townhouse. Her hot breath puffed out in visible clouds as she took off running.

"Thanks for tonight. I had a blast." Velar smiled but didn't say a word. "I can walk home by myself," I stated, but Velar didn't slow down. "It's fine, I don't mind the snow," his fangs glinting in the moonlight.

I started to pick up the pace through the wooded path when I heard him mumble, "Can't keep Daddy waiting." I smiled, thinking he was joking, but when I turned back to look at him, his expression was serious.

I couldn't quite place his facial expression, but it seemed like he was unhappy about something. When we reached the iron gate, it didn't open. I knew it was pushing me to ask the question that was on my mind. So, I did, "What did you mean... can't keep daddy waiting?"

"I just mean you have rules, and you must follow them, that's all. I didn't mean to upset you," he said, trying to play it off, but his tone told me otherwise. It was as if Velar was trying to convey a message, but didn't want to say it outright. I sensed a hint of tension in his voice, and his eyes seemed to hold a secret.

I looked down, pondering whether I was satisfied with his response. He didn't leave, and I sensed that there was more to it. "Is something bothering you?" My eyes locked on him. He quickly shook his head, his expression dismissive. "It's been a long night, a rather good one. I'm just a bit tired."

I nodded, accepting his explanation at face value. But as I glanced up at him, I couldn't shake off the feeling that there was something more beneath the surface. His eyes seemed to hold a hint of unease, a flicker of emotion that he quickly masked. I wondered if he was hiding something, but I didn't press the issue. Instead, I accepted the conversation for what it was, a gentle dance around the truth.

When I turned to face Casmira, the iron gate swung open, and I walked up the stoop. I didn't look back until I reached my front door, but Velar was already gone. The door creaked open, and I stepped inside, where Bellamy was warming himself by the fireplace.

"Back so soon?" he asked, feigning innocence. I walked closer, and he asked, "How was it?"

"It was fun." Bellamy started undressing me, hanging my snow-covered clothes by the fire. He could have easily dried me with his magic, but it was obvious he enjoyed undressing me piece by piece.

As he helped me out of my wet clothes, I felt a sense of comfort and intimacy. Bellamy's hands were gentle, his touch warm, and his smile soothing. I knew he had been waiting for me, and I was grateful for his presence. The fire crackled, casting a golden glow over us, and I felt my heart fill with love and contentment.

I stood before him, the warmth of the fire dancing across my skin. Bellamy's gaze lingered on me, his eyes burning with a tender intensity. I began to turn away, but he quickly snapped, 'No.' I hastily turned back to face him.

He pulled a pillow from the couch and tossed it on the floor in front of me, his movements deliberate. I didn't have to be told to get on my knees. His gesture was enough.

I knelt before him, my heart racing with anticipation. Bellamy's gaze locked onto mine, his eyes burning with a tender intensity. I felt a sense of vulnerability wash over me. I pulled down his pants letting him expose himself to me. Already hard for me. *He has been waiting for me all day.*

I took him into my mouth, opening wide. He guided me closer, his hands gentle yet firm, and I felt myself surrender to him. I needed to serve him. I felt his hand on the back of my head pushing me deeper onto him.

Drool fell from my mouth as he thrusted in and out of me. I was so aroused I sucked him so good hoping to be rewarded. I felt his tension build, his breathing quicken, and I knew he was close. This time he pushed me further down and held me there.

I couldn't breathe and it was useless to struggle against his grasps as he fucked my face. Tears filled in my eyes and my mascara ran with them. Bellamy let out a roaring moan as warm saltiness filled my mouth.

He leaned in, his lips brushing against mine in a tender kiss. I felt a spark of electricity run through my body, and I knew I was lost in the moment. I only got up when he reached for my hand. He pulled me close and kissed my lips. His hand made its way down further to my pussy and felt that I was excessively wet.

He raised his finger to his mouth to taste me. He moans in my ear savoring me, making my breath quicken. I wanted him to touch me more, I needed it. He pulled me close, his hand wrapping around mine, and led me upstairs. I knew where we were headed, the playroom.

As soon as we entered, Bellamy wrapped a soft blindfold around my eyes, and I was enveloped in darkness. He swept me off my feet and gently laid me on the bed. I tried to speak, but a gentle gag muted my words.

Then, I felt the soft restraints around my ankles and wrists, securing me in place. I couldn't move, but I didn't want to. I was eager to surrender to him. I felt him touching me.

"So wet baby girl, is this all for daddy?" I nodded, the only thing I can do.

"Good girl." He spent his time playing with me and making me feel so amazing, his fingers stretching me open. My hips grind towards him, showing I want more. I need more.

Then I felt him pull out of me. Leaving me dripping wet and panting. I was almost disappointed until I felt the intense pressure of himself inside of me, making me arch my back and catch my breath at the same time. I try to moan, but the gag restricts me.

I'm paralyzed with pleasure, unable to move as Bellamy's passion intensifies. The sensation builds, a delicious blend of pain and pleasure that leaves me breathless.

As I surrender to the moment, Bellamy's grip on me tightens, and I feel myself letting go. With a final burst of ecstasy, I cry out in joy, my voice freed from the gentle restraint that had held it back. In this moment, our love is the only thing that mattered.

The next day, the circus roared back to life, unleashing a kaleidoscope of wonder and awe upon a new city and new audience. Headlines screamed our arrival, and the circus became the talk of the town, drawing in crowds like moths to a flame.

After being dormant for the holidays, we were open year-round for the most part, and I was wrapping up my show, packing up my belongings in the backyard as the crowd dispersed like wildfire. Most of the performers had already vanished into the night, heading back to Jubilee.

I grabbed my bag and waited for Bellamy by the willow tree. And then, I heard shouting, loud and urgent. I crept towards the screaming, my heart racing with anticipation.

I came to one of the smaller tents in the middle of the circus. Coming from the inside I heard Marcella's voice, like a wild animal, untamed and ferocious. Velar stood still, his face a mask of calm, but his eyes betrayed a hint of tension. I hid outside, my ears glued to the canvas, knowing I shouldn't be listening but unable to resist the allure of secrets.

Her words cut through the night air like a knife, 'I won't be controlled! Are you fucking crazy? Get me out of here!'

The silence that followed was oppressive, and I held my breath, wondering if I'd been discovered. I stumbled backwards, straight into Bellamy's arms. He caught me with a questioning gaze, and I quickly stood up, adjusting my clothes.

Velar and Marcella emerged from the tent, their eyes fixed on us with an unnerving intensity. Marcella's face was a picture of embarrassment, but her voice was laced with defiance. 'I'm sorry for shouting,' she muttered, her eyes downcast.

Velar's swallow was audible, and his voice was low and urgent. 'Bell, I need to speak with you... alone.' I nodded, sensing a storm brewing, I kissed Bellamy's cheek. 'I'll see you at home.'

Marcella remained still, her feet rooted to the ground, her eyes flashing with rebellion. 'I'm not your property!' She spat under her breath to Velar, and then stormed past me.

I sprinted after her, desperate to understand her words that lingered in my mind, *'You don't own me...'* When I arrived at Jubilee, I scanned around but she was nowhere to be seen. The scene was a serene expanse of calm, still white snow. The silence was almost calming to my mind. A trail of small footprints etched into the pristine white surface. They were the only clue that hinted at her swift departure.

I started walking towards Casmira, but when I reached the snowy wooded path, my feet seemed to have a mind of their own, continuing straight ahead. I decided to follow their lead and check on Marcella instead. Hoping to find some clarity, I hiked up the hill towards the Emberlynn Forest.

Breathless from my climb up the hill, I entered the forest and made my way to Marcella's cottage, the newest and most distinctive one in the area. It stood out starkly from the others, its modern design and immaculate facade a stark contrast to the surrounding cottages, which still retained their Gothic Victorian charm from the seventeenth century.

As I approached, I noticed that all the lights were on. Hesitation gripped me as I stood at her doorstep, wondering if I should intrude. My head was screaming at me to mind my own business, but my gut was urging me to check on her, to make sure she was okay. But before I could even knock, the door swung open, and Marcella stood in the door frames, looking past me to see if I was alone before she welcomed me in with a gentle wave.

I'm not sure why I was expecting her home to be warm and cozy inside. Vampires never bothered with mundane human comforts like temperature control. I instantly rubbed my hands on my arms to warm them. Marcella noticed my shivers and swiftly set about building a fire in the clean fireplace.

"Sorry." Her quick reflexes had the flames sparking to life in no time. "Thank you," checking out my surroundings. I couldn't help but notice the tasteful decorations, like right out of a magazine spread. However, my gaze soon landed on an open suitcase that was halfway filled with clothes.

'What's going on?' Interrupting Marcella as she tended to the fire. She followed my gaze and walked over to me. With a loud sigh, she flopped down in the chair across from me. "I can't stay here anymore."

"What do you mean?" I sat on the chair across from her, my confusion wearing on my face. Marcella's expression turned stern, and she shook her head, her eyes flashing with anger. "Don't play dumb, Nicole," her voice firm but laced with hurt.

"Did you and Velar have a fight?" I asked, trying to understand the sudden tension. Marcella stood up, her movements abrupt, and began pacing in front of the fire. "No matter what I do, it's not enough, it will never be enough. I." Her voice cracks. "I will never be enough." Her voice trembled.

"What are you talking about?" I gently grasped her cold arm to stop her pacing. She turned to face me, and my heart ached at the sight of red tears welling up in her eyes. *Please don't cry*, I silently pleaded, *I can't stomach watching a vampire cry.*

"No matter how hard I try, I'm not you, and no offense, I don't want to be like you... you're submissive," her voice cracking. The phrase 'submissive' stung, and I felt a surge of defensiveness. "That's what Velar says anyway." She rolled her eyes at her words.

I felt like I'd been punched in the gut, my shock and confusion evident on my face. I never wanted Marcella to be like me or expected her to be like me. *But did Velar? Did he want her to emulate me? Why?* My mind raced with questions as Marcella dropped another bombshell on me. "He'll never admit it, but he's in love with you.

I was about to protest, but my voice caught in my throat as I stood there in shock. *All this time, Velar still has feelings for me.*

Nine years later, I looked back on the whirlwind decade with wonder. Time sure flies when you're surrounded by immortals, I thought back on the countless circus performances, the endless excitement of Jubilee, and the loving moments with my husband. We'd traveled the world, exploring new lands together. Were the signs there, was I just oblivious?

I was speechless, my mind reeling with the revelation. Marcella's eyes met mine, and I saw the pain in them. She quickly began packing again, her movements swift and determined. I wanted to tell her to stop, to beg her to stay, but my words were trapped in my throat. *Did I really want her to leave?* I couldn't seem to muster the courage to speak up. I simply watched as she packed her belongings. Just as I finally found my voice, the cottage door burst open, and Velar stood before us, his presence commanding attention.

His piercing emerald gaze met mine, and his eyes widened in astonishment. He clearly hadn't expected me to be there, and his surprise was written all over his face. 'Get out of here!' Marcella shouted at Velar. The smell of pine and leather filled my noise with his presence.

"Nic, please leave us." His curt dismissal sent me hurrying towards the door, my body language betraying a subtle surrender to his authority. As the door closed behind me, I felt a lingering sense of submission, as if my very posture had conceded to his dominance.

The tension was palpable, and I didn't want to get caught in the middle of their explosive confrontation. But I already was. Eavesdropping outside, I strained to make out their conversation as they continued shouting at each other.

'Where are you going to go?' Velar demanded. 'Far from this fucking place!' Marcella retorted. Their bickering escalated until Marcella spat out, 'If I never see a circus again, it will be too soon!' I felt a pang of discomfort at her words, but I continued to listen, curious about the outcome of their argument.

'I'll never be what you want...' she shouted with pain in her voice. Velar finally reached his breaking point and shouted, 'I know!' Then, suddenly, silence. It seemed he had hit a nerve, and the shouting match was over. It was over just like that. I quickly ducked to the side of the cottage as I heard someone approaching the front door.

Marcella stormed out, suitcase in hand, and before I knew it, she sprinted away, her speed a blur. I started to head home when the familiar vibration coursed through the land. Bellamy had jumped us to a new location.

A faint noise behind me sent a shiver down my spine, and I froze. I didn't need to turn around to know he was there, I could feel his presence.

When I finally gathered the courage, I slowly turned to face him, my voice trembling as I whispered, 'I'm sorry,' breaking the silence. Velar stood tall and unashamed. His expression was unreadable, but not sad.

"Sorry for eavesdropping or sorry for Marcella leaving?" He said flatly.

"Both." The vibration struck again, and with our knowing eyes locked onto each other we knew she was gone. Wherever Bellamy jumped us to, it was far away from Marcella.

CHAPTER
TWENTY-TWO

Just as I predicted, the snowy oasis came to an end. It seemed that everyone in our magical town had finally had their fill of the snow, and they shared their complaints to my unwavering husband. Eventually though, he relented, and with both hands raised to the sky, he transformed our winter white wonderland into a balmy seventy-degree sunny day.

It's only been a couple of days since Marcella's departure, and I haven't seen or heard from Velar. I didn't ask Bellamy where he took her, it wasn't my business, and he didn't volunteer the information on his own. I wondered if Velar knew.

We haven't opened the circus in a couple of days because Bellamy was getting anxious about the media attention. More headlines about us in the UK were popping up, and Bellamy likes to keep a low profile. Even though Darlington Circus is the most famous circus in the world, no one knows about the actual magic in the circus nor of the immortals who run it, and we need to keep it that way.

I've been trying to focus on my own work, but my mind keeps wandering back to Marcella. I hope she is doing well, wherever she is. With the circus closed, most people take time and enjoy Jubilee or travel outside of the circus.

I, on the other hand, nestled on a chaise lounge on the fourth story balcony, utterly absorbed in a dark romance novel from the local library in Jubilee. The words on the page had transported me to a far-off land, imagining the beautiful scenery of the City of Starlight. I was so engrossed that I didn't even notice Eve's approach.

"More smut?" she teased, startling me out of my literary reverie. I slammed my book closed and flicked her my middle finger in a playful rebuke.

"Let's get out of here!" her eyes sparkling with mischief. I rolled my eyes, knowing she meant outside of the circus and Jubilee which Bellamy would never allow unless he came with us. "Where are we anyway?" I asked, usually I never know where we are.

"Don't worry, Bellamy said it's okay, I made sure to ask him." She gave me a cheesy smile before answering me. "We're back in NYC,' I jumped up excitedly. I could finally visit my mom! It had been eight months since I'd seen her. Bellamy was gracious about letting me visit and keeping in touch.

Eve followed me down the stairs to my bedroom, where I quickly changed into fresh clothes. Just as I was about to head out, Bellamy burst in. 'Don't be gone all night, okay?' he cautioned. 'I want us to jump out of here before dawn. I don't want to see another news headline about us.'

I nodded in agreement, and Eve chimed in with a cheeky, 'Yes, Daddy!' Her sarcasm was thick as honey. Bellamy didn't skip a beat, shooting back with a grin, 'You wish, little girl!' The playful banter was like a familiar dance, and I couldn't help but laugh at their antics.

Bellamy kissed me goodbye, lingering a little longer than necessary in front of Eve, trying to prove a point. But I pushed him away, feeling Eve rolling her eyes at us, no doubt annoyed.

We made our way out of the house together, heading towards the weeping willow tree. Up at the circus it was quiet, some performers were rehearsing, but the gates remained closed. Little did the New Yorkers know we would be disappearing in the middle of the night while they slept.

As we stepped out of the circus gate, the bustling energy of New York City enveloped me. I missed every inch of this city! Eve called out, 'Hey, while you're at your mom's house, I'm going to do some shopping!' I nodded and began my journey out of Central Park, where the circus was set up.

I hadn't thought to bring any money for the subway, so I decided to walk to the Upper West Side. The snow in NYC was a far cry from Jubilee's Wonderland. Instead of being soft and fluffy, it was dirty and sludgy, wet and gross. The city streets seemed to suck the magic out of the snow, leaving behind a grimy mess that was more frustrating than festive.

As I stepped carefully through the snow-covered streets, I felt the city's unique magic pulsing around me. The blaring horns, the hum of conversations from passersby, and the wailing sirens in the distance. Each noise blended into a symphony of urban rhythm, a beat that seemed to match the thrumming of my own heart.

When my mother answered the door, her face lit up with a radiant smile, and she was so excited that she threw her arms around me, nearly squeezing the breath out of me! 'My baby's home!' she exclaimed, her voice trembling with joy.

"Where's Bellamy?" she asks, her eyes sparkling with fondness for her favorite son-in-law - her only son-in-law, for that matter. 'He's at the circus.' Her face falls, but she nods understandingly, aware of the importance of his work under the big top.

My mom lives alone now, she dumped her boyfriend a couple of years ago. Although they remain friends, she seems to be thriving on her own. She has a new mischievous cat who always hides whenever I come to visit.

She had recently discovered a passion for traveling, and I was thrilled to hear that my own adventures with the circus had inspired her. She mentioned that the countless pictures I mailed her sparked her own desire to explore the world.

It was like no time had passed at all, and we fell into our usual routine of giggles and chatter. Her hugs always had a way of making me feel like everything was going to be okay, and this time was no exception.

As we sipped our coffee and munched on sandwiches at the local bodega, I pulled out some pictures and described the recent performances I had done. She fussed over the costumes and sets and beamed with pride at my accomplishments.

After our late lunch, we strolled through the central park, stopping by our favorite Balto statue, window-shopping and chatting about everything from our favorite books to circus acts. My mom laughed at my silly jokes and teased me good-naturedly about my hair, which was sticking up in every direction as usual. I felt like I was 10 years old again, carefree and happy in her presence. Being with my mom was a welcome escape, a chance to temporarily forget about the circus and the men who ran it.

As the afternoon wore on, we settled into a cozy movie theater for a matinee showing Love Story, a romantic drama starring Ali McGraw and Ryan O'Neal. It was the perfect way to spend quality time with my mom, just the two of us, enjoying each other's company and making memories that would last for lifetimes. My lifetimes anyway.

As I left my mother's house, the sun had just set and the cold night air chilled me to my core. I knew Bellamy would be expecting me back by now. I strolled back towards Central Park, but my attention was diverted when I saw Velar entering a jewelry store. I quickly ran over towards the shop, and I peeked through the window. I watched as he spoke with a beautiful saleswoman, who appeared to be flirting with him.

She handed him a necklace, which I assumed was a gift for Marcella. I hid from view, not wanting to be caught spying. But then, Eve startled me by yelling my name. I quickly ducked away from the window, my face flushed with embarrassment.

"I've been looking for you!" Eve exclaimed, as I hurried towards her. "We need to go!" I didn't mention what I had just witnessed, and instead, we quickly walked back towards the circus.

Within seconds Velar appeared behind us, resting his heavy arms on both Eve and I's shoulders. No bag in sight, and I wondered if he hadn't made the purchase after all. Either way, I played it cool, pretending it was the first time I'd seen him tonight.

"Going back so soon?" he asked to which Eve replied, "Bell wants to jump tonight." Velar blurted, "Well, Bell can wait, let's hang out for a bit longer." My mind suddenly flooded with memories of our last outing together.

Marcella was with us that night, and we were out getting drunk, lost in the haze of alcohol and camaraderie. Bellamy was there too, a steady presence amidst the chaos. But then, Velar and I clashed, our words igniting into a fiery argument.

I don't even remember what sparked it, but our voices grew louder, more intense, until we were screaming at each other. The air was electric with tension, and I knew it was more than just a disagreement. The sexual tension between us was thick, a living, breathing thing that threatened to consume us. I knew everyone could feel it. If Bellamy hadn't stepped in, who knows what might have happened.

A pang of guilt hit me like a ton of bricks. *Was it my fault she left?* I couldn't shake off the feeling. Eve seemed hesitant, refusing Velar's request, but I agreed to it, "Just a little longer."

"I sure hope you know what you're doing," Eve whispered to me. Her cautionary tone hinted I was making a bad decision, but I was too enthralled by Velar's presence to heed her warning. Instead, I felt a rush of excitement. His face lit up with a smile flashing a fang at me.

Velar whisked us away to an underground nightclub, where the pulsating music and dim lights seemed to hypnotize me. A place he had obviously been to before since he knew right where it was in Greenwich village. I thought for a moment if he visited while I was living here with my mom.

Before I knew it, I was sipping on my third cocktail, my inhibitions slowly slipping away. Eve, too, let loose, dancing with a couple of strange men, while Velar kept a watchful eye on them. But his attention kept drifting back to me, his gaze intense as he continued to buy me another drink.

I finally slurred out, "Why are you getting me drunk Sir?" Velar's expression remained enigmatic, but a hint of a smile played on his lips. "You only let me in when you're drunk," his deep voice declared as he handed me another cocktail.

I set the drink down, my mind racing with uncertainty. Velar's words hinted at a desire that made my heart race, but I couldn't shake the image of him buying a gift for Marcella just hours ago. *Was he playing games with me?*

The alcohol spoke for me, "What do you want, Velar?" My words hung in the air, a challenge and a plea all at once. Eve drunkenly approached, oblivious of the conversation happening. She pulled on my arm, trying to steer me towards the dance floor, as she danced to Kung Fu Fighting. But I resisted, my eyes locked on Velar, craving the truth. Just as I gave in to Eve's tugging, Velar's response came, "You."

As I danced with Eve, Velar's baffling response swirled in my mind like a tantalizing puzzle. I needed answers, and I needed them now. With a sense of determination, I excused myself from Eve's grasp and scanned the room for Velar.

After searching everywhere inside the club including the bathroom, I found him outside, smoking a cigarette in the cold night. Without a word, I strode towards him, my heart pounding in my chest. I took the cigarette from his lips and tossed it on the sidewalk then stomped on it with my Frye Boot.

In case that wasn't enough to get his attention, I kissed him passionately, pouring all my pent-up emotions into the moment. Velar didn't hesitate; he matched my intensity, kiss for kiss, our lips dancing in perfect sync. Pulling away for just a moment, he gazed at me with desire.

"What took you so long?" he seductively whispered. The scent of pine and leather made up for his cigarette and whiskey breath. He deepened the kiss, leaving me breathless and wanting more.

His chilled hands drew me near, and I felt his aroused firmness against my stomach. Then, both of his arms wrapped around me, pulling me closer into his embrace. "Touch me," his voice deep with desire.

Nervously, I slid my arm from around his back lower, feeling his taut muscles beneath my fingertips. Slowly lowering my hand, I felt for his hard erection. My knees almost gave out when I felt his size.

As I felt him, my own arousal grew as I explored his length and thickness. "This is what you do to me," he groaned in pleasure as I stroked him. I squeezed him gently, and he deepened our kiss.

Velar's icy fingers wrapped around my neck, his touch sent shivers down my spine. His eyes blazed with desire, pinning me in place as he drew me in. The subtle glimpse of his fangs, peeking out from between his lips, sparked a sudden thrill throughout my body.

The air was electric with tension, our lips inches apart, when the sound of footsteps interrupted our moment. But Velar's gaze only deepened, his eyes burning with an unspoken promise. Without a word, he took my hand, his fingers intertwined with mine and led me back inside.

As we glided past the bar, Velar's pace slowed, his gaze scanning the room as if searching for someone. I followed his lead, my eyes sweeping the crowd, but Eve was nowhere to be found. The bartender's deft hand tossed a set of keys to Velar, who caught them with a swift motion, his fingers never releasing mine.

He pulled me along, his stride purposeful, and I found myself hurrying to keep up. The stairs flew by in a blur as he led me upward, his hand guiding me with a gentle yet insistent pressure. Only when we reached a door did he release my hand, his fingers fumbling with the keys before finding the right one and unlocking it with a soft click.

As the door swung open, Velar gestured for me to enter. I stepped across the threshold, nervous and intrigued. The room was dimly lit, the only sound was the soft hum of music from below. Velar followed close behind, his presence making my skin tingle. He locked the door behind us, the click of the lock echoing through the room.

I didn't care about anything else at that moment. I let go and was prepared for Velar to have his way with me. We were in a small studio apartment with a combined living area, kitchen, and bedroom. I waited for Velar to lead the way, unsure if we were heading to the couch or the bed. Then, he sat on the couch and for a moment, I was slightly disappointed it wasn't the bed. But Velar's eyes sparkled with mischief as he patted the space next to him.

I turned to face him, my eyes searching his emerald gaze. The desire took my breath away. He reached out, his hand cradling my cheek, his cold fingers tracing the curve of my jaw. I felt my lip's part, my body leaning into his touch.

'You're so fucking beautiful,' his voice husky with emotion. 'I can't resist you any longer.' His lips claimed mine, the kiss deepening even more than before. I felt myself melting into his arms, our bodies entwined as we moved to the music below us.

As I sat down beside him, Velar's arm wrapped around me, pulling me close. His fingers traced the curve of my neck. I felt my heart racing with anticipation.

Velar's lips brushed against my ear, his icy breath sending tremors through me. I felt myself getting lost in his embrace, my mind clouding with desire. Being close to him again was even better than I remember. Maybe because of all the built-up tension between us.

Suddenly, he stood up, lifting me with him. He carried me to the bed, his eyes burning with intensity. He gently laid me down onto the bed and then pulled his shirt over his head in one swift motion. "I don't know when I'll get another chance like this, " his voice low and wanting. He mounted me and I leaned back into the bed as his massive firm body covered mine.

I knew at that moment, I was his. Completely and utterly his.

As Velar's lips met mine, I felt like I was melting into his embrace. His kiss was passionate, yet gentle, and I couldn't help but respond with equal intensity. Our bodies moved in perfect sync, our hearts beating as one.

'I want you,' he whispered, his voice demanding. 'All of you.'

I nodded, my voice caught in my throat. *Bellamy. I thought of Bellamy and Velar couldn't have all of me because I belonged to Bellamy.* "Velar..." I began to say, but he stopped me with one finger across my lips before I could say anything at all.

He stood up and swiftly unbuttoned his black jeans and slid them down all while keeping his eyes fixed on me.

'I've waited so long to have you,' he whispered. 'And I'm going to cherish every second.'

As I laid watching his naked body move, I became so aroused. Piece by piece he slowly undressed me. Taking his time.

"I've waited patiently for you." He pulled my shirt over my head.

"I know you want to give yourself to me," He unsnapped my bra.

"I know you want me like I want you." He took off boots and then slowly pulled off my pants.

"Don't worry, I won't leave it up for you to decide." I shuddered as he took off the last piece of clothing. Black lace panties slid down my legs and I watched as he tucked them into his back pocket. *Dirty Rascal.*

He took a step back and observed me naked like I was a buffet. "You're so fucking beautiful,' I blushed, feeling a sense of shyness wash over me. But Velar just smiled, flashing his fangs. 'Don't be shy,' he said. 'You have nothing to hide from me.' I relaxed, feeling a sense of trust wash over me.

"I'm going to have you tonight" he moved in front of the bed and my legs were still together. I was nervous but so aroused. He went to spread my legs apart, but I kept them together nervously. "Open," he cooed, and I obeyed. Quickly realizing I had just obeyed another man instead of Daddy. But the thought of Bellamy disappeared when I felt Velar's tongue licking my clit.

I moaned in instant pleasure and arched my back as he licked and sucked on me like it was his last meal. I couldn't contain my moans, but I knew the music below was covering my cries. Velar slid his thick fingers inside of me curling to reach that special spot and within minutes I was reaching my climax. I orgasmed with his fingers still buried deep inside me. Only retreating after pleading with him to stop.

My legs trembled as I basked in the afterglow. He gazed at me with a fierce tenderness, his eyes burning with a deep connection.

I couldn't help but compare Velar to Bellamy. Both men were dominant and very aggressive. But being intimate with him was different. I sensed a hunger in him, a longing that went beyond words. He was a man consumed by his emotions, driven by a force he could no longer contain.

He climbed on top of me and straddled my welcoming mouth, "Open for me." He whispered deep. I opened as wide as I could. "I need to feel that wet mouth of yours." He moaned at the anticipation.

My tongue slid underneath his thick swollen shaft as I guided him inside my mouth. My eyes began to water as he pushed himself inside. He let out a primal grunt and it aroused me knowing I was pleasuring him. Slowly he began to fuck my mouth deeper and deeper until I was gagging and drooling all over myself and him.

His finger met his mouth, and I watched as he sucked it, and then reached it behind his back so he could touch me. He rubbed my clit slowly and I shuddered at his touch. A moan escaped me when I felt his fingers enter me. "So wet." He growled.

While fucking my face, his fingers danced inside me putting me in pure ecstasy. He thrusted into my mouth, and I bucked my hips into his fingers. Wanting more. Needing more.

I moaned loudly when I felt his fingers leave me, I watched as he raised them to his mouth and sucked on them. Locking my gaze, making sure I was watching him taste me. "Delicious," his velvet voice made me weak.

He mounted me again, but this time his massive dick was at the entrance of my dripping wet pussy. I spread my legs without being told this time. Taking himself in his hands as pushed himself between my slit.

"Uh" I gasped, holding my breath. He paused knowing I needed to take it slow. I knew it would hurt by the size of him. I looked at him with wide eyes telling him I was ready. His mouth met mine just as a pleasurable moan was escaping it. I was in a state of euphoria, feeling his girth stretching me with each thrust.

"Oh Nic," He moaned, pulling away from my lips. He thrusted into me, fucking me harder. "Velar." I tried to catch my breath as he plunged deeper inside me. His eyes were glazed over as he pounded me.

"Velar! Stop." I shouted but he didn't stop. I tried to push him away, but his heavy firm body pinned me in place. Tears escaped me just as he let out a primal grunt. It was so loud I believe everyone in the bar below heard us.

He laid next to me, but concern etched on his face when he saw my tears. 'Did I hurt you?' His voice concerned and worried. I nodded slightly, and he quickly sat up, his eyes scanning me with care.

'I'm fine,' I reassured him, but he pulled me close, kissing my shoulder and neck and then down my arms. It was as if he wanted to erase any discomfort, to make up for any pain he may have caused.

'I never want to hurt you,' his lips tracing gentle patterns on my skin. Then his eyes met mine 'Only the good kind of hurt." He grinned mischievously, 'I couldn't restrict myself any longer, I had to have you.' I nodded feeling this truth escape his soft lips.

Three loud thuds on the door made Velar and I freeze, the sudden interruption shattering the silence like a splash of ice water. *Oh my God, Bellamy's here!* I just knew he was on the other side, his impatience growing. I was waiting for him to wield his magic and burst through the door.

I scrambled to dress, my hands shaking as I fumbled for my clothes. Velar watched me with an amused glint in his eye, but I was too anxious to appreciate his humor at the moment.

As I struggled frantically to put on my underwear, my legs tangled in the fabric, and I tumbled to the floor. Strong hands caught me effortlessly just before I face planted. Velar chuckled, but his smile faded as he saw my distress.

Just then, Henry's voice boomed from outside, "Hey, Velar! Bell's ready to jump!" My relief was short-lived, as I knew we had to leave immediately to avoid Bellamy's wrath.

Before I could open the door Velar grabbed me around my waist snatching me into the air and setting me onto his lap. His hands remained wrapped around me tightly. "We have to go," I urged, trying to wriggle free.

"I know, but first, I want to give you something." His cool breath against my ear instantly stilled me, and I relaxed into him. As I settled into his lap, I realized how much I enjoyed being there. My resistance melted away, and I turned to face him, no longer fighting the moment.

Sitting on his lap I could feel his swollen cock pressing into my back. In a swift motion he handed me a small black box, adorned with intricate patterns. I opened it, and my heart stopped as I saw the beautiful gold locket inside. It was exquisite, but my shock was all over my face. *I thought he bought it for Marcella.*

His emerald eyes gazed into mine, filled with adoration, as if locking onto my very soul. "I've loved you in secret, but I can't keep this anymore."

I glanced at the locket, then back at Velar, and finally at the door, my mind racing with disbelief. My expression must have been a picture of dumbfounded shock, confusion, and shame, because Velar's eyes sparkled with understanding.

'Don't worry, I can keep it from the world, just not from you any longer.' I felt like I'd been rendered speechless, my only response a numb nod, as if my brain was struggling to process the revelation.

Thankfully, Velar didn't wait for me to respond or say anything at all. Instead, he started getting dressed, and I followed suit. Then, he took my hand, and we joined Eve and Henry, who were waiting for us outside the nightclub.

CHAPTER
TWENTY-THREE

As I spotted Eve, I hastily released Velar's hand, feeling a pang of guilt and shame. Velar's subtle sadness was evident, and I sensed a deep regret in letting go of him. Eve's raised eyebrow seemed to hold a knowing glint, but I was grateful for her silent understanding. Still, I wasn't ready to confront the emotions swirling inside me, and the thought of facing my husband at home felt daunting. For now, if Eve asks what I have been doing, I will tell her Velar and I were talking.

Eve and I hung back, creating some distance between ourselves and Henry and Velar. I was grateful for the temporary reprieve from Velar's intense presence. Eve leaned in close and whispered, "Why do you look like you just got laid?"

My eyes shot to Velar, knowing he could hear if he wanted to, but my eyes were telling enough. They conveyed a message that was loud and clear, I wasn't ready to talk about it. Velar's gaze turned back and met mine, and for a moment, we just stared at each other, the tension between us obvious. Then, I looked away, breaking the spell.

Eve cleared her throat, announcing her presence and drawing attention to my exchange with Velar. "Well, this is going to be fun," she mumbled, her words dripping with sarcasm and a hint of resignation. It was as if she'd been waiting for this moment with a sense of inevitability, like a storm cloud gathering on the horizon. She said it like she was thinking this is going to be a disaster but was too polite to say it aloud.

As we arrived in Jubilee, Henry dispersed quickly. He must have informed Bellamy of our return because within seconds we felt the familiar vibration as we jumped to somewhere else in the world, far from NYC. Eve headed to her townhouse, leaving Velar and me to walk alone.

He offered to escort me home, but I declined, feeling a sense of unease. Velar didn't object, and I think he understood my hesitation. When we reached the path that led to Casmira, Velar warped me in a tight hug and placed a purposeful kiss on my forehead.

I watched him walk into the darkness before I brought myself to walk home. I stood at the iron gate, knots formed in my stomach, and I couldn't bring myself to face Daddy. I felt so much guilt and shame for what I had just done.

"Come here, baby girl." Bellamy's gentle voice called out from the darkness of the porch. I hadn't noticed him waiting for me, but his words drew me in. I slowly followed the steps towards him, my heart heavy with emotion.

I climbed the porch steps and approached him slowly. Bellamy sat shrouded in darkness, his presence barely discernible except for the faint glow of his cigar. The red ember pulsed with each puff, casting an eerie light on the surrounding shadows.

As I drew closer, the smoke swirled around us, mingling with the night air. His low, smooth voice broke the silence, "Welcome home."

I stood there, frozen, as the warm night air in Jubilee surrounded me. I shrugged off my winter jacket, feeling the sticky humidity cling to my skin. I didn't respond. Instead, I watched as he patted his lap, a silent beckoning. I knew what he wanted. And so, I went to him, taking a seat on his lap.

I leaned in and kissed his cheek, my lips grazing the rough stubble of his jawline. Though I could only see his silhouette, his sexy, intense energy made me feel both intimidated and turned on at the same time. His body radiated a powerful allure, drawing me in with an irresistible force.

"Did you have a good time?" His tone suggested he already knew the answer. I felt a flutter of nerves as I quickly replied, "Yes."

"Were you a good girl?" My heart skipped a beat. I nodded, grateful for the darkness that hid my face. Thank God he can't see my expression, or he would know I was lying, if he didn't already.

The night air was sweltering, making me sweat and tug at my winter clothes. "Daddy, why is it so hot tonight?" I asked, trying to sound innocent. He savored his cigar, blowing out a relaxed cloud of smoke, "To make you sweat." I swallowed hard, and with that comment, Bellamy knew exactly what I had just done. His words held a hint of knowing, a subtle acknowledgment of my secret.

I swiftly rose from my seat, excusing myself to change, and surprisingly, he let me go without a word. I hastily retreated upstairs. As I burst into my bedroom, I was greeted by the sound of the shower already running in the bathroom. I couldn't get in there fast enough, my desire to wash away the guilt and shame overwhelming me.

I washed my body quickly, my eyes darting towards the door, expecting Bellamy to appear at any moment. I considered rushing into bed and feigning sleep, but then I remembered that wouldn't stop him if he wanted me tonight. I was completely at his mercy. He owned me.

I stepped out of the shower, and the water ceased its gentle patter, plunging the bathroom into an unsettling silence. I strained my ears, listening intently for any sign of Bellamy's presence, but the stillness was oppressive, eerily so. I swiftly donned a nightgown, my ears listening for any sound.

Instead of retreating to bed, I crept to the stairs, my ears listening for any sign of movement, but the silence was deafening. I called out, my voice trembling slightly, "Daddy?" The only response was more silence. *Where did he go?* I walked back into my room knowing he had left.

I slid into bed, waiting for Bellamy to return, but as the moments ticked by, my eyelids grew heavy, and I submitted to sleep.

I woke to the sound of Bellamy's gentle undressing, followed by the creak of the bed as he climbed in beside me. I lay still, curious about his whereabouts but reluctant to reveal my wakefulness.

His arm reached across the bed, pulling me across the bed to him, and I felt his warm, naked body against the back of mine. I sleepily murmured, "Where were you?" But Bellamy simply shushed me, his breath whispering against my ear, urging me to sleep. Just when I thought he'd never respond and I relaxed in his arms, he said "I owed Velar a visit."

The air was heavy with unspoken truths, and I felt like I was drowning in the silence. Bellamy's arm tightened around me, his grip possessive, as if he sensed my unease. I tried to calm my racing heart, but my mind raced with questions. *What had he discussed with Velar? Did he know I slept with Velar?*

The next morning as I slowly emerged from my groggy state, the haze of sleep still clung to me like a damp shroud. I realized I hadn't slept well, my mind tangled in a web of dreams. Bellamy and Velar, the two men who held a fragile piece of my heart, had haunted my slumber.

Just as I was struggling to shake off the fogginess, a steaming mug of coffee materialized on my nightstand. I took a sip, and instantly, my headache dissipated, replaced by a welcome sense of clarity.

Bellamy walked in, his timing impeccable, his eyes sparkling like sunlit waves. His radiant smile illuminated the room, banishing the shadows, but he made no mention of the previous night's secrets or his mysterious conversation with Velar. Instead, he asked, "Are you ready to perform today?" His enthusiasm was a contagion, infecting me with its energy. He was already dressed and ready, his hair still damp from his morning swim in the Opal Sea, the salty scent lingering on his skin.

Bellamy's magic always ensured I was ready, but today, my mind was a maelstrom of emotions, each one wrestling for dominance. He dressed me in a resplendent ring mistress outfit, but I felt like a puppet on strings. As he worked his magic on my hair, I felt too emotionally drained to muster the enthusiasm for today's performance, and the thought of facing Velar only added to my exhaustion.

Bellamy's gaze pierced through my facade, his eyes narrowing as he read my face like an open book. "Baby girl, what do you feel like doing today?" his voice filled with concern that gently probed into my turbulent soul.

I knew he could see the truth I hid, the secrets I kept, the lies I told myself. Shame washed over me like a tidal wave, and I couldn't meet his eyes, my gaze faltering like a coward's. Bellamy's hand gently tilted my chin, his fingers whispering against my skin as he coaxed me to face him.

"Anything you want to tell me?" He asked softly but firm. But fear held me captive, and I lied, "I just don't feel like performing today, Daddy," the words tumbling out like a weak excuse.

"I understand," he said. "Why don't you take the day to relax, and tonight, I'll take you out to dinner?" I nodded, a spark of excitement igniting within me. I genuinely wanted a date with him. It's been a while, and I wanted to be close to him. I felt that I needed him.

He leaned in, his lips brushing against mine in a long, tender kiss that left me feeling loved. As he pulled away, I couldn't help but smile. As soon as he left, I undressed and crawled back into the soft linen sheets. My bed seemed to be calling me, and I gladly surrendered, letting the softness cradle me in a sweet reverie.

Persistent knocking at the front door jolted me awake, and I rubbed the sleep from my eyes to see it was already noon. "Who is it?" I called out, as if Casmira would magically respond. The knocking grew louder, followed by Eve's urgent yelling of my name, "Nic!" I sat up and shouted into the air, "Open the door!"

I listened for the front door to open, and then Eve's footsteps hurried towards me. "There you are!" She exclaimed, bursting through my bedroom door. When she saw me in bed, her eyes scanned me as if searching for answers. She was confused why I was still in bed. I sat up quickly and asked, "What's going on?"

Eve's expression turned serious as she sat beside me, "Did you know Velar left? He left the circus this morning" My heart sank like a stone, and I felt a chill run down my spine. I knew Bellamy must have made Velar leave, and the thought terrified me. Eve's eyes locked onto mine, and I knew she sensed I was hiding something.

"I slept with Velar!" I blurted out, my voice trembling with guilt and shame. Eve's expression remained calm, but her eyes betrayed a deep concern. She stepped closer, her presence enveloping me in a warm embrace. 'Velar makes me feel alive,' attempting to justify why I was drawn to him.

"I knew it! Does Bellamy know?" she asked gently. I shook my head, my eyes welling up with tears. "I don't know, I didn't tell him." Eve's nod was empathetic, but her words were a gentle reminder of Bellamy's all-knowing presence, 'Of course he knows. He knows everything.'

I knew she was right, and that only made me feel more miserable. Earlier, I'd lied directly to his face when he asked if I had anything to confess. Now, I was consumed by guilt and wanted to disappear. Betraying him was bad enough but doing it with his best friend - someone he trusted like a brother - made it even more unbearable. "What have I done?"

"Well, I'll try to find out more," her tone reassuring. But we both knew Bellamy knew already. She glanced at her watch, her sparkling costume was a reminder to me that she still has performances to get to.

"I have to get back, but are you going to be, okay?" She asked quickly with concern. I nodded, and she hastened her departure, knowing she had to return to her acts.

Just as she reached the bedroom door, she turned back, her eyes locking onto mine. "Don't be hard on yourself Nic, Velar has been in love with you for lifetimes and honestly I'm surprised he waited this long."

Her revelation left me breathless. I had no idea Velar had harbored secret feelings for me for so long. As I reflected on our past, memories resurfaced - fleeting moments of us laughing, teasing, and playfully flirting. But while I had dismissed them as sibling-like banter, Velar's emotions had run far deeper. I had always seen him as a brother, but now I was forced to confront the possibility of something more.

The truth was, I was intrigued by the prospect of exploring a relationship with him. I felt excited. Yet, the thought of ever leaving Bellamy was unthinkable. My heart belongs to Daddy, and I couldn't imagine choosing anyone else. And given how possessive he was, I knew he wouldn't release me from his grasp even if I wanted to break free.

CHAPTER
TWENTY-FOUR

Later in the afternoon as I lounged in my favorite chair on the balcony, the performers and crew began to trickle back, their weary faces a testament to the day's grueling schedule. The circus's closure signaled the start of my date with Daddy and my heart fluttered with anticipation and anxiety.

I retreated to my room, my mind consumed by the weight of my confession about Velar. The thought of revealing the truth to Bellamy made my stomach twist into knots. I dressed in a stunning dark green boho dress, the fabric hugging my curves in all the right places. I curled my brown locks, the familiar ritual a comforting distraction from my nerves. Taking my time, I hoped that if I looked captivating enough, Bellamy might not mention Velar or my indiscretion. But deep down, I knew I couldn't avoid the truth forever.

"Damn, you're gorgeous!" Bellamy's sudden exclamation startled me, and I turned around to see him standing there, his eyes blazing with desire. I was in sheer shock, having not even heard the door open or his footsteps on the stairs. I must have been lost in my emotional turmoil.

Before I could speak, Bellamy approached me, his movements fluid and confident. He reached out, gently tucking a piece of hair behind my ear, and then his lips claimed mine in a passionate kiss. His salty sea scent from earlier was replaced by the tantalizing scents of the circus. The sugary aroma of kettle corn swirled together with the comforting smell of cinnamon that intensified our kiss.

For a moment, I thought he might skip dinner altogether and sweep me away to the playroom, but he gently released me. His eyes were still burning with intensity, "Are you ready?" As he offered his arm to escort me, I took it, feeling even more ashamed of my betrayal.

We left Casmira and strolled together to the town square, which was bustling with townspeople unwinding after a long day of work at the circus. The atmosphere was lively, with laughter and chatter filling the air. Bellamy led me to his favorite restaurant, The Gilded Goblet.

His creation was influenced by a charming seventeenth-century restaurant, famous for its mouthwatering dishes, which held a special place in his heart since he used to frequent it. He used it as a blueprint to craft his own culinary haven. It was a stunning Victorian Gothic tavern. The interior with intricate woodwork and stained-glass windows.

Bellamy gallantly pulled out a chair for me, and we sat in our favorite spot, the cozy table by the window. I settled in concealing my nerves the best I could. The soft light streaming through the window highlighted the warm glow of the restaurant, making everything feel even more intimate.

As the wine flowed, our eyes met, and I searched Bellamy's gaze for answers. 'How was the circus today?' I asked, taking a sip of wine. He smiled slyly, savoring his response, and I could sense him toying with me. Finally, he spoke, his voice low and husky, 'The circus missed you today, I'm hopeful you slept well?' I nodded, feeling a blush rise to my cheeks. He purred, 'Good girl,' his praise sending shivers down my spine.

As I sipped my second glass of wine, I finally mustered the courage to mention Velar, despite Bellamy's evident reluctance to discuss him. 'Where did Velar go?' I asked, striving for nonchalance but my voice betrays a hint of trepidation.

Bellamy's expression turned glacial, his eyes narrowing as if I'd crossed an unspoken boundary. 'He went to visit Marcella,' he replied, his tone clipped and dismissive. I forced a bright, artificial smile, desperate to conceal my shock and dismay.

'Oh, that's... that's great!' My voice dripped with insincerity. 'I'm thrilled for him.' But inside, I seethed with anger and hurt, feeling like a pawn in Velar's games. Why would he seduce me, only to pursue Marcella? The question burned in my mind, fueling my resentment and sense of betrayal. Bellamy's gaze pierced through me, as if he saw the turmoil I struggled to hide.

Bellamy reached across the table, his hand holding mine in a firm grasp. Leaning in, his eyes locked onto mine with an intensity that made my stomach twist in knots. With raised eyebrows he asked, 'Is there anything you want to tell me, baby girl?' I swallowed.

'As your Daddy Dom, I expect complete honesty from you. You know that don't you?' His words were laced with a subtle hint of authority, leaving no room for evasion.

I recall the early days of our relationship when Bellamy and I first began exploring our dynamic. It took a long time to get to where we are now. He guided me in understanding, and I eventually embraced my role with willingness and trust. I knew I had to be honest for our dynamic to work.

I took another sip of wine, then looked at him with a mix of emotions. 'I did something I am not proud of,' my voice barely above a whisper. I glanced around the room, ensuring we were out of earshot.

Bellamy's expression was stoic, tightening his grip on my hands, rendering them immobile. 'Look at me,' he firmly ordered. I obeyed and met his gaze. "I already know. Everything." I breathed a sigh of relief, grateful for him freeing me of the burden of saying it aloud.

That's when the tears began to flow from my eyes, and Bellamy handed me a napkin with a gentle smile. I took it gratefully, using it to wipe away the streaks of mascara that were running down my cheeks.

Bellamy subtly motioned someone away, giving us privacy. At that moment, I wished we were at home in private. I was too emotional to speak, but Bellamy simply held my hand, offering comfort and support. Despite my mistake, he showed me kindness and understanding.

When I finally composed myself, we got up to leave. Bellamy held my hand, gently guiding me out the door. Once outside, he wrapped me in a warm embrace, holding me close as tears began to fall once more.

The weight of my actions crushed me, and his peaceful acceptance only made the guilt and shame more overwhelming. I dissolved into tears, my body shaking with sobs as I buried my face in his solid, comforting chest.

The silence between us was unnerving as we walked home. It was the lack of anger in his eyes that really got to me. The fact that he wasn't mad at me only made me realize how much I must have hurt him, and that thought shattered my heart.

When we arrived back at Casmira, I was consumed by shame and hurried up the front steps, eager to escape the weight of my actions. But before I could reach the first step, Bellamy swiftly caught my arm and gently pulled me back. I stumbled backwards, my balance faltering, but he steadied me with a firm yet gentle grasp, preventing me from falling.

'Not so fast, baby girl,' his voice was soft, but authoritative. 'I'm not done talking to you.' I felt a bit of relief thinking that maybe talking it through would help me ease my guilt. Together, we strolled up the front steps of Casmira, but he paused before we entered.

The moonlight illuminated his face, making his eyes look dark and intimidating. His forehead and a furrowed brow, conveying a deep concern. He gestured for me to sit with him on the swing, and I waited for him to settle in before sitting beside him, our thighs touching.

As I looked down at my hands, awaiting his cue to begin the conversation, he lifted my chin with his finger, his eyes locking onto mine.

'Did you forget what it means to be owned, to belong to me and only me?' His eyes burned with intensity. I nodded, feeling a flutter in my stomach.

'I think you need a reminder,' releasing his grip on my chin. I was surprised by his sudden gesture.

'I'm sorry,' I whimpered, his hand moving to my thigh, his fingers squeezing gently. 'You think you are, but you will be." His words sounded like a threat.

"I own you, Nicole Darlington. Make no mistake, I will remind you of that, even if it means using pain to do so.' His words made my blood run cold. He stood up, adjusting his clothes, then gazed down at me.

'Am I clear?' I nodded slowly, still processing his words. "Yes."

"Yes, what?"

"Yes Daddy."

"Good girl." He offered his hand, and I took it, allowing him to lead me inside just as the door opened for us.

"I'll meet you in the playroom," his voice commanded.

I waited upstairs, my heart raced with every tick of the clock. My usual submissive position felt suffocating tonight.

As the door creaked open, I hastily adjusted my position, my head bowed in submission. The lights slowly dimmed, plunging the room into shadows, and I listened to his footsteps. The soft creak of the floorboards beneath his feet was like a death knell, signaling his approach. And then, his black boots came into my view.

When Bellamy began to undo his belt, my eyes remained downcast, avoiding his gaze. The sound of the belt swooshing out of its loops made my back arch. 'Stand,' he ordered. I quickly obeyed, not wanting to keep him waiting.

He took the belt and wrapped it around my neck, pulling it through the loop to create a tight, unyielding collar. He tugged on it, leading me to the black leather couch, where he positioned me with precision.

Above the couch, a hook beckoned, perfectly placed to accommodate the belt's end. He secured it, leaving me no room to move, the belt's tension a constant reminder of my submission.

Bellamy walked over to a stand with drawers and returned with zip ties. I remained silent, not because I wanted to, but because the belt around my neck held me in a position that made speaking impossible.

He methodically tied my hands behind my back, then moved on to my feet, securing them with swift efficiency. I was now completely immobilized, my naked body vulnerable and exposed. The zip ties dug into my skin as I sat helpless.

As Bellamy undressed, my eyes devoured every inch of his chiseled physique. His body was a masterpiece, honed to perfection, and I couldn't help but feel a surge of arousal. I longed for him to inflict pain upon me, to take away the hurt that I had caused him. I yearned for him to claim me, to mark me, and to erase the pain of my transgression.

He approached me, his movements deliberate and calculated, and I knew I was in for a reckoning.

'You have been a very naughty wife,' his voice low and sultry, his words dripping with menace. He reached out and trailed a finger over my cheek, his touch sending shivers down my spine.

'You are mine, Nicole. Mine to punish and to pleasure.' I tried to speak, but the belt around my neck held me silent. I tried to struggle, but the zip ties held me fast. I was completely at his mercy, and he knew it.

He reached out and grasped my chin, his fingers digging into my skin as he tilted my head back and leaned into me. His breath was hot against my ear. 'You are mine, Nicole. Mine to protect. Mine to punish.'

Tears welled up in my eyes as Bellamy's words pierced my soul. Before I could even process, he swiftly attached two clamps to my nipples, causing me to cry out in agony. The pressure was excruciating, making me feel like I was bleeding, but I couldn't move my head to see. The clamps were like vice grips, squeezing my sensitive skin with an intensity that left me gasping for breath.

Bellamy's eyes seemed to gleam with a sinister light as he watched me struggle against the pain. He approached me and released the belt that had been suspended above my head, freeing me from its constraining grip.

I gasped for air, desperate to catch my breath, but my respite was brief. He was already pulling me towards him, his intention and desire clear. His hard dick was already pushing against my closed mouth before I could open it.

Not waiting for me to catch my breath he held the belt tightly as he fucked my throat. Drool dripped from my mouth to my tits as he fucked my face over and over again. As the air escaped, I struggled to breathe. I couldn't push away because of the zip ties. He pulled out and pushed deeper into my throat but held himself there. I couldn't breathe. Everything went dark.

When I regained consciousness, I found myself bound to a table, my stomach flat against the surface, and my limbs tied separately, rendering me helpless. A ball gag muted my cries, and I realized I must have been drooling for some time, as a puddle had formed on the floor in front of me.

Without warning, a sudden strike across my ass made me shriek in agony, and the pain radiated through me as the belt struck me again. This time even harder.

I screamed in anguish, my body convulsing in agony as the belt struck me again. The sound was muffled by the gag in my mouth, but my tormentor's sinister whisper cut through the darkness: 'Shhh.'

I trembled, anticipating the next blow. It came without mercy, the leather searing my skin like a branding iron. My vision blurred as tears streamed down my face, my moans and grunts of pain filling the air. This was no pleasure; it was unadulterated torture. And I knew it was far from over.

My body felt like it was on fire, the pain radiating through every nerve ending. I thrashed against the restraints, desperate to escape the agony. But they only dug deeper, cutting into my skin like razor wire.

I felt a hand grasp my hair, yanking my head back. My tormentor's face loomed before me, his eyes gleaming with a sadistic light.

'You're mine,' he hissed. 'Mine to break and to shape. Mine to own.' I tried to scream again, but my voice was hoarse from the gag. My throat burned, my lungs aching for air. I felt like I was drowning in my own despair.

Suddenly, the belt struck again, the impact sending shockwaves through my entire body. I felt my consciousness slipping away, the darkness closing in like a shroud.

I thrash and beg through the gag, but my pleas fell on deaf ears. The torment continued, each blow landing with precision and cruelty. "Daddy." I mumbled over my gag.

Just as I was about to succumb to the agony, he finally removed the gag from my mouth, and I watched in relief as it dropped to the floor. Then, I felt the tingling sensation from his magic releasing the restraints on each of my limbs.

I was trembling with weakness and pain, I almost fell off the table just when Bellamy was there to catch me in a gentle embrace and carried me to the bed that was in the center of the playroom.

He laid me on my back and then mounted me. Desire and rage filled his eyes. He pushed my legs apart, almost rushing like he couldn't wait to be inside me a second longer. He plummeted inside me not caring about the pain he was causing. I cried out but he swiftly covered my mouth with his hand.

He fucked me slow and deep at first, his hard his dick stretching me open, I felt myself getting wetter each time he sunk deeper into me.

"This is my pussy and I'm going to fuck it when I want and how I want." He thrusted deeper to make his point clear. I moaned in pain and pleasure.

"Who do you belong to?" He pounded into me. "You." I answered.

"Who do you belong to?"

"Daddy!"

Reaching towards my tits, he hastily pulled the clamps from my swollen nipples, causing me to scream out in pain.

My cry alone was enough to push him over the edge. He let out a primal roar and released his load into me with such force that my head smacked against the headboard.

Before drifting off to sleep that night, Bellamy and I had a heartfelt conversation about our relationship and the dynamics between us. I intentionally avoided mentioning Velar, sensing that it was a sensitive topic for Bellamy, and not wanting to stir up any unnecessary tension.

CHAPTER
TWENTY-FIVE

Only a handful of days had passed since Velar's departure, but the reprieve from his all-consuming presence was already a blessing. The constant thoughts of him, which had plagued me mere days ago, were finally beginning to subside.

With Velar's absence, I saw an opportunity to distract myself from the lingering emotions I had for him. I didn't know how long he'd be gone, but with him out of sight I redirected my focus towards Bellamy to nurture our relationship.

Today was the first day I didn't fall victim to intimate thoughts of Velar. I found myself back in the spotlight, performing alongside Eve once again. I was finally able to channel my energy into a dazzling performance for the circus guests, and it felt exhilarating to be back in control.

Yet, amidst this triumph, guilt lingered. I couldn't shake off the feeling that I'd betrayed Bellamy, even though he'd already forgiven me. But alongside this guilt, a spark of anger ignited within me, directed towards Velar. His words still echoed in my mind - 'I love you' - yet he'd so easily returned to Marcella.

The inconsistency gnawed at me, refusing to make sense. Why had he professed love for me, only to revert to his old ways? The question swirled in my head, fueling my frustration and confusion.

As our final act of the day reached its crescendo, Anise's cue sparked a thrill of excitement within me. I stood atop the platform, gazing out at the sea of faces below, my heart pounding in my chest like a drum.

Across from me, Eve shone like a radiant star in her shimmering black and white outfit mirroring mine. Our eyes locked in perfect synchrony. With a deep breath, we leapt into the silks, our bodies entwining like tendrils of a vine as the crew members beneath spun us around with a gentle yet firm touch. The crowd below became a colorful blur, their gasps and cheers a distant hum as we twirled and spun, our silken wings beating the air.

When the spinning slowed, I summoned every last ounce of strength to climb higher, wrapping the silk between my legs as I ascended higher. Eve mimicked my movements with grace and precision. In perfect harmony, we released our grip on the silks and plummeted towards the floor spinning the whole way with the silks unraveling our bodies.

The crowd's collective gasp a deafening roar. Just before hitting the ground, we stretched out our sleeves like wings, the fabric billowing around us like a cloud, and the crowd erupted into a frenzy of applause.

As Eve and I met in the center of the stage, hands clasped, we bowed in unison. And that's when I saw him - Velar, his emerald eyes gleaming like a beacon in the crowd, his gaze fixed intently on me. When I quickly rose from my bow, he was gone, leaving me wondering if I'd imagined the whole thing.

I scanned the crowd, searching for Velar. But he was nowhere to be found. I felt a sense of unease. *Was I hallucinating?* I pushed the thought aside, focusing on the applause and cheers that still echoed through the tent. Eve and I took one final bow, basking in the adoration of the crowd. But my mind was elsewhere.

As we left the stage, Anise approached me, her eyes sparkling with excitement. "That was incredible!" she exclaimed. "You and Eve are a perfect pair!" I smiled, feeling a sense of pride and accomplishment wash over me. But my mind was still reeling believing Velar is back.

I quickly gathered my belongings and exited the tent, my eyes still scanning the surrounding area. I searched every nook and cranny, peering into nearby tents, but my efforts yielded nothing.

Eventually, I conceded defeat and decided to head back to Jubilee. Though I knew Bellamy was still performing under the big top, I couldn't muster the energy to join him. My heart wasn't in it, and my mind was preoccupied with the lingering thoughts of Velar.

As I approached the weeping willow tree, I noticed Henry deep in conversation with someone, but the person's identity was shrouded by the tree's drooping branches. As I drew closer, and my eyes widened in shock when I saw Henry talking to Velar.

I froze, my feet seemingly rooted to the spot, as if time itself had paused. Henry's eyes met mine, and he nodded discreetly at Velar before taking his leave, disappearing into the magical tree.

Velar's piercing gaze locked onto mine, and I felt like he could see right through my very soul. When Henry's footsteps faded down the stairs, I finally found my voice. "You're back." Velar nodded curtly, his face a mask of neutrality.

Velar took a step closer, his voice low and gentle, "Nic, I am—" But I cut him off, anger and hurt fueling my words, "What? Sorry? I don't want to hear it! Go back to Marcella!" I turned and ran, dashing down the stairs and out into the magical world of Jubilee. I didn't stop running until I reached Casmira, my heart still racing from the encounter.

Later that night, Bellamy returned, and I greeted him with a glass of our favorite rich, full-bodied red wine. I was wearing a stunning black dress that hugged my curves in all the right places, the short hemline and long sleeves making me feel like a seductress. The thin line of white trim around the seams added a touch of innocence, but I knew I looked anything but innocent.

Bellamy's eyes seemed to agree, as he purred, "You look delicious." I smiled, knowing I had dressed for him, and him alone. The dim lighting in the room highlighted the sharp angles of his face, and his sea blue eyes seemed to burn with an inner fire.

"You didn't come see me after your last act." he stated, taking the glass from my hand and kissing me softly on the lips. I took a sip of wine, feeling the tension build between us. "I wanted to change out of my work clothes."

Bellamy followed me into the dining room, where I had laid out a feast fit for a king. The aroma of roasted meats and fresh herbs filled the air. He took in all the dishes that were spread out on the table. "I'm so hungry," His gaze locked onto me, and he growled, "This will have to wait."

He strode towards me, his eyes burning with desire. He tilted my chin up, and our lips met in a fierce, passionate kiss. My body pushed against the head of the dressed table.

His hands on my thighs had me quivering as he felt for my panties to pull them down, but to his surprise I wasn't wearing any. "Good girl." A soft, velvety purr vibrated in the back of his throat.

He hastily hoisted me on top of the table. I gasped when I felt my ass land on the dishes full of food, spilling them over, but Bellamy didn't care. He stood between my thighs and slowly pushed my chest, lying me down onto the table, pushing dishes out of the way for my head to lay.

I looked up at Bellamy as he gazed at me with intensity as he spread my thighs further apart and pulled a chair right up to me like I was his meal. A rush of excitement filled me as he yanked my body closer to him, knocking glasses onto the floor. My legs draped over his muscular shoulders, and I felt his breath on me. Lightly licking me, making me moan in pleasure. Then he began licking harder and sucking on my clit.

At that moment nothing else mattered. "Oh Daddy" I screamed in pleasure as he roughly devoured me. Not stopping, he placed a finger inside me as he licked me, making me moan in pleasure.

Wetness ran out of me as Bellamy pleasured me, making me reach climax. He kept going even as my legs were shaking. I almost forgot how to breathe when he finally stopped.

I lay on the table, basking in the afterglow, my body still reeling from the intensity. As I finally caught my breath, I pushed myself up, my eyes locking onto Bellamy's. He was sitting back in the chair. His eyes intently on mine as he licked his lips clean.

We never made it to the playroom. Bellamy's desire was too strong. He swept me onto the table. The delicious dishes went spilling onto me and the floor as he thrusted into me, making the table shake and drinks spill.

Mashed potatoes coated my hair, and my hand landed in the gravy boat. Bellamy didn't miss a beat, raising my hand to his mouth and slurping off the gravy. Mashed potatoes coated my hair, and my hand landed in the warm gravy. Bellamy raised my hand to his mouth and sucked the gravy off, his eyes locked on mine.

Then, he flipped me over, and the centerpiece went crashing down, unleashing a mini flood as white roses landed in the biscuits. I gasped as the cold water seeped into my dress, the chill of it contrasting with the warmth of Bellamy's body behind me. The water trickled down my chest, as Bellamy's movements became more insistent.

Bellamy, without pulling himself out of me, pulled me onto his lap. I bounced up and down, taking my time to feel him deep inside. His growl vibrated through his chest, like a wild animal ready to unleash its fury. His moans sent me tumbling over the edge, and I gripped him tightly with my wet, trembling body. I felt his weight press against mine as he held me close, his explosion of passion leaving me winded. After a few moments, he released me, and I slumped into his lap, resting my head on his chest, spent but sated.

As I surveyed the dining room, I couldn't help but laugh at the chaos that surrounded me. Broken dishes and food littered the floor and walls. Even the Persistence of Memory, painting by Salvador Dali had been splashed with wine, the melting clocks now coated in red. But I didn't fret - with Casmira's magic, I knew that in no time, the room would be restored to its former elegance, and all would be right with the world. My world anyway.

As we savored the remnants of our meal, the warmth between us was comforting. But the tranquility was short-lived, shattered by a knock at the door. Bellamy's eyes met mine, and he nodded reassuringly before rising to answer it.

'Stay and finish your dessert, I'll answer it,' his voice was low and soothing. I nodded, but my appetite vanished as soon as I heard Velar's voice. My fork clattered to the plate as I froze, my heart racing.

Bellamy's response was firm, but laced with a hint of wariness, 'This isn't a good time, Velar.' The tension escalated, and I found myself holding my breath as I strained to listen. Velar's words made my mouth drop open, 'Bell, please. I need to speak with her.' My heart pounded in my chest as I wondered what Velar wanted, and whether Bellamy would relent.

I sat motionless, as Bellamy and Velar's hushed conversation continued. The tension was suffocating, and I felt like I was drowning in the silence. Suddenly, Bellamy's voice rose, firm and commanding, ' I said no. This isn't the time.' A pause, and then Velar's pleading.

'Bell, please. Just a minute.' *What did he want to tell me?* Bellamy's response was resolute, 'No, Velar. You can't just barge in here and demand to talk to her. She's been through enough.'

I was about to confront Velar and demand to know what he wanted to tell me, but just as I stood up, the front door closed, and I knew he was gone. I heard Bellamy returning to the dining room and quickly sat back down, trying to act nonchalant.

Bellamy walked in, 'It was Velar.' I nodded, and asked, 'What did he want?' I knew Bellamy wasn't going to volunteer any information. He brushed it off, saying it was just about the circus, and I didn't press the issue further.

Bellamy leaned back in his chair. He flashed me a smirk, "Do you have feelings for Velar, baby girl?" His question slammed into me like a surprise wave, sending my wine careening down the wrong pipe.

I gasped, my airways rebelling in a fit of coughing spasms. My eyes watered, my throat burned, and my dignity momentarily vanished. Finally, after an eternity, I regained my composure and coughed out, 'No.'

The word felt like another betrayal, but I couldn't bring myself to admit the truth. Not even to myself. Bellamy's eyes narrowed, studying my face as if searching for any hint of deception. I met his gaze, determined to convince him of my loyalty. I wanted him to know that I was only his.

Even if I did harbor feelings for Velar, I could push them aside. After all, Velar had returned to Marcella. I would be his friend, nothing more. Bellamy's eyes seemed to bore into my soul, as if seeking the truth.

Finally, he nodded, appearing satisfied with my response. "I just want you to be honest with me, about everything, like you have always been in the past," his voice tinged with a hint of vulnerability. I saw the hurt in his eyes and nodded fervently, trying to convey that I was his, and his alone.

Bellamy's gaze lingered on mine, as if searching for any crack in my facade. I held my breath, worried that he might see through my lie. *He can always tell.* But after a moment, he seemed to relax, his expression softening. 'Good,' he said. 'I need to know that I can trust you, just like I always have before.'

I nodded again, feeling a pang of guilt for deceiving him. But I pushed it aside, telling myself that it was necessary to protect our relationship. 'Always,' I said, trying to sound convincing. 'I love you baby girl, in every way." I smiled back, feeling a sense of relief wash over me.

CHAPTER
TWENTY-SIX

As the predawn darkness slowly gave way to a hint of sunrise, the circus came to life. The crew and performers stirred, bleary-eyed, as they began setting up for the day's performances. Vendor stands filled the air with the sweet scent of sugary treats. Clove took Orlow to the backyard for a bath.

Meanwhile, Bellamy moved with purpose, his eyes scanning every detail as he fine-tuned the preparations with his magic. With a flick of his wrist, he made minute adjustments, ensuring everything was absolute perfection before the excited crowd pours in.

As Eve and I huddled in the dimly lit tent, sipping our morning tea, Velar burst in with an air of urgency, his eyes blazing like hot coals. He exchanged a curt nod with Eve, who swiftly gathered her belongings and made a hasty exit, leaving me alone and uneasy. I muttered a bitter "Bitch" under my breath, but before I could process what was happening, she left the tent. Velar's intense gaze pinned me in place.

'I tried to come see you last night...' he began, but I cut him off, my heart racing. 'I know.' I tried to brush him off, gathering my belongings with a pretense of nonchalance, but Velar's grip on my arm was unyielding.

'Whatever you think you know about Marcella and me, you're wrong,' he growled, his eyes flashing with a dangerous intensity. I tried to deflect him, 'I know you went to see her. It makes sense, she's a vampire, you're a vampire...' My words trailed off. Velar's expression turned feral, his fingers digging deep into my skin.

'I only want you,' he snarled, his voice dripping with possessiveness. Then, his head jerked up, as if he'd heard a distant call. 'Let's talk tonight, after Bell leaves,' before hastily disappearing out of the other side of the tent.

I stood frozen and confused. *Why did Velar just run off so fast?* I didn't even know Bellamy was going somewhere tonight. *And what did he want to talk about?*

Just then Bellamy walked in, and I knew instantly that's what Velar had heard, Bellamy's footsteps heading towards me. I could tell the sun was rising now with the light that followed him inside the tent.

"Are you ready, baby girl?" his voice bubbling with genuine excitement to open the circus. I nodded, but my mind was already wandering to Bellamy's mysterious plans for the night. Where was he off to? I pushed the thoughts aside as Bellamy checked the tent and equipment, his eyes scanning every detail with a seasoned showman precision.

Before departing, he turned to me, "After the circus closes tonight, I need to head to the Undying Council for a meeting.

I shouldn't be gone too long." I nodded in surprise as if he just read my mind. He flashed me a reassuring smile before exiting the tent, his voice lingering. "It's showtime!"

The circus was abuzz with activity in the afternoon. The accents around me were a dead giveaway that we were somewhere in Australia. Eve and I had already put on five shows, and I was ready to call it a day. Eve still had one more performance to go, but I was done.

Before I headed home, I went to my favorite stand to indulge in an elephant ear. The line was long, but it moved quickly. As I approached the stand, Miss Poppet's familiar white hair came into view, and she greeted me with a warm smile. Before I even reached the front of the line, she was handing me a warm elephant ear, its sweet aroma filling the air.

A few grumbles arose from the crowd about my skipping ahead, but Briar's booming voice quickly silenced them, 'That's Mrs. Darlington!'

The sudden attention made my face flush bright red as the crowd erupted in cheers and applause. I smiled and waved hesitantly. *I will never get used to this.* Their enthusiasm left me feeling grateful for this strange, wonderful circus family.

After indulging in the sweet treat, I made my way to the majestic weeping willow tree, its drooping branches beckoning me towards its secret hideaway. I cautiously scanned my surroundings, ensuring I was unseen, before slipping inside. Just as I reached the bottom of the stairs to enter Jubilee, Velar's sudden presence startled me, making me jump.

"Velar!" I exclaimed, trying to sound indignant but failing miserably as I jumped in surprise. His eyes sparkled with mirth as he burst into laughter, his deep chuckles so contagious that I couldn't help but join in, giggling at my own foolishness.

'You're such a sneak.' Velar just grinned and shrugged. 'Hey, someone's got to keep you on your toes.' I laughed again, feeling a warmth spread through my chest.

As Velar's arms encircled me, his lips met mine in a tender yet passionate kiss. The familiar scent of his skin filled my senses, transporting me back to the memories of our first intimate time together. My heart raced, and my knees weakened, as the desire to be close to him again overwhelmed me. But I knew that giving in to my desires would be a mistake, and the image of Bellamy flashed in my mind, giving me the strength to pull away.

Velar's eyes sparkled with persuasion as he tried to convince me, but I shook my head, my resolve firm. 'No, I can't see you tonight,' I said. 'I'm sorry, it's not a good idea.' The words felt like a lie, as every fiber of my being yearned to be with him. But I knew that I had to resist, for my own sake and for the sake of my relationship.

As I walked away, a part of me was surprised that Velar didn't follow me home. But another part of me, a part that I didn't want to acknowledge, felt a pang of disappointment. I couldn't help but wonder if he would have followed me if I had given him a sign, if he would have pursued me with the same passion and intensity that he had shown before.

Later that night, Bellamy returned, gently rousing me from my slumber on the couch. I hadn't intended to drift off, but the emotional exhaustion from my encounter with Velar had caught up with me. As I opened my eyes to find Bellamy standing over me, a warm smile spreading across his face, I knew in that moment that I had made the right decision.

"My love," he said, handing me a single white rose. Its heady scent filled the air, transporting me to a place of serenity.

Our lips met in a tender kiss, and I felt my heart skip a beat. But amidst the passion, a twinge of guilt crept in, knowing that just hours before, I had been in another man's arms.

Bellamy's eyes sparkled with desire as he gazed at me, his words sending shivers down my spine. 'You are so sexy, I would make love to you right now if I had the time...' He trailed off, his hands roaming my body, leaving a trail of fire in their wake.

As he stood to leave, adjusting his suit, his eyes locked onto mine. 'Eve and I are departing tonight, our meeting is tomorrow, and we shall return thereafter.' With that, he nodded, and a sleek suitcase materialized beside him, as if conjured by his words. I watched, still reeling from our encounter.

A few seconds later, the vibration was felt, and I knew we were somewhere else in the world. I looked out my window towards the Emberlynn Forest, wondering what Velar was doing, but still I told myself I made the right decision.

WHILE I WAS DEEP IN SLEEP I FELT BELLAMY'S GENTLE touch on my thighs, but I kept my heavy eyes closed. I was too tired to respond, but I couldn't help but enjoy his tender caresses. He slowly undressed me, and the cool air danced across my skin, leaving me naked and cold.

'No, Daddy,' I whimpered, still keeping my eyes shut tight. But his slow, sensual touch ignited a fire within me, and I couldn't resist. I slowly surrendered, spreading my legs and inviting him in. His fingers rubbing my growing wetness, making my body want him inside me.

He positioned himself between my legs and rubbed the head of his cock against my slit. I spread wide inviting him in. I let out a moan as he slid in slow and deep. The smell of pine and leather filled my nose. Instantly I opened my eyes to see Velar fucking me. Before I could say a word, he covered my mouth with his hand and fucked me deeper, pinning me in place.

It wasn't long before I was grinding into him, wanting more of him. He must have known because he removed his hand from my mouth. I moaned as his emerald eyes locked onto mine. 'Someday, you will belong to me,' he whispered.

He caressed my breast, making my nipples hard. As he made love to me, his movements slowed, and he paused to kiss my body, his lips lingering on my neck. I knew what he wanted, and I nodded, pulling the hair away from my neck.

I wrapped my arms around him just as his fangs sank into my skin. Blood ran down my chest as he sucked the blood from my neck.

The sensation was both exhilarating and terrifying. When he finished, he laid me back on the bed, his mouth stained with my blood. I watched, mesmerized, as he licked his lips on my blood.

It seemed to only fuel his desire more because without warning he flipped me over on all fours and fucked me from behind, his hands holding my hips in place. My screaming didn't faze him as he fucked me like a savage. He flipped me over without any effort and mounted me. Velar whispered, "Come for me baby."

I was grateful when Velar reached his climax, my body surrendering to the intense pleasure. I lay there, spent and trembling, my senses reeling from the passion we shared. The room spun, and I felt lightheaded either from getting fucked or from the loss of blood.

Having sex with a vampire is scary and intense. *I highly recommend it.*

After our passionate lovemaking, I finally mustered the courage to ask Velar about his intentions and what had driven him to visit Marcella. Velar's expression turned serious as he sat up in bed and flicked on the light.

'What do you mean I went to see Marcella?' I raised an eyebrow, skeptical of his sudden naivety. 'Bellamy told me you went to see her, that's why you left,' I replied, my voice firm.

A sly smile spread across Velar's face as he revealed the truth. 'Of course he did, No, Bellamy sent me on some bogus errand, but I knew it was because I slept with you.' My eyes widened in shock. 'You told him?' I asked. Velar shook his head, his eyes glinting with amusement. 'Bellamy knows everything, don't you know that by now?"

I leapt out of bed, my heart racing with panic. 'Bellamy will find out!' I exclaimed, my voice trembling. My mirror reflected the blood trickling down my chest from two prominent bite marks on my neck. 'How will I hide these?' I shouted, desperation creeping in. Velar approached me, his calm demeanor only fueling my distress. 'Bellamy will find out,' he said nonchalantly, his eyes gleaming with amusement.

'My bite looks good on you.' I glared at him, incredulous. 'Velar!' I shouted, pleading with him to understand my distress. Just then, a glass appeared on my nightstand. I grabbed it and took a hasty sip. Rushing back to the mirror, I gasped in relief as the bite marks vanished. 'Oh, Thank you, Casmira!' I called out, gratitude flooding my voice.

As soon as I was fully healed, I firmly told Velar to leave. But he just laughed ignoring my request. He pulled me back into bed, his grip gentle but insistent.

'Bellamy won't be back for another day,' he whispered. "We have all day. Finally, we can be together, just us.' His words were like honey, sweet and tempting, and I felt my resolve weakening. I knew I should resist, but Velar's pull was too strong, and I found myself surrendering to his embrace.

We didn't sleep a wink, our conversation flowing effortlessly as we took our time to play, make love, and cherish each other's company. The hours slipped away, and before we knew it, the first light of dawn was creeping through the windows, casting a warm glow over our entwined bodies.

We watched the sunrise together on my third story balcony and then Velar picked me up and carried me back inside my bedroom. As we lounged in bed, Velar's voice became my favorite serenade. He read to me, his words captivating my heart and soul.

His reading was my favorite part of our time together, a treasure I cherished deeply with him. He loved to read as much as me and I loved that about him,

With each word, he wove a spell of enchantment, transporting me to far-off lands, fantastical realms, and emotional depths. I was entranced by the way his voice danced with the words, his inflections and pauses like a gentle caress on my skin. In those moments, time stood still, and all that existed was Velar's voice, the stories he told, and the love we shared.

We surrendered to the bliss of each other's company, spending the entire day ensconced in my bedroom. Our hours were filled with tender lovemaking, savoring the delicious treats Casmira lovingly prepared for us, and getting lost in the pages of our favorite books. The world outside melted away as we indulged in our own private paradise.

As the day drew to a close, I clung to Velar's strong, tattooed arms, reluctant to let him go. I walked him to the front door, my heart heavy with the thought of separation. But Velar's reassuring smile and gentle kiss eased my anxiety, reminding me that we would reunite soon.

Yet, as I watched him leave, a pang of guilt crept in, knowing that Bellamy would return tomorrow. Velar, however, seemed unfazed by the situation, his confidence and passion leaving me breathless. He pulled me in, his kiss and touch igniting a fire within me, making me feel like his alone. It was as if he claimed me, marking me with a possessiveness that only my husband should have.

'I'll see you soon,' Velar whispered, his eyes locking onto mine as he slipped out the door. The promise hung in the air like a gentle caress, leaving me with a sense of longing and anticipation. I stood there, frozen in the doorway, my heart still racing from his touch, my soul craving more of his presence.

CHAPTER
TWENTY-SEVEN

When Bellamy and Eve arrived around mid-morning, I greeted them with a mix of excitement and nervousness. Bellamy filled me in on the details of the Undying Council meeting, while Eve chimed in with her characteristic bluntness, "It was so boring!" Eve's curiosity then turned to me, "What did you do yesterday?" My mind raced as I tried to come up with a convincing response, but before I could think, I blurted out, "Read, I read a lot." Eve raised an eyebrow, "More smut?" I shot her a defensive look, "It's called fantasy!"

Bellamy's piercing blue eyes locked onto mine, and I quickly looked away, praying that he wouldn't suspect anything about my secret tryst with Velar. I still wasn't sure what we were doing, and I couldn't bear the thought of Bellamy finding out.

Thankfully, Bellamy changed the subject, announcing that the circus would open tomorrow and that I was free to do as I pleased. My heart skipped a beat as I exclaimed, "I want to perform!" The thrill of the circus and my desire to perform clouded my mind, temporarily pushing my worries about Velar and Bellamy aside.

The next morning, Bellamy woke me up with a gentle nudge, and I sprang out of bed, eager to get ready for the circus. I was thrilled to be back in the swing of things and decided to perform on the silks, feeling an exhilarating rush at the prospect. However, my excitement was momentarily dampened when Eve informed me that Anise wouldn't be helping us, but Velar would be instead.

A knot formed in my stomach as I processed this information, but Eve's keen eyes noticed the lingering excitement still etched on my face. "I know you were with Velar yesterday," I shot her a wary look, wondering how she'd figured it out, but she just shook her head and said, "You aren't that hard to figure out."

I rolled my eyes, trying to play it cool, but the truth spilled out of me in a whispered confession, "Velar makes me feel excited!" Eve's expression softened, and she offered a gentle smile, but I could sense a hint of concern lurking beneath the surface.

As we arrived at the tent, Velar's eyes locked onto mine, and he strode over to me with a confident swagger. He wrapped me in a warm embrace, his arms wrapping tightly around me, and I felt a rush of excitement. His scent, a heady mix of leather and spice, filled my senses, and I couldn't help but lean into his touch. But as I pulled away, I remembered we were in public and glanced nervously at Eve, who was watching us with raised eyebrows.

"We can't do that here," I whispered to Velar, my cheeks flushing. He just flashed me a mischievous smile, his fangs gleaming in the light, and I knew he was enjoying the thrill of our secret. Eve's gaze lingered on us, her expression a mix of curiosity and concern, but I quickly looked away, trying to play it cool despite the butterflies in my stomach. Velar's hand brushed against mine, and I knew I had to keep my composure. I took a deep breath and focused on the performance ahead, trying to push aside the distraction of Velar's captivating presence.

After my first performance, I took a break, strolling around the circus to soak in the vibrant atmosphere. The smell of sugary treats and the sound of laughter filled the air, and I felt carefree, until Velar approached me. His eyes locked onto mine, intense and piercing, making my heart race. He didn't touch me, aware of the crowd and crew surrounding us, but his gaze spoke volumes.

"I need you again," he whispered, his voice low and husky. I tried to walk away, but he grasped my hand, his grip firm but gentle. "Let's head back to Jubilee early?" he suggested, his eyes sparkling with desire. I shook my head, trying to resist his charms. "I still have three more shows," I replied, my voice firm but my heart betraying me. Velar's gaze lingered on mine, his expression a mix of understanding and disappointment, but I knew he wouldn't give up easily.

During my next performance, my mind wandered to Velar, and I couldn't shake off the desire that had been building up inside me. He wanted me, and I wanted him with every fiber of my being. There was something about Velar's intensity that set my soul on fire.

The way he took me was different - more primal, rawer, and more intoxicating. I felt a deep sense of submission when I was with him, like I was surrendering to a force beyond my control. The thoughts made me weak, and I struggled to focus on my performance. But the more I tried to push Velar out of my mind, the more he consumed my thoughts, leaving me breathless and wanting more.

After my performance, I couldn't wait any longer to see Velar. I didn't bother telling Eve where I was going or what I was doing - I just left. I made my way to the backyard of the circus, my heart racing with anticipation. Velar was there, carrying a huge bundle of ropes, but when he saw me, he dropped everything. Our eyes locked, and without a word, we walked together quickly, trying not to draw attention to ourselves. We slipped away from the circus, our pace fast and purposeful, until we reached Jubilee.

Instead of heading to Casmira, Velar suggested, 'Let's go to my place.' I agreed, my heart racing with anticipation. Together, we walked towards the Emberlynn Forest, the trees growing taller and darker as we approached his cabin. I felt a thrill of nervousness mixed with arousal, my body craving the intensity of Velar's touch.

I couldn't wait to feel him inside me again, to surrender to his passion and lose myself in the fire that burned between us. Velars eyes locked onto mine, his gaze burning with desire. I knew I was ready to surrender to the flames that Velar had ignited within me.

As we reached the forest edge, Velar's patience wore thin. With a sudden burst of speed, he scooped me up in his arms and whisked us away to his cabin, the world blurring around us as he employed his vampire swiftness to get us there in an instant. I felt a rush of exhilaration as the trees and foliage blended together, my heart racing with excitement. Before I knew it, we were inside, the door closing behind us with a soft thud. Velar's eyes gleamed with desire as he gazed at me.

Velar's lips crashed against mine, his kiss devouring me whole. I melted into his embrace, our bodies entwined as he carried me to the heart of his cabin. The world outside faded away, leaving only the two of us, lost in the inferno of our passion. His hands roamed my skin, setting my soul ablaze with every touch. I surrendered to his caress, my heart beating in harmony with his.

As we reached the bed, Velar's gaze locked onto mine, his eyes burning with adoration. He laid me down, his body covering mine, and I felt the weight of his desire. His lips traced the curve of my neck, his fangs grazing my skin, sending shivers down my spine. I arched my back, inviting him in, and he accepted with a gentle bite. The pain was fleeting, replaced by a wave of pleasure that left me breathless.

Our bodies moved in perfect harmony, our love a symphony of passion and longing. Velar's movements sent me over the edge and I let out a long moan in his ear.

Velar's gentle fingers traced circles on my arm as we lay together in his bed, basking in the warmth of our love. Our deep conversation about life and dreams had led us to a crossroads. The possibility of running away together and leaving the circus behind.

I had hinted at the thrill of becoming a vampire, but Velar's expression turned serious. 'That's not the life I want for you, my love,' his emerald eyes shining with concern. 'You deserve to bask in the sunlight, to feel its warmth on your skin.' I smiled, knowing he was right.

Our gazes locked, and I knew in that moment, I was exactly where I was meant to be.

Bellamy's voice thundered through the room. 'I knew you couldn't keep your fangs away from her!' he bellowed, his eyes blazing with rage. In an instant, Velar sprang into action, positioning himself protectively in front of me. But Bellamy's rage was unstoppable.

With a swift gesture, he sent Velar flying across the room, his body suspended in mid-air by the force of Bellamy's magic. Velar struggled against the invisible bonds, his face contorted in a mixture of pain and helplessness. I watched in horror, frozen in place, as Bellamy's magic encircled Velar, holding him captive.

Bellamy's magic swirled around him, its familiar dark tendrils writhing like living shadows. I'd only seen it look like that once before, when he was fighting the dark angels. Now, it seemed to pulse with an otherworldly energy, as if fueled by his rage. Velar, still suspended in mid-air, struggled against the magic's hold, his eyes flashing with a fierce determination.

Bellamy's anger boiled over as he approached me. His magic swirled around him, and he grasped my legs, pulling me close. "You want to be a little slut now?" I trembled, feeling a mix of fear and shame.

He slapped my leg, and I turned to face him, tears welling up in my eyes. "You're hurting me, Bellamy," I pleaded. But he just pulled me closer, his grip tightening. "You're mine," he hissed, his eyes blazing with fury. I cried out in pain and fear, feeling overwhelmed and trapped.

Velar struggled against Bellamy's magic, but I knew it was futile. Bellamy's powers were too strong, overwhelming Velar's vampire abilities. I braced myself for the worst, waiting for Bellamy's anger to subside, but it only grew fiercer.

Then, a sudden, sharp crack echoed through the air. Velar's scream followed, a heart-wrenching cry of agony. 'No!' he pleaded, but it was too late. I felt my own neck snap, my body fragile as a twig.

As Velar's despairing cries echoed through the air, my fragile existence unraveled, thread by thread. Bellamy's magic had snapped the delicate chain of my life, shattering the dreams we'd woven together. Memories of our whispers, our laughter, and our tears now taunted me. My vision faded like a dying ember, and I beheld Velar's anguish-ravaged face, his emerald eyes pleading for me to stay.

UNTIL NEXT TIME...

EPILOGUE 1

I stared at Ambrette, my eyes pleading with her to bring her back. 'Please, I beg you, do something!' I shouted, my voice cracking with despair. When I finally regained control of my body, I realized the horror of what I had done.

A dark force had taken hold of me, and I had lost myself to it. Seeing them together had unleashed a fury I couldn't contain. My gaze locked onto Velar, still trapped in my magic's grip. I released him with a swift motion, and he rushed to her side, cradling her lifeless form.

'No, no, no!' Velar cried, voice shaking with anguish. 'Come back to me, baby!' I stumbled backward, my mind reeling with the consequences of my actions. 'Look what you did!' Velar snarled, his eyes blazing with hatred. 'You'll pay for this!' But his love for her overpowered his rage, and he sprinted out of the house to get help, leaving me alone with my guilt.

I approached her cautiously, my heart heavy with regret. I gently brushed her hair aside, and the sight of her bruised neck made my stomach churn. I felt like I'd been punched in the gut. I couldn't touch her, couldn't bear the thought of causing her more harm.

I couldn't meet Velar's gaze, my shame and guilt consuming me. Ambrette's expression was grim, his eyes filled with a deep sadness. 'You have to fix this,' Velar spat, his voice venomous. 'You have to bring her back.'

I slumped against the wall, my mind racing with thoughts of what I had done. I couldn't undo the damage, but maybe... just maybe... I could find a way to make it right. I looked at Ambrette, pleading for help.

Velar's anger slowly gave way to despair, and he cradled her lifeless body in his arms. I watched, helpless, as he whispered sweet nothings to her, begging her to come back. My heart broke for him, for what I had done to him.

I knew she would reincarnate once more because of the Samsara ritual, but now we had to endure the agonizing wait. And it was all my fault. I couldn't escape the weight of my guilt, knowing that Velar would never forgive me. I didn't blame him; I was unforgivable.

My actions had made me a monster, unworthy of her love. I didn't deserve her, and yet... I held onto hope that I didn't fuck up the ritual and it would still restore her to us. I will find her again and I will make it right. I have to find a way. I must.

EPILOGUE 2

I'm going to fucking kill Bellamy Darlington. I'd already stormed out of there, my anger and grief boiling over. I couldn't bear the thought of being in the same space as Bellamy Darlington, not after what he'd done. The pain of losing her was still a fresh wound, and Bellamy's presence was salt rubbed into the open sore.

As I walked away, I knew I'd never be able to go back. The rage that burned within me was too intense, too all-consuming. I wanted Bellamy to pay for what he'd done, to suffer as I was suffering. I'm going to make him pay, no matter what it takes.

The Ritual is all that's keeping me going, the promise that she'll return to me. But even that's not enough to calm the storm raging within me. I need revenge, and I need it now. Bellamy Darlington, you may be immortal, but I'll find a way.

My rage towards Bellamy simmered just below the surface, but it was nothing compared to the self-loathing that consumed me. I knew that sneaking around, taking her without permission, and making her sneak away was a reckless game. Bellamy knew everything, and I was playing with fire.

As I fantasized about snapping his neck, draining his blood, and watching him writhe in agony, my anger reached a boiling point. But it was the memories that replayed in my head, memories of Nic, of finally confessing my love to her, only to have her taken away. The pain was a palpable weight, crushing me beneath its oppressive force.

That night, Ambrette and Bellamy had shown up at my door, demanding that I erase her memories of this lifetime. I was forced to comply, my hands trembling as I stood over her lifeless body, erasing our memories together. The agony was overwhelming, and in that moment, I knew I was done with Bellamy and his orders.

But I knew the truth - the truth of our love, of our connection that spanned lifetimes. And that was all I needed to keep going. She will be back, and I will be waiting for her. Bellamy may think he has the upper hand, with his power and his magic, but he's not the only one who knows a powerful witch.

ABOUT THE AUTHOR

SK Hinkley, a seasoned media professional with a passion for storytelling was born and raised in Lancaster, Pennsylvania. She made the bold move to New York City, at the age of 20, to pursue her dreams in broadcast media.

SK has worked with some of the biggest names in the industry, including NBC, MLB, CNN, Aljazeera America and Court TV.

When she's not behind the camera or creating engaging media content, she can be found exploring the great outdoors with her husband and children in her home state of Georgia.

SK finds inspiration in nature and the beauty of the world around her. And that inspiring love of adventure shines through her writing making her a compelling voice in the world of fiction.

You're invited to come on in and find a seat... It's Showtime!